VISIONS OF FIRE

The Seer's Blessing: Book 2

Jana Sun

This book is dedicated to everyone
who's ever looked for magic.
I hope you find it.

Contents

CHAPTER ONE

FALCON

Low key, I did not think that falling through a portal into Obius, the realm of magic, would feel like my atoms were being ripped apart and then put back together. Ignorance on my part there–it's a portal, it's magic, and the link was thready at best. So I fell through the sky, through the universe, through a black hole. My skin was heavy on my bones and everything compacted in me. I didn't know which way was up or down, or if directions even existed.

Centuries could have passed and I wouldn't have known. Everything in the tunnel was a void, and I was hollow, so very hollow, hollow and empty, and utterly alone–

"Falcon," Jack Hawthorne said. Her voice mighty, and sounding mighty angry. And that anger was a hundred percent on me; I pushed her through the door–portal, tunnel, galactic funnel–to Obius, and she dragged me with her. I know how the evidence looked. Big, bad, evil Falcon tried to kill the woman of his best friend's dreams that he had been waiting on for literal *centuries*.

But that's only half the tale.

When the Goddess of Justice, whom you've pledged your life to, screeches *kill her* in your head so loud it could burst an eardrum, you listen. Her perfect scales were tattooed on my forearm and would dip when I wasn't following the right path. Her path. Her words echoed through me, and I caved. I wasn't a killer. I *was* a grade-A asshole, but I wasn't a killer, and I sure as hell wouldn't kill Jack. So I did the next best thing.

I booted her to Obius. I just didn't anticipate her *dragging me along*.

Laying flat on my back, I stared at the sky. Jack hovered nearby, her fury like a tangible thing, and I stayed there. The sky was incredible. It was blue, but not a human blue. It was a hue I'd never seen, like this was the truth of the color, and every variation on Earth was a lie. Everything here felt like a lucid dream: too sharp, too bright, intensity dripping from every color.

"Get up," she said.

I obeyed, my feet unsteady from the fall, and kept some space between us. My insides didn't feel like they were all exactly where they should be, and being aware of that made not blowing chunks everywhere difficult.

I was keenly aware that being here was my fault, but the devastation of the field in front of us wasn't my doing. Jack's staff–of course the damn thing came with us–floated next to her, bobbing gently up and down. The sparkle of the crystal sent chills through me. The magic in it burned, just like this field had burned.

"Snapdragon burned the forest," Jack said, sinking to her knees. She dug her fingers into the scorched earth and her arms trembled. I wanted to comfort her, oddly; she looked like she was shattering too, but there was zero chance of me seeming like the good guy right now. I noticed that her legs and feet were bare. Jack's hair was in the same floppy bun that she had on Earth, in the same oversized t-shirt she wore as a nightgown. I shoved her through a portal in her pajamas. The staff laid itself across her lap like a dog offering comfort.

Forest. It was hard to imagine this place as a forest. It was desolate and bleak. Patches still smoldered. Small embers and little whooshes of smoke still lingered from an epic fire. Jack's words came back to me then, before we made the leap, and before her own home burned to the ground. It seemed like a lie then; something to draw Diego in to her more, but now—

She sobbed. She didn't cry like this for her own house going up in flames, but for this forest, she cried and cried. I wasn't a complete asshole, I did want to help her. It wasn't my place to ease her pain and trying wouldn't help. Nothing would fix this destruction. I picked a flower that was unscathed next to me. The petals were gold with flecks of red and orange in them. It smelled like smoke and honey.

"Where are we?" I asked, my throat was overly dry and the words cracked. Her head snapped up, assessing. Her eyes were made of ice, and the magic that pooled around her crackled with power. The tears had slowed but leaked down her cheeks. The sadness in her was so visceral; was that part of Obius' magic too? The staff hummed, and the heat reached me from several feet away.

"Trellis, where do you think? This was Diego's home, and Snapdragon burned it to the ground."

I really took in the sights when she said Trellis. Diego wasn't tight-lipped about his home, but he didn't enjoy strolling down memory lane. It caused heart aches, and he didn't have a lot of heart left to handle it. He told me about the rainbow forest, where the tree trunks were alight with colors and the leaves were in matching shades. The only thing alight here now was the embers that refused to fully go out. Too bad Peony Hawthorne, the older one with more of an attitude than my current Hawthorne, wasn't here to drench the forest.

The more I looked, the more I saw the colors. They were muted, like a burnt painting.

Jack's tears had nearly stopped now. Little drops still rolled down her cheeks but the heaving had stopped, and she dabbed at her eyes to get herself back under control. I was thankful for that. She had the feel of a nuclear reactor, and I didn't want to be caught in the meltdown.

"If this is Trellis, then the castle should be somewhere nearby. Diego talked about that a lot. There's a small town near the gates too. He used to visit there a lot," I said.

Diego got a little tipsy one night and talked about his home for hours. He told me about the fountain in the center of the main plaza that was dedicated to his mother. Diego was a not-so-secret art lover and went on for ages about the tapestries that filled the halls of the castle and how he made stained glass and jewelry for the folks at court. He didn't mention the locket with the piece of his heart in it, but Diego was choosy about what he wanted to say most of the time, even tipsy. It was one of my favorite memories with him; he felt alive. I didn't even know he could get drunk, but something about the drinks that night made him chatty. It was a year or so before Jack entered his world. Our worlds.

Now I was standing in *his* world, his true home, only he wasn't here.

"I miss him too," Jack said.

"Huh?"

"Your thoughts are like a loudspeaker here dude, I can hear everything." Jack tapped the side of her head and the staff bobbed faster. Jack creeped me out, but the staff was in a league of its own. It responded to her emotions and magic like an extension of her mind. I didn't want to piss her off—again—and find out what that thing could do.

"I'm not planning on *zapping* you. Calm down." The staff spun slowly in wide circles. She grabbed the shaft and jammed it into the ground. Magic poured through the forest floor and waves of warmth filled me. It started in my feet and rose up through my chest. It was a healing spell but grander. It didn't want to heal bumps and bruises, it was a balm on the soul. The forest responded, some of the color coming back, flitting in and out like it was trying to revive itself.

The spell didn't stop. Wave after wave of magic rolled against me. It felt like Jack was hitting me with all of the years of therapy I should have attended.

"Girl, what the hell is that spell?"

"Healing spell. I'm trying to comfort the trees," she said.

"I feel like I need a cigarette and a hug, damn." I rubbed my arms, and wondered how much past trauma Jack could see tumbling around in my head.

"The trees are dying," she whispered.

"I don't think any healing spell is going to fix that, Jack," I said. I tried to say it gently. I wasn't great with gentle.

Little orbs of light floated up and came closer to Jack. They swirled around her, and she opened her hand, letting them all gather at her palm. The orbs danced in the air, moving in time with the beat of Jack's magic. It was rhythmic, like a heartbeat. She closed her eyes and when she opened them again, her eyes shone green. Emerald green. Too bright to be anything other than magic.

"Hey, Jack, they can't go to rest. There's no link to Sanctum–"

She dropped the spell immediately. The orbs fell back to the ground, and her eyes were shiny with tears again.

"I'm gonna find Snapdragon and make her pay for this." The staff spun violently. I took another look at the forest ruins. The tattoo of the Judge's scales was perfectly balanced on my arm. Justice. Rightness. The way forward.

I blew out a sigh, "Alright, alright don't twist my arm, I'm coming too."

JACK

My heart was shattered. Was this how Diego felt for all those years? How he still felt? The forest was in ashes. I tried to pull the souls from the trees, to heal their dead branches, but it didn't work. Of course it wouldn't. I didn't know what I was doing as a so-called Priestess, and there was nowhere to send the souls *to*. Falcon was right, and admitting that made my anger worse.

This was the real face of anger: it gnawed at me, consumed me, the blackness of it sucking at every light inside me. It raged in my chest, begging for me to cast something to lash out at all of the destruction. I wanted to scream until I was hoarse, and scream for every soul that died in this hellscape. There was so much *death* that it made the air stink of it, and I felt it seeping into my pores. I wanted to cry until there was no air left in my lungs without Falcon here to pretend like he cared. My crystal ball, Harold, glittered at the top of the staff. Magic was alive here, and seeing Harold react to my every thought made it seem alive too.

Was the heaviness that I felt from Diego in those first visions of his anger or sadness? I thought that it was just sadness that ate at him, but now I wasn't so sure. Harold showed me a picture of Diego smiling at me in my shop before it had been burnt down. The pain in my chest eased but just barely. I leaned my forehead against the crystal; it was cool, the magic rising to greet me. For a moment, I could pretend that Diego was here with me.

My head was pounding, but it wasn't just from the crying; now that I stopped I knew what it was. Every thought that entered Falcon's head blared through my mind. It was deafening. *I'm not a killer, I'm not! Fuck, I've messed up. She's gonna kill me. Irony. That staff is gonna kill me. Nope, it's her. She's gonna get both of us killed looking for that crazy bitch.*

Snapdragon.

The rage flared up again, and magic pulsed in my chest. Everything was so *green–*

Falcon grabbed my shoulders and shook, bringing me back to the present. He immediately let go and backed up, hand in the air in surrender. He stumbled over a tree stump and that lump of sadness jumped up in my throat.

"No nuclear reactions. There's enough destruction," he said.

I opened my mouth to respond, but Falcon motioned for me to listen. I felt his nerves through his words, and I stayed quiet.

"For what it's worth, I'm sorry I didn't believe you about the forest. This is... well, shitty." He was thinking about Diego, looking at each ruined tree, and my heart sank.

"How am I going to tell Diego that his home is gone?" My lips trembled. *Don't cry, do not cry.*

"Let's not worry about that too much right now. Maybe let's find you some pants and figure out how to get back home." Falcon glanced down at my bare legs, and the skin on my thighs turned to gooseflesh. I wasn't even cold until he mentioned pants; a light breeze brushed across my skin and I shivered. It wasn't late fall here. I didn't know if Obius even had seasons, but it was much warmer than in Cape Margaret. Maybe that was just the leftover heat from the fire.

"I'm not going anywhere until I find Snapdragon." My staff stamped into the ground like a post, and I crossed my arms for more of an effect. I imagined how ridiculous the scene was, but Falcon didn't react. He sighed and rolled his eyes. I heard his thoughts mumble something along the lines of *we're both gonna die* before he threw his hands up in defeat.

"Alright, fine." *This is so stupid.* He didn't *say* the words, but he didn't have to. Not here, not in Obius where I was drowning in magic.

I spoke very, very slowly, "It's *your* fault that we're here, and *we* are going to find her and bring her to justice."

"Justice?" he scoffed, "What the hell do you know about that? What are we gonna do, Jack? Bring her to Earth and let her stand trial? This isn't our wheelhouse!"

My staff spun faster and faster, reacting to the anger that refused to settle, and a little nagging thought danced in the very back of my mind. The surge of magic jolted through my body and raced through my mind. It was coming alive.

Oh yes, it is.

CHAPTER TWO

MARI

Morning came fast considering that I didn't sleep. I couldn't sleep. Jack's house was gone. The shop was gone. Her *everything* was gone because I burned it to the ground. There were too many twisted souls everywhere. She was weak and then Snapdragon was reaching through the veil some-how–

So I burned it all down. All of it. Abuela vanished. Falcon helped me hold the cube spell until Peony rescued us. I don't know how she got us out or handled all the firefighters or got Jack settled in a hotel, but that was Peony. She fixed all of the problems while the rest of us fell apart, or in my case made it worse. Like always. I turned over in my bed, pulling my blanket tougher around my shoulders. *Fucked up, Mari, great job.*

Once I saw that everyone was alive, I just slunk back to my apartment. I couldn't face Jack after burning down her house. I couldn't see the com-passion in her eyes when she scanned my thoughts and knew I didn't mean it. Did it fucking *matter* that I didn't mean it? Some things couldn't just be forgotten. Tears stung my eyes so I squeezed them shut tighter, curling up to make the world have less of me in it.

And as the night shifted to morning, I still couldn't face her.

It didn't help that I was setting fires all night, either.

When Jack started getting the visions of Snapdragon and Diego, her magic shifted. The worlds' threadbare links had shifted, and everyone's magic changed. Mine went erratic. Too weak, then it fizzled out, then came back like a wildfire of magic burning through me. And now I couldn't *stop* it. I lit candles and burned little pieces of paper, shot small flames into a bathtub full of water or under the kitchen spigot because I had to cast, I *had* to get it out. Sparks leapt from my fingers, so I kept my hands balled up, containing the fire as much as possible. *Why couldn't I just stop!*

I was going to burn everything down because now I couldn't stop the fire. I got up, feeling the flames igniting in my chest and paced around my apartment. I wouldn't burn my blanket–Peony spent ages on it and I could at least not screw that up.

I opened my hands and a flame burst from them. Just a small one, like I was my own personal candle. The flame danced in my cupped hands and I sighed. *Don't look too closely. Don't enjoy watching it dance. Stop before you–*

"Marigold Groves, what are you doing with that spell?" Puddin said. I blew the flame out, it came back, I did it again, and I felt that cat arching an eyebrow at me. I never knew cats had eyebrows until this one crossed my path.

"Just practicing. See how well I can control it?" The lie came out easy, quick. Probably too quick. I schooled my face; the last thing I needed was to be scolded by a housecat.

"Your energy is frantic. Are you sure you're okay?"

"I mean, are any of us okay right now?"

"That's what I wanted to talk to you about," she purred. Puddin's tail flicked back and forth. She hovered at eye level, flopped over like she was laying on something solid instead of just air.

"I'm not really feeling a heart to heart," I said, waving her off.

"I was hoping to find Jack here," she deadpanned. The fire in my palm fully went out. *Find* Jack? Alarm bells sounded in my head.

"Jack isn't here. Did you call her?"

"With what opposable thumbs? I don't have a phone." She rolled her eyes. Puddin had so many human expressions.

"I'll call her." I pulled out my phone, a little charred on the case, now that I was looking at it, and speed-dialed Jack. She was the second on my list, even though my mama's phone had been turned off for over a decade. I couldn't bring myself to delete the number.

Straight to voicemail.

I sent her a text–just a few emojis. The text came back undelivered. Puddin rested on my counter now, like a real cat, and I desperately pushed the fire magic back down into my body. Smoke was gonna come out of my ears any minute now.

"She could be sleeping," I said as a sinking feeling spread through me. I knew that wasn't the case even as I said it. I tapped my fingers on the glass screen, chewing my lip. I *knew* she wasn't sleeping.

"I checked her hotel room; the door was unlocked."

Panic made another small flame pop from my thumb and I shoved my hands in my armpits. Jack never left anything unlocked. Sometimes, she would forget to unlock the store until a customer would bang on the window to be let in. After she had one creeper demand that she rewrite his future and change his fate, she never forgot to lock a door or window again. Peony was on him instantly, punching so hard he lost two teeth.

"Have you talked to Peony?" I asked.

"No, between the two of you, Jack would come here first." *So would Peony,* I thought to myself. Peony crashed at my house just as often as she did at Jack's. Past tense–Jack's house was *gone* thanks to yours truly, and Peony should have been *here*. My heart was racing and as I felt my temperature rise, I worried I'd combust. *No more fire, no more fire, no more fire.*

"Wait, where is Peony?"

"I'm guessing she's with the man," Puddin said. *The man.* The guy Jack buys herbs and plants from, Sherwin. He was a nice dude. A little flighty, but not catastrophically so. He seemed like an alright egg to me, but I'd never ping him as Peony's type.

I took a breath, calming the storm in my chest, and sent her a text too. *Is Jack with you?*

Peony, in true Peony Hawthorne form, responded in seconds. I could hear her crunching an antacid. **No, she's at the hotel.**

"I'm not telling her," I said. The magic in me faded fast. Just thinking about Peony's reaction doused the fire burning through me, and relief from the heat practically oozed from me. I could breathe.

Puddin curled up on the counter, ducking her head between her little fuzzy feet and covered her eyes with her tail.

"Good luck, Mari. You'll be fine." And just like that she went to sleep. My phone dinged and dinged and dinged. Peony had gone back into panic mode. I tanked Peony's whole morning within seconds with a four word text.

Ok I called the hotel and they said she didnt answer the phone in her room

She isnt answering me either

OMG i cant even leave her for ONE NIGHT

Meet me at the shop

Wait

No i'll just come to you

I have Sher with me, hope that's okay

I'll get us some coffees

Did you call Diego? Do you have his number? He might know something

I didn't respond. Peony would only read every third word at most when she got like this–which was often–and it wouldn't do either of us any good. I sent her a thumbs up and immediately texted Falcon.

Yeah, he sorta tried to kill Jack, but it wasn't his fault. No one that worked so hard to keep us alive would really want us dead. He left after I did, and I didn't see where he went. He had to be with Diego; they were joined at the hip like I was to Jack. I wondered if he ever felt like he was standing in the shadow of a giant too.

He didn't respond either. Maybe he wasn't a texter. Falcon had the chaotic energy of someone who actually used his phone as a phone. The knot forming in my stomach tightened. Something was up. Bad vibes circulated through me and I shivered. The asshole part of my brain told me it was my fault and I did my best not to cry, because only people that *didn't burn their best friend's house down* get to cry.

I leaned against my kitchen counter, mindlessly rubbing Puddin's head. She let me, and I was glad I didn't have to explain my need to do something other than light another fire. My house smelled like smoke now too. So, I opened up my creaky windows, and let the icy air in. It was too cold to keep the windows open and too windy for it to be comfortable. I needed the air though. Fresh, cold, and crisp. It settled my nerves, until the wind picked up, catching my pale blue curtains and whipping them around.

Mama always told me that the wind would tell you how your day would be if you bothered to listen. Abuela always talked about listening to the wind too, but now I understood it. The wind was wild. It ripped through my house and left a line of chaos. The junk mail I was fixing to throw away was all over the floor. A small plastic vase with artificial flowers got knocked over. The curtains were disheveled and brushed against the picture frames I had hanging on my wall.

Puddin perked up, quietly watching as the wind got stronger.

"Mari," she purred, hopping down to weave through the mound of junk mail on the floor, "I think we should close that window before we invite anything else in."

Peony chose that moment to knock on my door, opening it without a response. She half-dragged Sherwin behind her before stopping to look at the mess. At least it would distract her from any lingering smoke. I stuffed my hands in my back pockets, trying to keep them out of sight. I didn't want her to see the magic. I didn't want her to notice that my skin was flaking and charred in places. I just wanted to be invisible again.

"What happened here?" she asked. Peony had a bag of bagels in one hand, Sherwin in the other, and he was precariously holding all three coffees.

"Just some spunky wind. Felt a little claustrophobic in here," I lied again. It was getting easier, and Peony didn't react.

"I'll help you clean it up. Go eat darling, you look sunken." Peony kissed my forehead, the big sister I never had but always wanted, and started on the junk mail. Sherwin unloaded everything on the counter, waving awkwardly as he went for the window. Even after it was closed again, the chill hadn't left the house. I had chill bumps on my arms and a fire burning in my chest.

"So what's the plan, P?" Sherwin said. He reminded me of Falcon, all easy smiles and shiny teeth. His energy was like the promise of summer, and I saw why Peony fell for him. She needed a lot more summer in her life.

"First we're gonna finish these coffees, then we're gonna go find Diego and Falcon," she said.

"Falcon didn't answer his phone either," I said. I sent a text to Diego too, but I had the feeling it would also go unanswered.

"Yeah, something about this isn't sitting right. Where did they go?" Sherwin said. Peony brought me a large iced Americano. A few sips in and my nerves settled, the fire spell churning through me slowed, and the calm that only caffeine can bring hit.

"I don't know where their hotel is, but it's within walking distance of Jack's, so that's something. Let's swing by her place first."

Peony tucked one of my braids behind my ear, "Mari, it's all torched. It's probably best that we skip her place–"

"No," I said. I took another swig of the coffee, cold and crisp just like the wind that blasted through my window, and grabbed my purse.

DIEGO

Everything in me ached. It wasn't a surface level ache either; this pain went deep into the tissues and into my heart. And I would know that better than anyone else. My heart was shattered so many years ago when I broke the bonds between the realms for the woman I loved. I thought I was saving her. I thought wrong.

I thought I was saving my kingdom. I thought wrong.

I thought Falcon was my family, my brother, my friend.

I thought wrong.

Each beat radiated a new wave of pain through my body, and I couldn't bring myself to sit up. I was flat on my back, looking up at the morning sky. I'd been here all night. It took several minutes to feel anything other than pain. I was wet. Cold. Stiff. Falcon stabbed me with something and I collapsed, right after the fire at Jack's home died out. He dragged me into the only untouched bushes and left me there.

"You'll be okay, D. Not like, immediately, but you will be. I'm sorry. Truth be told, I don't know what's in this shit, but she promised it wouldn't kill you, and that's all I'm really asking for." His words echoed through my mind, and I wondered why he cared whether he killed me or not.

The ground was still damp from Peony Hawthorne's staggering magical display to put the fire out once and for all. She called the tides and held the ocean in her hands. It was magnificent, and I would have appreciated it more if I wasn't lying on the very cold, very wet dirt. I willed myself to move but nothing happened. My limbs felt like lead.

What the hell did Falcon put in that syringe? I don't know why he would attack... what did he say? I couldn't remember now. I'd been stabbed before a handful of times, and this was worse than any stabbing. There were drugs and magic interlaced in whatever he dosed me with. The magic clung to my blood. Having a heart that functions made me more aware of my blood pumping. When Jack had fused the two pieces together, I could breathe again. That was harder now, because of this spell. My blood felt thick, sticky, like it struggled to circulate through me.

When I opened my eyes again, the sun was fully up and I still was not. My legs stiffened when I tried to move, but this time they did bend a little. I groaned and grunted like an old man just to sit up, but I finally was upright. My head spun from the movement, and I rested my head on my knees until the world stopped moving. It took several more agonizing and embarrassing minutes to crawl out of the bush fully. By the time I was on my knees, my arms tried to give out. I was too aware of the nerves in my back, the aches and strain of muscle as I moved.

I leaned against Jack's large white fence that was warped and stained by the fire, and it groaned louder than I had. The only remaining bushes scraped my arms and snagged on my sweater.

The beeping of a car alarm got my attention, and I searched for Falcon. It had to be him—returning to the scene of the crime—

But no, Mari Groves, Peony Hawthorne, and a man I didn't know headed up the sidewalk to where Jack's front porch should have been. Mari dug something out of the rubble; it was part of the psychic eye sign that hung from Jack's window. Jack told me that she loved that sign; she got it at a yard sale as a teenager and had it hanging in her bedroom before she opened the shop. The frame was mangled, but still eye-shaped enough that I could see it. Mari dropped it, the clanging bringing me back to the present.

Where was Jack?

"H-hey," I croaked out. My throat cracked with dryness and I doubted they could hear me. The man with Peony lifted his head sharply, staring right at me. He tapped Peony's arm, and then the three of them were headed my way. I'd spent all of the energy I had sitting up, so I stayed on the ground. This should have been embarrassing, but I was past caring. Caring took too much energy.

Peony hovered over me, and the dryness in my throat turned to a lump. Goddesses above, she looked like her younger sister. Peony was blonder, fairer, but everything else was the same. No freckles, but instead had huge, pink glasses that matched the pink ends of her hair. Where Jack was soft, Peony was hard. Her eyes never missed a detail, and her mouth was made for barbs.

The heart link on my wrist warmed, and I felt Jack's heart beating softly through my wrist.

"Diego, can you hear me? Sherwin, come help me get him up," Peony said. Sherwin. Sherwin. The name sounded so familiar. He studied me, and I saw the otherness about him. Another Fae trapped on Earth. He ducked his head, averting his eyes.

He seemed so familiar.

"Where have you been?" she asked.

"Not answering his phone," Mari mumbled. She bit at her fingernails, a habit I'd seen from her over and over in the short time I'd known her. The three of them studied me, and I wondered what mess they saw.

"Diego... What happened to you? Were you injured in the fire? I thought I saw you afterwards and you were okay." Peony even sounded like Jack when she wasn't trying to command the tides.

"Falcon. That's what happened to me. He stabbed me with something, and I've been struggling to get up for the last... what time is it? I don't even know how long I've been here. Where's Jack? Is she still resting?"

"Wait, Falcon *stabbed* you!" Peony tried to fuss over me, looking for signs of injury. I gently waved her off; nothing she could do would make the spell wear off any faster. I couldn't focus on their words because my attention was on Sherwin. He stayed a few steps back and to the right. Something nagged at my memory, something about him was *so* familiar.

"Hello? Diego?" Mari snapped.

"Ah, sorry, I'm still foggy," I said. My eyes returned to Sherwin.

"Why would he stab you?" Mari asked. She chewed on her nails again.

The yard was truly destroyed. Jack's square flower beds filled with flowers were torched. The garden gate was warped and the flower pots were smashed. None of the bushes except the one I was in survived. Jack had a metal bench in the center of her garden where her circle had been drawn. The stones of the circle were still there, but the bench had either been moved or blown away. It wasn't long ago that I'd first seen Jack in this garden, looking like she belonged more in my forests than in this world.

Falcon's words were coming back in bits and pieces. He stabbed me. He had a reason. He wouldn't attack unprovoked–

"I think Falcon was looking for Jack. Where is she?"

"We don't know where she is," Mari said. Her words were always so flat and emotionless, but the storm that raged in her was plain as day. They didn't know where Jack was?

"What?"

"We can't find her," Peony said. I wondered if she knew just how similar she was to Jack.

"I don't understand." My head throbbed. The heart link on my wrist was tight and Jack's heartbeat was steady–she was safe. I struggled to keep my eyes open, and I felt myself slipping forward before I could stop it. Firm arms held me steady, and it was Sherwin. He moved so fast, encasing me in an embrace before I face planted in the dirt again.

"*My king,*" he whispered in my mother tongue. The sound of my language jarred me back when our eyes met and he smiled. I knew him. *I knew him.* He winked and for a second, I could see the slight curve of his horns and remembered the color of his feathers. My friend, my true friend. My mind filled in all the missing pieces: the feathers on his arms, purple, not blue like mine, short, stout horns, the beard with irises braided into it, the golden rings on his eyebrow.

Sherwin. *Shēr-win.* The King's Shadow.

"Sherwin?"

His lips twitched up in a half smile; the Shadow answered simply, "Yep, that's me. Howdy." He lifted me easily, bringing me to my feet. Shēr-win was a titan of a Fae. He was the rock that I could lean against, and often did.

I hugged him.

"All good, bro, all good. You're alive, we got you," he said. *I won't say a word to them until you say so, my king,* his voice played softly in my head and I remembered the thousands of words said silently in court, in the forests, the towers, in lands faraway.

"Thank you," I said mostly to him, but I turned to Peony and Mari then. Mari *hmmmed* at me.

"You look like shit," she said.

"That's about how I feel. Have you checked Jack's hotel?" I asked. I ran my hands through my hair. It was tangled and also wet. My clothes clung to my skin, and now that I could really feel the rest of my body, I realized how disgusting I was.

"She wasn't answering her phone either," Mari said. She kicked at some rubble. I promised Jack I'd help her find any crystals that survived the fire; I wondered if Mari had already found a few.

"So that's a no?"

"We headed here first. We thought maybe she wanted to come by," Peony said. Sherwin was silent and hovered close to Peony. I'd never seen him smitten with anyone, but he was glowing around her. I tried not to let it sting that he was standing with her instead of me.

"And there's no sign of Falcon?"

"Nooope," Mari said. She rocked back on her heels, and I watched as her eyes scanned over the mess. Fire was a nasty spell. It was meant for the Creator to play with, and no one else. Jack's home was proof of that.

The twisting feeling in my gut wasn't just from the spell, it was Falcon himself too. He was gone. Jack was gone. I knew that meant nothing good for her. Falcon was not a man to give up on anything.

"We're gonna go to Jack's hotel and go up to her room. We can drop you off at yours," Peony said.

"What? I want to go too, Jack could be–"

"Diego, you need to change and get warmed up. Your hands are like ice, and you're shivering. If Falcon spelled you right after the fire, you've been laying out here for like eighteen hours straight. I'll keep you posted, but you have to get cleaned up. Can you walk?" Peony tucked her hair behind her ears, and Sherwin was already next to me, an arm looped around my waist, hoisting me up.

My knees gave out. I couldn't walk. I leaned heavily on Sherwin, and the concerned words from everyone were muted. Sherwin's grip tightened and the last thing I heard was my name before passing out again.

PEONY

Crisis mode was reactivated upon seeing Diego. He looked like death warmed over, and that was generous. The facts stated that: A. Both Jack and Falcon were missing; B. Falcon wounded Diego without the intent to cause permanent damage or death; And C. I was going to eviscerate Falcon when I got my hands on him.

Sherwin loaded Diego into the backseat of my car like he was weightless. His arms didn't bulge. His back was straight and strong. Practiced grace. That was it. His coy smile played on the corners of his lips and my insides melted. A little. Crisis mode overrode everything else, but Sherwin smiled and the bubble of panic eased. A little. His eyes were laser focused on me, and my cheeks heated. A little.

Diego's hotel was easy enough to find. I dug through his wallet and found a room key. Sandy Days Inn. It was an older hotel about three blocks from Jack's front door. I also happened to work there as a teenager and knew the owner. Cape Margaret was large and small—big enough to have some space, but close enough to know your neighbors and their gossip. And being the town's favorite witches had its perks. It took no magic at all for the clerk to give me Diego's room number. Sherwin hauled him into the elevator and plopped him on one of the beds. Diego was flat on his back, but he needed some help. I took his shoes off and covered him with a blanket. He needed to get out of those clothes and into the shower, but we hadn't reached the pants-removal level of acquaintanceship yet.

There were two beds. Two sets of things. Two small suitcases and backpacks. Diego's suitcase was obvious—black, sleek, practical. Falcon's was sky-blue and covered in stickers. Some peeling, some not. Same with the backpacks. One clean, boring black backpack, and another with five keychains hanging from every possible zipper.

What kind of man had a unicorn plushie keychain but would stab his seemingly best friend? What kind of man would try so hard to appear carefree and lock the main compartment of his backpack? There was a laptop on the desk, perfectly centered. Diego's. Chaos threw up on the other side of the desk. Falcon's. I opened Falcon's suitcase and saw the mess of clothes stuffed in it. Unfolded but laid on top of each other. Brighter colors, but still mostly neutral. Blue and green instead of gray and black.

"See anything?" Sherwin said.

"Not sure yet. Falcon didn't take his things. He didn't go far, if he went anywhere at all."

"You think he's still here?"

"I don't think I have enough information to make a decision." Sherwin kissed my forehead, and I left a note on the nightstand for Diego with my phone number and a promise to text him once I had been to Jack's hotel room.

Mari was in her own world by the time we got back to the car. Sherwin was quiet, but he was always sort of quiet. This was different though; intentional, purposeful silence. I used this tactic a lot when questioning a defendant. I didn't like having the tables turned. I could drown in this silence faster than the ocean could ever take me. Mari asked to be dropped back off at her place before we headed on, and I agreed. She needed to move and I needed stillness. Her thoughts were chaotic and loud, and mine were chaotic and quiet. We processed our disasters differently and found each other equally exhausting.

Jack's hotel was a few more blocks down; here at the beach, there were more hotels than houses, and this time of year was bleak for the hotel owners. Lots of vacancies until the Christmas Parades would start.

I didn't have to sweet talk anyone here because I knew exactly where Jack's room was. I booked it and got her checked in.

Sherwin held my hand like I would break, so I squeezed it. He squeezed it back. The hotel elevator took all of twenty seconds to get to the second floor, and within a minute we stood in Jack's room. I forced my emotions to stay in check. There were clear signs of a struggle. Jack wasn't the neatest person in the world, but she wouldn't leave her things on the floor. Or a towel on the bed. Or the lid off of her lotion.

My lips trembled and Sherwin hugged me from behind. I reached with my magic, looking for anything that would tell me where Jack was, but there was nothing. I felt the traces of her magic, green like life itself, and then it was just gone.

"Let's go to my place. Diego is going to be out for a while longer, and you need to not be here."

"I can't make a missing persons' report. It hasn't been long enough."

"Breathe counselor, let's take it one step at a time." Jack's phone was still plugged into the charger. She wouldn't leave willingly without it.

"Come on, I don't think we're gonna find anything else here."

We left in silence. Rode to Sherwin's apartment in silence. Climbed the stairs in silence. He unlocked the front door and took my coat in silence. I sank into one of the barstools and he immediately went to the kitchen, starting to cook something. Sherwin liked his hands to be busy. It took me a second to realize that he had made a place for me here already. Space on the coat rack. Two mugs on his breakfast bar. Another blanket on the couch where there had been one before.

"Sherwin?"

"Peony." My insides got a little mushy every time he said my name, like a blessing, reverent and a little too steamy to be decent.

"I don't think we are going to find Jack," I whispered. It was an admission; forever I pulled the truth from others' lips with my magic, while I held every one of my thoughts as closely as I could. Sherwin worked his own kind of magic to pull them from me.

"Hey, no, don't go down that road. We are going to find her. How far could she have gone? Like no shade, but Jack isn't what I'd call wildlife friendly. She isn't going to just vanish."

I smiled, and realized how little he knew about my sister. Jack was more than wildlife friendly. She *was* wildlife. She would fall in love with trees. She befriended every animal she ever met, including a freaking black bear, and had no fear of them. We would go to the zoo as kids and the animals would try to reach her from their enclosures. Jack cried and cried, telling me and Mama that she could hear them asking her to be their friend. She wandered through this world like a tourist instead of a native, and it always sent my panic to record highs.

"Yes, yes she would."

"So, what are you thinking? We put up lost posters and hope for the best?" He was joking, but he wanted me to spill my thoughts, and I couldn't help myself.

"Falcon has her. That's the only conclusion, and what Diego didn't want to believe." I searched through my bag and grabbed my antacids. I crunched them up quickly, the chalky tablets drying my mouth out for the thousandth time.

"Can you take me back to Diego's hotel?"

"Yep. Do you want some food first?"

I really did; I didn't sleep all night, I was starving and thirsty and tired, but the thought of food made me feel sick.

"No, I'm good," I said. Sherwin slid his hands up my arms, around my shoulders, and pulled me into a hug. He messed my hair up and nuzzled against my cheek. I felt safe and seen in his arms. It was exhilarating that someone looked close enough to see me and my instinct told me to cut and run, so I hugged him tighter.

"Liar," he said as he kissed my ear.

DIEGO

This was the third time I'd woken up this day. I assumed it was the same day. The morning was foggy but I remembered seeing Peony, Mari, and Sherwin. I glanced out the window and the sun was higher in the sky. Now I'm back in my hotel room alone laying on Falcon's bed, instead of my own, with jeans that were stiffer than stone still on. I could sit up easier this time; the spell and poison must have finally run its course. My shoes were by the door, but I don't remember taking them off. Or getting a blanket.

I rolled my shoulders, cracked my neck, and peeled out of my stiff, dirty clothes. Turning on the shower, I grabbed some fresh clothes and saw my reflection in the mirror before the steam filled the small bathroom. My human face really was like my true face; maybe a little slimmer from the years, but the same nose, same eyes. My facial hair here was a little darker, coarser, but not altogether different.

I was still me.

Hornless, featherless, and homeless, but still me. The water from the shower beat on my back, scalding hot, but my nerves weren't fully awake yet to notice. My palms were red from the heat. The heart link charms glowed, and I wondered if I had imagined it. The magic swelled in the slim bracelet, and for a second I felt like Jack was standing there with me. The water ran down my face and into my eyes, but it felt like Jack was there.

Her heartbeat ricocheted through my arm, and her heart rate climbed quickly. Her panic became my panic through the link, and I couldn't do a damn thing to help her. She wasn't here. Her magic was faint and only noticeable because of the link. Falcon's magic wasn't around either. I could always feel exactly where Falcon was, but now he was gone too. How far had he gone for me to not feel my best friend?

"Diego, can you hear me? Please, Diego, I'm so sorry—"

Jack's voice unfolded in my mind, and I tried to really listen. She was so distant, so far away that it was hardly a whisper. But I heard it. I heard her!

"I tried to stop her, I'm sorry—"

"Jack? I'm here," I whispered to the shower walls. I ran my fingers down the glass door, like she was there to feel it. The pull of her magic, like when she would call to me before we met, sucked at me. My eyes got heavy, blackness tinting my sight, and I held on to the wall as her magic wrapped itself around me. Was this what visions were like for Jack? I saw Jack in some other hotel room. Falcon hovering behind her. Blinding light. The tug in my belly that came from falling, and I saw Jack falling through the sky. Her arms were outreached with my name on her lips as she slipped farther and farther away from me.

Then the vision shifted again. Bare feet and bare legs, she stood in the center of a field that was smoldering, just like her home. Trees moaned and everything was charred and black and crumbling. She turned then, looking straight at me and her lips trembled. Jack pushed the hair out of her face and hid behind her hands.

"I tried to stop her, Diego."

The forest was gone. Falcon was just barely in view, head bowed. Jack's magic scratched at the inside of my head, forcing me to look around a little more, to see what she was seeing.

The castle in the distance.

I didn't need to look any further.

Jack Hawthorne was in Trellis, whatever was left of it.

"Stay with me, my Blossom. Stay—" The words never left my mouth. They were lost in my throat, unable to find their way out, just like Jack stuck in Trellis. I hung my head in the shower, letting the water hide the tears I knew were coming.

"I can't hold this much magic. Diego—"

The hot water had lost its heat. I stood there letting the hum of the shower echo around me while the grip of Jack's spell released itself. Her voice disappeared to the lull of the water until I heard her cry out again.

"Bring me home."

"I will, I promise." I pounded my fist on the wall, knowing I had just lied to her. My newly formed heart broke a little; I had no way to bring her back to the Earth.

Chapter Three

JACK

Being in Obius was giving me a magic high. My magic flirted with my thoughts, willing me to cast more and more and more. I didn't. The magic would be too joyful, too light when the forest deserved my sorrow. White, searing anger coursed through me as we made our way through the forest. The forest grieved and I wanted to grieve with it. Someone had to. I wanted it to be me.

Falcon desperately tried to calm my rage, mostly so I wouldn't blow a magical fuse, but he did have a valid point: what good would hunting down Snapdragon do if I accidentally did more damage to the forest? Magic here was reactive. Every spell was like the world tried to suck the magic out of you, and the more you fed into that feeling–the power of it–the more it wanted. The land felt dead, not just because Snapdragon fried it, but there was nearly no magic. Except for us.

In a moment of weakness, I called for Diego. I knew the heart link had us bound together, but I didn't think it would *work*. The link between Obius and Earth was essentially nonexistent, but the heart link didn't care about that. It was tied to souls, to magic, and it wouldn't stop until the souls could touch again.

So I pushed my magic, calling for Diego, and he heard me.

His voice was sweet and featherlike, feeling like drops of water on my face, but he *heard* me. For a second I thought that I saw him, standing in the rain with water pouring down his face.

Obius *liked* my magic, so that probably helped. The land was dying and my magic must have felt like a lifeline.

"Stay with me," he pleaded, and my heart ached. I couldn't stay with him. In all likelihood, I'd never see his face again–

Nope. Not going down the road. I wanted to go home, but I didn't *have* a home anymore. I shook the tears from my eyes, clearing my head and my throat, and focused on the task at hand.

Pants. Shoes.

Falcon was kind enough to give me his sweater. It was huge on me, but my legs were cold, and my feet were sore. I tied leaves to the bottoms of my feet with vines like I was on some survival show. It sucked, for the record. Do not recommend leaf shoes.

My staff floated and bobbed in the air next to me, like it enjoyed being around so much energy. It reminded me of Puddin, how she would float and dance in the air when she was really happy. Falcon marched along, close but out of reach, and stayed mostly silent. His thoughts here played through my mind easily and loudly.

She's just as crazy as the dead one.

D sure can pick 'em, that's for damn sure.

Why would the scales be balanced now?

When's the Judge gonna speak to me again? Is she angry? How do I apologize to a goddess?

Jack's gonna kill me, prolly.

At least I won't die a murderer, that has to count for something.

"Care to share what's on your mind?" I asked, rubbing my temples. His thoughts were so *loud*.

"Huh? Oh, me? Nothing. Just wondering if moss still grows on the north side of a tree here and if that means literally anything at all." He flashed a smile, and turned back to walking through the ruined forest.

"I can hear everything you're thinking. Loudly."

"Well, honestly, that's just rude. You're worse than a peeping tom." *Fuck. Me.* He cracked his neck and stopped.

"I'd really rather not. Not really my type." This time I flashed a smile and he cackled. The head-back laughter that always seemed a little unhinged.

"Same," he said. Falcon tugged at the bandana tied to his arm, and it drew my attention. The bandana itself was old and a little threadbare. Red, paisley. Classic bandana print. The tattoo of the scales on his arm was indeed balanced again.

"Look," he started.

"You don't have to tell me anything you don't want to." I did mean that, mostly because I would hear the unabridged version regardless of his preferences, but it sounded polite at least.

"I don't regret it." Falcon grabbed a stick and drew a circle around himself. It was flawless; no bumps or uneven spots. He dropped the stick and closed his eyes, but the stick moved on its own. The sigil for the Judge appeared in the center of the circle, and he held his hands at his heart, like he was praying. Maybe he was.

"You don't regret booting us here?"

"I don't regret choosing not to hurt you."

"I don't understand. I *told* you–"

"–what you think I'd wanna hear. Try listening now and hear what I have to really say. What I *really* did say."

The circle lit up gold with the sigil shining bright, and I tapped into the spell. I touched the lines of the circle, and Falcon's memories came to me fast. I saw his birth, the death of his mother, the absence of a father, I saw Abuela holding him gently and another woman that sort of favored him drawing sigils on his face. I saw him fighting, getting his ass beaten, I saw a city full of life and lights, and then Diego. They stood on a busy street together, little shops and vendors lining the way. It was dusk and I could smell the smoke from the cigarette between Diego's lips. He was grinning, easy and vicious, and the sound of his laugh filled my chest until I thought I would burst from holding it all in. They talked–I couldn't hear the words, was it English?–and Diego was different. His energy didn't feel like sorrow, but danger. He was dangerous. This was a man I would be afraid of on the street. His eyes were dark, not golden, and he posed himself like a predator. Falcon too. They meshed together, two sides of the same coin, and I felt the roots between them. I saw them running, some kind of boat blowing up, and Diego howling with laughter. The energy there was incredible, and I remembered Diego telling me about his time in Rio de Janeiro and how much he loved it. He didn't mention the boat or how Falcon's eyes lit up just like his, but I saw it all here.

Falcon laid his life's story bare before me.

I saw him stroking a man's face, his thumb caressing their bottom lip. I saw them kiss and felt Falcon falling in love for the first time, and I saw Falcon kissing a small Asian woman, and someone with long, blond hair. I felt the love he had for all of them, and how deeply his love ran. I felt his love for Diego, and then I saw him crying and begging in his car. I saw him sitting on Mari's couch, eating popcorn and pizza, and them laughing together. His vision was rosy and warm when he looked at her, and the same feelings filled me too. Falcon rubbed tears from his face and he pleaded–for mercy, mercy for me. The command to kill burned through every part of him, and he agreed. It all stopped them, and the relief that washed over me—us—was immediate. The scales tipped further and further when he *did* try to kill me, but now they were balanced, and he was lost.

Falcon closed the circle then and waited. He didn't leave the circle, knowing that it was now a stronghold for him, a place of safety. He just waited for me to leave his thoughts, to release him.

"I'm sorry," I said. I didn't mean to look so deep, to dig through every little detail of him, but he offered, and my magic responded in kind.

"Don't be. I'm not asking for it and I'm not apologizing. I'm just sharing."

"Are you in love with Diego?"

"Loaded question there, Lefty. Love is a complicated thing," he said. I thought of all the kisses he let me see, and the genuine affection for Diego. The warmth around his memories of Mari, and what that could mean.

"Indeed," I laughed. Falcon stayed in his circle, and I kept my distance.

"I'm not interested in D the way you are, but he's my family. And I love him more than I think you could ever really get." I held my hand out to him in a truce. Falcon hesitated, stepping outside of his circle before he accepted and shook my hand. My staff lit up bright gold, the same color as the circle that he held. Harold was opening up to Falcon too.

"Truce?"

"Truce." His smile was real this time; not so large, not so many teeth, and really reaching his eyes. This was the look I saw in his memories, with Diego. He slung an arm around my shoulders, and his weight nearly toppled me over. He caught my arm before I really stumbled and chuckled. "This is why I'm gonna call you Lefty. Girlfriend can cast some badass magic, see the future, see across the worlds, but can't stop tripping over *her own damn feet.*"

"I'm not *that* clumsy!"

"Whatever you say, Lefty."

Falcon tried to put the walls of his mind back up like he had on Earth, but they'd never hold here in Obius. I tried my best to allow him his privacy after letting me dig through his memories, but my magic was fully alive here. Energy crackled in the crystal ball, and the galaxy of stars I'd see in it now felt even more expansive. If I were to scry here I'd never find my way back to my body with that many stars to touch.

He let go of me, and the physical distance helped me create more mental distance too. Falcon's wall spells were back up in full force and instead of it feeling like fish netting to hide his thoughts, it was more like a chiffon curtain between me and his emotions.

A glimpse of color caught my eye.

Magic.

Life.

Emerald green eyes. Emerald skin. A gown fit for a queen if it wasn't ripped and singed. Wild, messy vines. Leaves and dying blooms down arms.

"Who the fu–"

"Snapdragon," I hissed. Enough rage scorched through my heart that I could have burned the forest again, if there was anything left to burn. Falcon grabbed my arm, pulling me back. My feet were already going. The staff responded in kind–all of the electricity that flowed through my human body was magnified in the crystal. It blistered with energy; sparks flew from it and Falcon jumped back. The staff spun in front of me, fast enough that it felt like I was looking at her through fan blades.

"Bring that magic down, Jack. Don't start something you can't finish," he said.

Snapdragon smiled, her own staff hovering beside her. It didn't spin like mine, but that was about the only difference. The branches looked the same. She had a few more charms hanging from it. The magic in her crystal glittered green, emerald green, the same tone as everything else about her.

"It's her," I said more to myself than anyone else. She held her chin up, defiant and daring.

"That's D's girl? Not quite what I was imagining," Falcon said. His words made the rage in my staff snap and spit. *His* girl.

"Not anymore."

Snapdragon was only yards away from me. Close enough that I could see every detail on her face, far enough that I couldn't strangle her with my bare hands.

"Welcome to Trellis, False One."

Falcon's wall spells fell then, and I lost my focus on Snapdragon.

False One. False One? False One! Fuuuuuck.

One glance away and she was gone. Falcon flinched, the walls of his mind trying to rebuild themselves as quickly as he could cast. I searched the area, running between the tree stumps and husks, climbing over the debris of the forest, digging through the ashes.

Snapdragon was gone.

SNAPDRAGON

She really was here. I felt the shift between the realms, the opening and the surge of magic that came with it. She was nothing to laugh at; her magic responded like it was born of Obius. Jack Hawthorne.

I saw the heart link on her wrist. Who was she tied to? Whose life path was linked to hers? My leaves curled into themselves, causing the delicate veins to crack. As my foliage crumbled, I snarled.

I *knew* the answer.

My human messenger boy stood next to her like some faithful dog. His magic was dark, dark green. What power must lie in those pious veins. He prayed in such earnest to his Goddess, but She didn't listen to him. They never listened to anyone.

But I did.

I tuned my attention to the Earth to look for Deign, to look for another link. I did so in secret, sometimes even hiding it from myself. *Don't look for him*, I'd curse myself. He was gone. This was what I wanted: the throne of Trellis, the jewel of Obius. And it was mine. The Seer had turned Her back to us, but I'd never abandon my people the way that Deign and the Goddess did so easily.

I'd see it destroyed before I handed the reins back to anyone. Especially *her*.

Jack's magic was unwieldy and untamed. She didn't know how to control the endless fount of energy that was buried deep in Obius. This was the realm of magic. All magic came from here, and she was walking through these plains like it wouldn't consume her.

She was right about that; the land wouldn't consume her before I did. She stomped around, looking for where I went.

I found a tree with enough strength in its branches still, and I hid there, just watching. She was a child. She stomped around, a child having a temper tantrum. From my vantage point, I could see how deeply Wildfire had ravaged the forest. It was burnt all the way to the lake in the west, all the way to the market center in the east, and south to the castle walls. The walls I used had protected very little of the forest now that I could see it from up high. I saw the rock that I liked to meditate on by the lake.

Once I had taken as much of Jack's magic as I could from her, I'd pull her soul apart and revive the forests. Death magic was beautiful, really. As a Priestess, I sent souls to rest eternally in Sanctum. And with death magic, I could push and pull the soul wherever I wanted it to go, however twisted or intact that I decided it could remain. Death magic was never used by a Priestess; why send all of that magic to rest when I could bend it to my will?

The messenger boy would be great fuel for the forest too, his magic was ancient and pious. The trees would love him, and it would be a lovely gift for their sacrifice.

The tree I hid in rustled its leaves, trying to shrug me off.

"Don't make me burn you too," I growled. The tree stopped moving, and Jack had lost all sense of where I'd gone, so I took that chance to leave.

I'd felt something else when Jack pried open the links between the worlds.

Deign.

I heard him cast the Shattering again before then, but now I could see that his heart was stronger. His magic shone through the links.

I knew my next destination.

Trellis Castle. I had something to retrieve there. Going back to the castle was going to be an ordeal. Arturo had the Trellian Guard on alert looking for me. They had to be shaken by Wildfire, so I could use that as my opening to slip back into the castle. I needed to get to my rooms.

Arturo would sense the moment I entered the castle which would be an obstacle. I wouldn't cast Wildfire in the castle; there would be too much damage. The tree shook its branches and I lost my grip. I slipped but hit the ground easily. As a tree nymph, I was light on my feet, even when surprised. As I connected with the ground, my toes tried to take root in the soft soil. It had been so long since I had let my roots grow again, but this wasn't the season for me to take root.

I needed to get back to the castle, to my chambers. My tower was divided into several specified areas. After the Shattering, I moved myself from the lower bedroom to the one at the top of the tower; I couldn't sleep in the bed that Deign would visit me in. He'd sneak up into my tower, my *forbidden* tower, and spend the nights with me. Deign would wake early and return to the central tower. He'd pretend that no one noticed, but our little affair was the talk of the castle.

It took nearly a hundred years before I could walk by that room and not feel the sting of tears in my eyes.

Jack and the messenger boy had wandered off in the same direction as the castle. It was hard to miss now, especially without the cover of the forest. The three towers loomed over me. The flag on the central tower was tattered. I couldn't make out the emblem anymore. I was about a day's walk out from the castle now, less if I really moved quickly.

A vine curled around my ankle and I stooped down to unhinge it from me. The vine curled around my fingers instead, looking for magic to revive it. It was a survivor; Wildfire didn't kill it off completely, and now it was looking for any scrap of magic it could find. I ground the vine into the dirt. Its small leaves ripped under my foot, and I pushed harder until the vine snapped.

I needed every fragment of magic I could find.

Chapter Four

MARI

Thud. Thud. Thud.

I banged my head against the steering wheel of my car. It was an old coupe that was once a bright blue; it was sorta sky blue now. Spring sky, not a summer one. Puddin was in the passenger seat, curled up, pretending to be a house cat. The end of her tail flicked, and I just knew she had something to say.

"Out with it," I said.

"This is a terrible idea," the cat said.

"That's why I brought you as backup."

I was parked outside of an old thrift store. It was the wrong day for the traveling crystal markets, but my gut said that she would be here, and that was enough for me. Abuela reminded me constantly to listen to the wind. Well, I was done listening. It was going to be *her* turn to listen. I rubbed my hands down the steering wheel and little sparks came off of my fingers.

"Are you going to talk about that too?" Puddin purred.

"Nope."

I saw her little table set up near the entrance of the store. Normally, Abuela was set up in the parking lot, but not today. It wasn't a weekend or an afternoon. It was lunch time, the store was full, and Abuela was making small talk with a lady holding a poodle.

We waited. Puddin walked beside me. She meowed and rubbed against my leg, trying to really sell the house cat act, and it made me antsy.

Don't think about that, girl. Stay focused before you light something on fire.

Before I got halfway through the parking lot, Abuela made eye contact with me. Her eyes were cold and unfamiliar, and the barrier spells she had around her would have kept a Goddess out. Raising my hands in mock surrender, I walked up to her table. She was all smiles and I hated it. A spark escaped from my fingers, and I balled my fists. Of course she noticed. Her eyes darted fast, but I saw them trace a line from my face to my hands.

"Hi, Abuela," I said. Puddin curled in and out of my legs, gentle healing and warmth spells lacing through me. I noticed the protection spell that knitted its way around us too, but she purred louder, bringing attention to the warmth she provided.

Any warmer and I was going to ignite myself.

"Marigold, so good to see you." She tucked her hands in her pockets, and that hurt. No hug. No outstretched arms. My throat felt like it was closing in on itself so I grinned back at her. I wanted to shove my hands in my pockets, but I was worried they would catch fire.

"Why did you leave?"

"What do you mean?"

The fire in my belly was about to burst. No amount of calming spells would get the fire to stop at this point. I remembered the anger in her eyes when she attacked us, when we tried to seal her magic, and when she finally left. She teleported, just like Puddin. I'd never seen her do that; I'd never seen anyone other than Puddin have that magic.

"Do you want a play-by-play?"

"Marigold, we are not doing this. Why are you here?"

"Why *aren't* you here!"

"Because Snapdragon had her claws in me, and I would have killed you all if I hadn't left."

"And you–"

"Stayed away, because I want no part of that nightmare that you've raised." There was no magic in her words, but they cut through me nonetheless.

"Mari," Puddin said, low and laden with a purr. She'd rather not draw attention to herself, but needed me to focus on anything else. My hands were smoking.

"What have you done now, child?"

"What are you talking about?"

"I have nothing left for you. Figure it out on your own." Abuela practically spat at me. There would be no basket of empanadas today.

"Jack's missing," I blurted out because everything always led back to her. Abuela stopped. She closed her eyes and sighed. Puddin growled low in her throat, and I scooped her up. I needed my hands to do something, something that would force the sparks to calm.

"Falcon too," I added.

"Falcon is gone?"

I tried my best not to let her words hurt. Puddin's claws dug into my hand a little to ground me back.

"Yep," I popped the *-p*, making the word feel pointier than it was.

"Leave. I need to think," she said.

"Abuela, why are you shutting me out?" The wind picked up then, breezing through her wind chimes and overturning the packaged bracelets and peace spells displayed on the table.

"Child," she had the decency to look a little pained, "it's time for you to go."

"So you won't tell me *anything!* I don't understand–"

"Mari, let's go." Puddin spoke clearly, and Abuela didn't even glance at her. Abuela grabbed my arm, and I flinched. Her grip was painful, and her eyes were emerald green again.

"Take this and go." Abuela handed me another amber stone, but it was small and already cracked.

She let go of my arm, went back to her chilling smile, and I left before she could see me cry.

PEONY

Sherwin drove my car now, whenever we were together. Which was a lot. As soon as I was in Cape Margaret, I found myself in his arms, in his space, and not wanting to leave. We arrived at Diego's hotel in minutes. This part of town–our part–was small. The boardwalk was not huge, but the temperature was too low for me to want to walk anywhere. Sherwin held my hand as he easily maneuvered around all of the parking lots, narrow roads, and jaywalkers.

Diego loitered in the lobby when we walked in, Sherwin and I still hand in hand. He paced back and forth. He'd walk in little circles from the little seating area to the elevator, then back, and back again. The bracelet that Jack gave him was still on his arm. He touched it constantly, and I studied him. Sherwin stayed back, just slightly behind me, letting me lead. I liked that–I didn't have to ask for the lead, he just assumed I would take the reins.

Not having to fight for my independence made me want to give it all to hi
m.

After the fire, I picked this hotel because it was only three blocks from
Mari. Jack needed an anchor, and while I wanted it to be me, her truest
source of calm was Mari. Sherwin nodded a quick hello to Diego, and it
struck me as odd. It was a *nod*. Deferential, courteous. Subservient. Diego
smiled back at him, quick and tight as if I didn't see it, and then gently
bowed his head to me. Also deferential, courteous, but not acknowledging
that his place was below me. Which, I supposed, was true. He was a king in
Trellis, but here he was just a man. Sherwin stepped a little closer to me, his
hand on the small of my back–maybe a little lower, honestly–and I leaned
into his touch.

Diego's shoulders were up to his ears as he paced. He didn't stop when
he saw us, and just continued in his little circle.

"I wanted to go to her hotel, but then I realized that I didn't know which
one it was. I was going to just start checking them all. I asked here but they
wouldn't answer my questions because why would they? I'm no one to
her," his words trailed off. Diego ran his hands through his hair a few times
before looping them together at the base of his neck.

I followed his eyes as they searched the lobby, glancing at the outdated
magazines, to the ceiling, to the ugly carpets, trying so hard not to look at
us. When he finally stilled for a minute, the magic that rolled off him was
suffocating. Jack mentioned a heaviness to being around him, like there
was a black hole in him where his heart should have been.

"We came here first to grab you so you could come with us," Sherwin
said. Diego was pointedly keeping his eyes closed and turned his body away.
I touched his arm, and he jumped.

"Diego? Are you okay now? Feeling a little more like yourself?" I kept my
tone as gentle as I could manage. He needed softer words than Jack did; her

heart was so fragile, but Diego was already fractured. Anything too harsh and he might shatter completely.

He swallowed hard, his Adam's apple bobbing painfully slow. His eyes were still closed, and when he opened them, I saw why.

Magic.

His dark eyes were glowing gold, and he wobbled a bit on his feet.

"Th-they're in Obius. Trellis. My home. And I can't reach her. She's trapped there and it's my fault–"

He blinked the magic back, but only just. "It's not your fault, Diego," Sherwin said. It was a simple declaration. Diego shook his head, disagreeing, and Sherwin held a hand up. Diego stopped mid-shake.

Familiarity. That's what I noticed between them. Sherwin was still just slightly behind me, not quite edging forward around me. Diego was laser focused on him, on listening to his words, and I wondered who could hold a King's attention like that.

"Sher?"

"Peony," he said. His voice was liquid gold in my ears. It was my turn to be laser focused. I refused to use my magic on him. I refused to force any truths from his mouth that he didn't want to give.

I took in the details of his face. The scruff on his dimpled chin, thin nose and full, pink lips. His perpetually sun-tanned skin gave him a couple of extra wrinkles around his eyes that only made them more enticing to look at. His hair was surfer blond and waved, just barely to his ears.

I touched his face, reminding myself that he was real. "Tell me who you are?"

He smiled, stole a quick glance at Diego, and I already knew then. Fae. Of course. How could a man be this perfect?

"I'm just me, Pea," he tucked my hair around my ear.

"You're Fae?"

He grinned. "I am."

"And you know Diego, don't you? From Obius? You knew him there."

"Yes." Sherwin turned to Diego then. I tried not to be offended; there was more to their story than I had the rights to, but I wanted to know.

"Sherwin, tell her the truth," Diego said. He smiled and hugged Sherwin. Really hugged. Diego's fingers were digging into his shoulder, and Sherwin let go of him, grinning wildly. I missed feeling like I could hug Mari and Jack like that, like I was holding onto the other pieces of my heart.

"Pea, I was part of Deign's court. I was called the King's Shadow. We were always together. After the Shattering, I leapt through the links before they fully broke. I was going to find him, but I never did. Until now, anyway." His smile was so large it looked painful. My lips felt like they were cracking just watching him. I tried to picture them as kids, as having a whole other life that didn't begin here on Earth.

"Please forgive him for keeping this from you, Peony. I don't think he was intentionally hiding anything–"

"I understand, it's a lot to unload on you." Sherwin smoothed my forehead with his thumbs, trying to get my eyebrows to relax. I unbunched my face, but my nerves weren't settled. I listened for hints that the words he spoke so easily, so softly when we were alone, were all true.

"I know what you're thinking, Peony, but it's real. The only magic happening here is chemistry. I swear."

I searched his eyes, using as much of my magic as I could, and he let me. Of course he did. Sherwin would let me do anything that I wanted, and he stayed put as I pushed through everything.

I found only truths in his eyes and on his lips, but I didn't feel the knot in my stomach fully release.

Diego cleared his throat, politely trying not to look at us. He was truly the most awkward man I'd met. "Was he like this in Trellis?" I asked.

"Worse," Sherwin said and Diego laughed, loud and brisk. He threaded our fingers together, and I searched his face for the truth. Sherwin promised he wouldn't lie to me, he promised me the world with each little touch, and I wanted to believe him. So I did.

"Let's go to Jack's. Maybe we'll find something there," I said. Sherwin squeezed my hand a little, nodded to Diego—was this going to be a thing now?—and we were off.

DIEGO

It took longer to get into the car and out of the parking lot than it did to get to Jack's hotel. Heart of the Sea Inn. The building was reddish with an ocean mural on the side. Nothing about this place reminded me of Jack. Her essence was green, not the harsh tones of this place. Peony led the way into the lobby, waved at the clerk, and pushed the button for the elevator.

"She was within walking distance to me," I said.

"Well technically, but you were passed out in the bushes," Sherwin said. Peony elbowed him in the ribs, and I tried to imagine how that scene would have played out in the castle. No one was brazen enough to rebuke the Shadow, not even me. Sherwin's job was to keep me in line and keep me safe. That usually involved a lot of glaring before I said too much.

The elevator dinged, opening its doors, and I felt like I was walking to my execution. She wasn't going to be there. The room would be a mess. Falcon wouldn't magically appear either. The room would only tell us that I wasn't there to help her.

Room 215.

The door was closed. Peony unlocked the door and my heart sank.

The room was wrecked. There were scorch marks on the carpet. The lamp was on the floor. Towels on the floor. Jack's bags of clothes were untouched. The bathroom door was open, and her toothpaste didn't have the cap on it. The mirror was cracked too.

I walked around the room and stopped at the burnt carpet. Traces of her magic lingered in the air, and I could still smell Falcon's magic. Did he use the same poison on her that he did me? Maybe she got the jump on him—

The marks drew my attention again; Sherwin and Peony were chattering on, but their words were muted. The marks on the carpet were familiar. I got down on my knees and looked closer; they were sigils.

The binding spell.

Falcon and Jack opened the link to Obius here in this damn hotel room. He amped up her magic, and she was able to tie a link close enough together to wedge it open. The sigils repeated themselves over and over in a larger pattern: the symbol for binding. Two lines interweaving. It was sharper, more jagged than it should be, but that came from the intensity of the spell.

"Sherwin, do you recognize this?" I asked. Sherwin kneeled and scratched at the marks. I saw the flicker of a memory in his eyes. He knew it too.

"Yeah. Binding spell. Did they really—"

"Yes, Jack and Falcon are in Obius." The door to the room opened then, and for a second I hoped that it was Jack, but then Mari and Puddin stepped into the room. Everyone was silent, and I wondered if they heard me. Peony dug through her purse and put some medicine in her mouth.

"Obius. As in, the magic realm. As in, the place that *we can't get to because you shattered the links*?" she asked. Peony's voice was deadly.

"Well Pea, there has to be some links still there. Between Snapdragon's shenanigans and now Jack's, there has to be something that we're missing." Sherwin inspected the markings too, and nodded. "You know, I've heard rumors over the years that there's some spell books that have all of the old magic in them. Like, pre-shattering Obius shit."

"Where would we even find one?" Mari asked.

"We don't need one," I said. Everyone looked at me, Puddin's tail flicking back and forth. A warning or a challenge, I couldn't tell and didn't care.

"What do you mean?" Peony asked.

"I know the spell, but I don't have enough magic to cast it."

"So we need... what exactly?" Peony tied her hair up in a bun, the pink ends of her hair hidden enough that it was like staring at Jack.

"I need another piece of my heart. Ideally, I need it to be bound *to* me, but without Jack, that isn't possible."

"How many pieces do you have?" Sherwin asked. This was something that I didn't enjoy talking about. My heart was shattered into nine pieces, and from what I understand, some of them are in the other realms, Obius and Sanctum. I didn't want the number known. I didn't want anyone to have that power over me, to see how frail I had become, how easily overwhelmed I could be. Sherwin likely knew, but I didn't need to be specific. Not even a Shadow knows everything. He folded his hands behind his head, pointedly not looking at me, and I felt the urge to spill the truth to him.

"Two," I said. Partial truth. Enough. Sherwin nodded, satisfied with my response. Only seven more pieces until I was whole again.

"And we have no leads on any other pieces?" Mari asked.

"I was hoping the psychic would have more insights," I said. Mari plopped down on Jack's bed and hugged a pillow.

"So we're back to square one?" she asked.

"Maybe not. I've got an idea," Peony said.

Chapter Five

FALCON

Jack was vibing at a twelve on a ten point scale. Her magic was wild; it roared in her eyes like a flashbang, shaking her body like the impact of the blast hit her. It was too strong for her to control, and her emotions wrecked what little control she did have. I cast every calming, soothing spell on her that I could think of, while still maintaining my shields. It wasn't that I thought she would actively, purposefully try to kill me; it was more that she could lash out and not realize how strong the magic was.

Now Jack was struggling to get the staff under control. A lightning storm ignited in the crystal, and every thought and emotion she felt made the storm stronger.

"Look, I know this is the worst thing to say to someone upset, but you *have* to calm down. You're gonna light one of us on fire, and it's prolly gonna be me. And I have to say, not really lovin' that plan."

"I let her get away!"

"No, she just bounced, Lefty. Like, I couldn't even keep track of her, and I've been doing this shit a lot longer than you. It's not your fault. None of this is." I gestured to the forest. We'd been walking toward the castle spires for hours now, through nothing but a ravaged landscape. The fire took no mercy on the trees and Jack took no mercy on herself.

"I want to contact Diego again," she whispered.

"Didn't that, like, wipe you out?"

"I think seeing Snapdragon in person wiped me out more than Diego did."

Seeing Snapdragon shook me to the core too. Her voice was familiar. I'd heard it and mistook it for a Goddess. How could I have been so easily fooled? The intensity of her voice in my mind was nothing like I'd ever experienced. I'd never heard of anyone being able to direct thoughts like that. Did I imagine the whole thing? Bitterness flooded my mouth, flooded my senses, until I couldn't see straight.

"Falcon, you didn't imagine her. She... she just manipulated you. She manipulated Diego too. Her magic is fading, just like the rest of the world here. Can't you feel how lifeless it is here?" Jack put her hands on my arm, right where the scale tattoo was. The edge peaked out from one of her hands, and I could tell it was still balanced. It stayed balanced with her.

"I thought we talked about mental privacy?"

"It's hard when you're standing next to me and your thoughts are practically screaming," she laughed and released my arm.

"I really am sorry," I said. I wasn't great at this. I spent so much of my childhood apologizing for existing that I just stopped altogether once I grew up. The muscle memory wasn't great anymore.

"I know. Snapdragon was the one forcing you to attack me, wasn't she?" I nodded. Snapdragon forced my hands to wrap themselves around Jack's neck and squeeze. I flexed my fingers without thinking, and Jack held my hand.

"So you're gonna try to reach Diego again? What can I do to help?" I stepped away. I needed to be disconnected from her. The walls in my mind needed to reknit themselves together. Jack seemed to realize this too and started drawing a circle in the dirt.

"Yep. I'm going to cast a Full Circle to contain the magic. I wasn't really trying last time, so now that I am, I think it might be a little more intense."

"Say no more, girl. I'm gonna start adding some layers." The Cube. It was the best containment spell I knew, and it saved our butts before.

The Cube here was more like a fortress. It built itself within seconds of me starting the dance. Dance was an exaggeration. It was tracing and guiding the magic to follow sigils with your body. Were they even called sigils here? They were just words here, the language of Obius.

Jack was encircled in magic. Her eyes were emerald green again, and for a second, she really *did* look like Snapdragon. The magic radiating out of her was blinding. The Cube dulled the glow, but only just. Her staff spun at her side.

The wind picked up, and it ruffled the edges of her t-shirt nightgown. Her hair had slipped out of her bun, and she hugged the bracelet to her chest. I hoped it worked. And I hoped Diego wasn't still out of it from whatever the hell was in that syringe I dosed him with. Didn't feel great about that either, but I needed D out of the way. I knew he would try to stop me.

Now I wished that he had.

Jack was in a whirlwind of magic. Her eyes were still open, still emerald green, but far away.

A growl caught my attention, and I shifted. There were no trees around for cover, but something was prowling. The growls were low and deep. Movement to the left and I reached for my knife. You never knew how magic would affect someone, but everything bleeds. I twirled the knife through my fingers, a skill I'd done a thousand times before, getting my fingers loose and my hands nimble.

"Don't worry, Lefty, I got this," I said. My words wouldn't reach her through the layers and layers of magic, but I knew that I meant them. Nothing would get through. The cube held out, and I stepped outside of i
t.

A beast stood at the top of a small hill in the distance. It was red. Vaguely wolf-like. Too big for a wolf; if it was this massive in the distance, it would be hell up close. I braced myself, keeping my eyes trained on the dog-like creature.

Nothing gets through, I repeated like a mantra.

The sigil on my arm stung a little; I got it when I was a kid, shortly after my seventh birthday. I didn't know what it was. I'd looked, but as far as I knew, it was unique to me. It wasn't a tattoo–more like a brand. Nana used some spell to sear it into my skin. Sounds worse than it was; it felt like a bee sting, and lasted about as long. It was about two inches long, with lots of curling pieces.

"Don't you worry, my boy. This will keep the well of magic ever-burning in you. You are special, Falcon, never forget that."

I didn't need artifacts like other alchemists because of it, which was quite handy, I had to admit. It just stung when I was casting something heavy, like holding a Cube while focusing on the beast in front of me.

The creature brayed, the sound echoing in my bones, and then turned tail and left.

Jack was next to me then, closer to the edge of the cube instead of inside her circle. Her cheeks were flushed but her eyes were back to their normal hazel.

"He heard me," she said, "Diego really heard me."

JACK

I didn't have a clue how to reach Diego, so I just started speaking to him like he was next to me. The heart link warmed against my skin, like he had wrapped his hand around my wrist. Magic wrapped around my body like a hug, and then I could smell the sandalwood of his skin near me. I remembered how he cradled me against him during the fire. The feel of his hands on my face when he kissed me like he was dying. I saw his dark, dark eyes and how they changed when he was charged with magic. I saw how they changed when he had me in his sights.

"Diego?" I called.

Nothing.

"Diego?"

Nothing.

"Please, can you hear me?" A tear welled up in my eye, but I couldn't remember where my body started and the magic stopped. I was larger than life in this spell; all essence and no flesh, and I wanted to reach as far as I could, stretching myself thinner and thinner until I was small enough to fit through the links–

"Jack?" Diego murmured, and a chill raced down my arms. It was voiceless, silent; the touch of sound in my mind, but I knew it was real.

"You heard me!"

"Where are you? My Blossom, are you safe?"

The magic swelled in my chest, and I thought I might burst from it. "I'm okay," I said. I don't think the words came out of my mouth; every word resounded through my nerves. I couldn't see anything. My sight was clouded with magic and I saw nothing but whiteness.

But I felt everything.

Diego stood behind me in this space, this chasm of magic that we created through the heart links. The heat of his body, or maybe it was just his magic or his energy, warmed me through. When I chased after his essence, little stars formed in the whiteness, taking the shape of his face, then his neck, and shoulders. Diego built himself out of stars until he could raise his hand and wave at me.

"There you are," he said, warm and hushed. His voice felt like a wave of steam coming from a sauna.

"Here I am."

I wasn't sure what this star-encrusted version of him was, but it felt like the truth of him. Maybe this was what a soul looked like if you looked close enough. My breath hitched in my throat, as I took in the details of Diego. Deign. Here that was his name. The truth of him. He reached his hand forward until I reached back.

I realized that I was in my star form too. When our fingers touched, the heart link tightened around my wrist. The two links touched, and I felt the longing they had for each other; two halves split apart to keep two other halves linked together.

"You're twinkling," Diego said. I laughed. Twinkling. I imagined him singing me a lullaby, and felt the smile blossom through me. I hoped my stars lit up brighter for him.

"Same to you. Are you okay? Falcon told me about what he did."

"Getting there, it took a while to feel human again."

"Oh, so you feel human now?"

Diego put his hands on my face, and even though we were only made of stars, the softness of his hands sent shivers through me. His breath came through the star lights, gentle on my cheek. I wanted him to be human, I wanted him to be here holding me. The star lights were like touching his soul, but I wanted to be reminded that he was real.

"I feel alive."

I didn't want this moment to end, but I felt the distance coming. His stars were dissipating and mine floated away too. The heart links could bring us together even with the worlds hanging on by a thread, but we couldn't maintain it for long.

His fingers slipped out of mine, his hand on my face pulled away. I had to tell him about Snapdragon before I lost the connection completely.

"I saw Snapdragon. I'm going after her."

"What? No, please, you'll get—"

The connection snapped, and I collapsed in my circle. The circle had held, and the Cube shone brightly around me, so that I needed to close my eyes. Falcon was on high alert; I saw the knife in his hand.

Releasing my circle, I approached him slowly, and put my hands on his arm.

"He heard me. Diego really heard me."

"That's great, we need to move. Something's here and I don't want to find out what it looks like up close."

"What?"

"Big. Red. Beast. He was chilling on that little hill, and he looked *huge* from there. We don't want to meet that thing up close. Did D tell you anything other than sweet nothings? Ideas? Plans? Something?"

I swallowed. No, he really didn't. Diego wasn't exactly the most chatty man that I'd ever met—that honor probably went to Falcon—and he didn't offer a lot of insight. He was just relieved to talk to me.

"Well, no, but I did tell him about seeing Snapdragon."

"Great, at least you gave him an ulcer during your little mental huddle." Falcon cracked his neck and put the knife back in his boot. A sigil on his arm had a soft glow to it.

"What's that?" I ran my fingers over the raised skin.

"Nothing to worry about. You use your staff to cast, I have an artifact etched into me. The well never runs dry for me," he said, flashing a smile. "So, if we don't have a plan, I vote that we look for shelter. The sun is going down, and I don't want to be out in the open at night. Who knows how long the nights are here. Start looking for a house or something."

"What about the castle?" I asked.

Falcon shook his head. "Too far for tonight. We need to be safe in case the big bad comes looking for you again. Let's work on limiting the magical display here, okay?" Falcon's eyes surveyed the scene, and he nodded for me to follow. I did, but slower. My makeshift shoes weren't the best for hiking.

My stomach dropped. "Why do you think it was looking for me?"

"Well, Lefty, I'm not the one with the funny green magic that shines like a beacon."

"Oh."

Falcon surveyed the land, one hand shading his eyes before he released a bone-deep sigh.

"So, got any ideas?" I asked.

"I like anything that takes us further away from where that thing was. D mentioned a small town, or like a market square near the castle grounds. He told me stories about how he used to sneak out there when he could get away and spend the days in the square. Let's see if we can find that. There's bound to be somewhere we can rest, assuming it's still standing."

"What kinds of stories did he tell you?" I asked. I wanted to know about his life before the Shattering, when he was a king, when the worlds weren't broken.

"Mostly just how much he loved it here. I pray that he never has to see this," Falcon said. He lowered the Cube spell and gestured for me to stay close. His spell clung around us, following his lead just like I did. Night was falling quickly; my staff was the only light that we had to guide us.

"Take us to the square, Harold," I whispered, "I need you to be my eyes."

"Did... did you just call your staff 'Harold?'" Falcon laughed. I laughed. It was the first time I'd said its name out loud for anyone to hear.

"Yes. I named my crystal ball Harold ages ago when I bought it."

"So it's not alive, right?"

"Don't think so?" I shrugged. Actually, I had no idea if Harold was alive. Before landing in Obius, I would firmly say no, but watching it happily bob along, I wasn't certain. It felt rude to ask such a question, too.

"Lefty, you are by far the creepiest chick I've ever met, and that's saying a lot. One day, I'll tell you about Tuyen."

Harold lit up, showing me what looked like a small map, and we both leaned in to look at it. Falcon looked up between the little map and the road ahead.

"Hot damn, magical GPS. Good work, Harold." The staff shimmered. Maybe it did like the attention. I let go of the staff, and it led the way.

"Any chance you can find me some clothes too, Harold?" I asked. It shimmered again. There was hope for pants for me yet.

ARTURO

The castle was untouched by Wildfire. That insane woman brought forth the Creation Goddess's Holy Flame to our forest. She called it like it was nothing. How had I misjudged her magic so poorly? I couldn't bear looking at the forest, so I locked myself behind the castle walls. What few soldiers were left took turns watching for Snapdragon's return and sobbing over the loss of the forest.

She burned the Rainbow Forest down.

It was the worst crime ever committed in Trellis, possibly the worst crime in our entire history. My horns were going to molt before the season called for it at this rate. Grief settled in my shoulders, the weight causing me to hunch over.

The mage-hounds were expected to return soon; I sent them out to see what they could find. They were part of Deign's guard; animals bred to be excellent trackers, not deadly in the least, but the best hunters Obius had ever seen. Unless the animal was raised and trained by you, they could completely disappear. They communicated with magic, sending little images to whomever they wanted to speak with. It was interesting magic that Deign designed. I only prayed that they could hide themselves from her. We all felt the shift of magic, and I wanted to know what hellish thing Snapdragon was planning so we had time to prepare. My instincts told me she would be back, and that was not good for anyone.

Next time, I wouldn't hesitate.

No one wanted to stay in the castle grounds once the King was gone, and I wouldn't force them. I walked through the towers, taking in the details of the castle. The castle was decaying, just like the rest of the world here. It had been so long since I bothered to look anywhere other than just the floor but I noticed there was dust on top of dust and the stained glass windows were covered in grime. Even the sunlight that filtered in felt stagnant and stale. The halls were empty, the royal artifacts and tapestries either ruined or in tatters. How far the castle had fallen from its former beauty.

My bones ached. It would have been easier just to let Snapdragon burn everything to the ground instead of trying to save it. Was there anything even worth saving at this point?

"Captain, a mage-hound is back," Bitterroot said. He was one of the soldiers in Deign's personal guard with me. We grew up with Deign. All of us. Deign's guard was chosen shortly after his birth, when we were infants and toddlers. Assigned to the King's Guard before our horns, wings, or roots ever formed. I loved being a part of his guard; Deign never acted like he was above anyone. He was with us during all of our training, while we played and ate, while we slept. Deign didn't need to do any of those things, but that never stopped him.

"Just one?" I asked. I prayed that the others weren't hurt.

"For now. They went in different directions. I'm sure the others will come back soon," he said. Bitterroot was part of the tree folk, a sprite. His wings were small but strong; the delicate webbing of his wings had gotten thicker with age and injuries that healed.

"What did he find?"

"Captain... the hound thinks there's another Priestess. It wasn't Snapdragon." My heart stopped. Another Priestess? How was that even possible? Bitterroot kept speaking, but I didn't hear his words. Another Priestess. That would mean—

"We have to find her. *Immediately*."

"The hound is going back out. I'm sending some soldiers with him. Do you want to see his images before he leaves?"

"Yes, take me to him."

The hounds were kept on the castle grounds, in one of the courtyards. Deign called it their playground, and it was an apt description. He hated the idea of them being bored or lonely, so there were several kennels for them to rest in, toys to play with, and several options for treats and foods. He treated these beasts like they were his own children. They were ugly things too—red and orange fur, three tails, large teeth, drooling constantly. But he loved them, and they were useful. They all had names relating to fire magic, because the young prince insisted that they be themed.

Smokey rolled on his back in the courtyard, resting but looking like he might be dead. They played dead too convincingly.

"Smokey, come," Bitterroot said. He sat up, wagging his tails irregularly. Smokey was the least coordinated of the mage-hounds and also the largest. The tails slapped against each other at his rump, but he didn't seem to care. "Show the Captain what you showed me."

He howled, and then the images of a woman wrapped in green magic came to me. A human woman. She had no horns, no wings, no vines, but I recognized the magic around her immediately. It was the Seer's magic. She was blessed by the Seer, there was no doubt. No one in Obius or beyond could hold magic like that. No one other than Snapdragon, at least. She had a staff too that moved just like Snapdragon's but was less decorative. I didn't know the spell she was using. Perhaps it was a human one.

"Captain! Come quick! The Priestess is back! She was seen heading for her tower!" another soldier yelled. He was so young, his feathers hadn't fully come in yet.

"To the Priestess' Tower! Everyone! Smokey, gather the guard! Go!"

I *knew* that damn nymph would return.

SNAPDRAGON

I'd been found out. A guard turned the corner right as I hopped over the castle walls. I snapped his neck and grabbed his soul for later use, but not before he screamed for help. Someone would have heard that. The castle was empty by its former standards, but Arturo recruited more and more soldiers every year to keep the castle alive.

I ran.

I needed to get to my chambers before anyone else did. Howling in the distance made my skin crawl. Mage-hound. Probably Smokey. I hated those beasts but Deign didn't. I always kept my distance, but it was never enough. Once Deign was gone, I required them to stay in their space. They were not allowed in my presence.

The wall I scaled was closest to my tower; barring the need to execute anyone else, I could make it to my rooms in minutes. I climbed. This was the same route I used to flee the castle grounds. The balcony I jumped from was several stories up. There were no trees now to help me, so I needed to climb to a window to get inside. The doors would be too guarded.

Footsteps behind me made me quicken my pace. I had forgotten how much I loved to climb. My vines extended and wrapped around footholds to keep me going. I scaled the castle quickly, and without running into anyone. Even though I hadn't stretched my limbs and vines like this in ages, I still moved as gracefully and gently as petals in the wind.

Once I made it to the window, I used my staff to smash it. It was locked from the inside, and I needed to keep moving. The noise would draw attention.

"There! It's her!" a voice called out. I flinched; who could have possibly heard me?

I'd been found.

I ran.

The stairs to the upper portions of the tower seemed so far away. The hall would be filled with soldiers soon, so I pushed myself to run faster. I needed to get to my old room, to the jewelry box Deign's mother once gave me. I hadn't opened it in centuries.

"After her!" Soldiers clambered through the hall, their steps deafening in the quiet corridor.

I ran.

It wouldn't be ideal to set the tower on fire—there were too many price-less artifacts, too many memories of Deign—but I would if I had to. My tower contained so much history of the Goddesses; the Seer's jewels and the old spell books alone were reason enough not to set the tower ablaze. My favorite tapestry of Deign hung limply on the far wall, too neglected to hold itself up. The folds covered most of his face now, and I was glad for it. Seeing his smiling face gazing down at me would make the fire all that more tragic.

Two more flights of stairs and then I'd be there. The soldiers were heavy on my trail, trying and failing to cast spells to contain me. Their magic was too weak to have any effect, and my staff soaked in all of their attempts like a cloth blotting water. Tendrils of magic surged forward and went right through me; I couldn't even feel the brush of their magic anymore. I siphoned each spell, each sigil invoked.

"Y-you're not allowed in here," a young soldier said. He was an adult judging by his wingspan, but only just. His body trembled and I smiled my most wicked grin. My vines snaked down to the floor, making him nearly jump. Nearly. He forced his feet to stay in place. Arturo's ridiculous training must have stuck with him.

"And you plan to stop me?" I snarled.

"Y-yes!" He pointed his spear at me. My staff glowed bright with magic and a bolt struck him through the heart. He crumbled, his soul still clinging to its body, refusing to believe that this was its end. I stepped over him and pushed through into my bedroom. Stilling the energy thrumming through me, I focused on my staff. The soul floated up in a small, silvery bubble until it merged with the rough cut gem on the end of my staff.

The air was stale. It was like a memory trapped in time; the bedsheets were crumpled, a dress was thrown on the floor. A glass of water still sat at my tables with likely new life growing in it. My throat closed up as I stared at the crumpled sheets. The ghost of Deign's fingers tracing my jaw or the swell of my hips or trailing lines down my back made me shudder. He wasn't *here*.

None of that mattered anymore.

The jewelry box sat pristinely on my vanity, though covered in dust and the mirror was obscured. I saw my image in the mirror and looked away. My beauty faded like a waning moon. My leaves darkened, my vines wrinkled and heavy. I had paled too much. My staff smashed the mirror, and once the image was gone, I felt lighter again. The hinges of the jewelry box creaked when I opened it, but my treasure was still there, just as I knew it would be.

A sunstone, cracked and fragile.

A piece of the King's heart.

CHAPTER SIX

DIEGO

Peony's idea was terrible. I'd been searching for pieces of my own heart for half a millennia, and bringing Falcon and Mari's sort-of a grandmother into the mix would not help anything. Mari, thankfully, agreed with me. We needed to focus on stabilizing the link between the worlds and getting Jack and Falcon home before we focused on fixing me. I had two pieces of my heart, and they were going strong. It would have to be enough.

"I might have an idea," Sherwin said. I heard the question in his words even though he asked nothing. Sherwin could twist the truth out of anyone; no wonder he was so infatuated with Peony.

"Let's hear it," Peony said. She and Mari sat shoulder to shoulder on Jack's bed. I put as much distance from everyone as I could, leaning against the desk near the window. I still took up too much space; my human body felt so awkwardly large compared to the other humans, and too tight for me. Stillness and silence lessened the strain.

"Back in Trellis, you were always partial to sunstones. Is that what we're looking for?" he asked.

I nodded. I was made of flesh and blood like everyone else, but when the Goddesses shattered my heart, they turned it to stone. Sunstone, specifically, because I had a natural affinity for them. My magic blended well with the structure of the sunstone, and when I practiced my alchemy, they were my go-to material.

"There's something that I need you to see then. Pea, will you be alright for a while? I can drop you, Mari, and the cat off somewhere, if you'd like."

"I could use a nap," she admitted.

"Take us to my place, Sherwin. Peony is gonna have to deal with Jack's house stuff too," Mari said. Puddin blinked at me. I wanted her approval, just for the sake of having it. She stared at me so critically, but I couldn't blame her. I was the reason her human was gone.

"Can do. Anything else we need here?" he asked.

I looked around Jack's hotel room again. Everything of hers was lost in the fire, and standing in this oddly sterile space just emphasized that. There were no suitcases either; just plastic bags filled with whatever Peony grabbed for her.

"No, I don't think so," I said. The heart link warmed against my wrist, and I wondered if Jack would try to reach for me again.

PEONY

I didn't love that Sherwin immediately ditched us once he revealed their little bromance, but I needed the space as much as he needed to be with Diego. Annoyingly, I missed him, but I realized how co-dependent *that* sounded, so I stamped those thoughts out. I laid my head on the tops of my knees and hugged them to my chest. My clothes smelled like Sherwin, pine and autumn morning. It was nice relying on someone but it made my stomach acidic.

Mari and I sat on her old brown couch, and it was my first chance to really look her over. Mari looked rough. Her eyes were red-rimmed, and she had deep eye bags. Her braids were messed up too and the little charms she normally had were missing.

"You holding up okay?" I asked. No magic.

"Not really, but what can we do?"

Mari stretched, pulling a quilt from the end of the couch to cover her legs. Puddin curled up in her lap, purring loudly. She sensed the same storm in her that I did.

"Well?"

"I think we need to call in the troops."

"The troops."

"Mama and Abuela—"

"No, not her. She don't give a shit about us anymore." Mari's words dripped with venom, and I saw the flash of magic in her eyes. Fire.

"Mari—"

"*No*, Peony. Abuela is out, and you don't even know where your mama is." The words stung because they were true. Mama had turned off her phone and disappeared. She cast some heavy magic—death magic—and then left. She had to purge the magic out of her system before it corrupted her or did something worse. I didn't know the specifics, and she left before I could ask.

"She went to the mountains, that's where she always goes. But she was in bad shape, so I doubt she made it all the way to the Rockies—"

"Please don't tell me you're suggesting a road trip to some forsaken mountain slope looking for Jazzy Hawthorne." Mari groaned and pulled the blanket over her head.

I yanked it down. "Of course not. I'm going to use a locating spell."

Puddin got up, stretching and making Mari wince from her nails. "I'll find her," she said.

"You know where she is?" I asked.

"Peony, do you honestly think I would let anyone that Jack cares about truly out from under my paws?" Puddin's tone was predatory, her eyes sparkling with mischief and magic. I reached for my bag and popped another antacid.

"Let's get moving then. I'm still using the locating spell."

"Whatever makes you happy," she purred.

DIEGO

Once the girls were safely at Mari's place, we walked the few blocks to Sherwin's home. He ran in quickly and came out with a duffel bag. I stayed put; my body was still exhausted, and it felt odd to follow Sherwin to his home. Was I still welcome in his life?

Sherwin held my shoulders after he tossed the bag into the trunk and looked me up and down. He hugged me, and I sank into it. We grew up together, from the time that we were babes. He was part of my official guard, but I considered every one of them my friends. My closest friends, Sherwin and Arturo, became my Shadow and the Captain of the King's Guard. Sherwin was my confidant; he knew my secrets, my fears. He was a living diary.

And he was *alive*. Here.

"I never thought that I would see anyone from Trellis again," I said.

"It was just me that got through," he said quietly.

"I'm sorry." The words had so much ground to cover. Being alone. Following me. Shattering the links. I didn't even tell him about my plan. It was the only thing I ever kept from him; I wondered if I had told him if things would be different.

"So am I. I knew something was up, but I didn't press you. I should have," Sherwin's words stung; each one was barbed and dug into me. He cracked his neck, not looking at anything, and I remembered him doing that a lifetime ago when he was upset with me.

"I got my just desserts," I laughed. The breath left my lungs, remembering the Shattering. I didn't see Sherwin anywhere that day. I didn't remember much of what happened anymore.

And then, the links were broken.

The Goddesses shattered my heart, rendering me all but magicless, and with just enough of the organ to sustain life. I moved through the years praying for death and praying for life, but mostly just praying for Snapdragon to piece me back together. Only instead of Snapdragon, it was Jack. She was my true north. Whenever I felt strong enough, I'd cast something to try to reach Snapdragon. Anything that could reach through the veil. Sparks. Messages. Prayers for a priestess to send souls to rest. Anything.

Every spell went unanswered.

Then Jack found me with her visions. She showed me who she was, and Falcon found her. A priestess. A real, living priestess on Earth. It was a dream come true. I had a chance at life again.

"Come on, I need to show you something," he said. Sherwin patted me on the back and we headed off. His station wagon had seen better days and was covered in stickers. The rack on the top still had a surfboard on it, and I smiled despite myself. He always loved the water. Sherwin drove easily with me in the passenger seat. It felt like before, with Sherwin taking the lead to make sure I was safe. His ever-easy nature had returned and the guilt climbed up my throat. He had been alone for so long.

"Where are we going?" My voice cracked. His lips quirked up.

"A Fae market. One that never closes."

"Is that the same as the crystal markets?"

"No, this is for Fae only. The crystal markets are for the humans, most-ly."

"Why does it never close? That seems like quite a market."

"Because the Fae needed shelter from the humans. I sorta helped build it." The topic was closed for discussion, but I wondered what he had faced to make him create this shelter.

I'd spent much of my time on Earth in the presence of good humans. I sought out countries full of sun and stayed there. I stayed out of sight and on the fringes of every society, only mingling with the humans for short, brief periods. I'd seen the evils that the humans could commit—I don't think I'll ever be able to forget what they now call the Dark Ages—but I've seen the beauty, too. These last few years with Falcon have been the best. We traveled through all of South America and most of the United States. Falcon was the first human that I felt truly understood the essence of Obius. My side ached, and my heart ached, and I pushed those thoughts away.

Had Sherwin missed all of the goodness? Where had he spent all these years on Earth? Sadness welled in me when I thought how many years alone we both spent instead of being able to survive in this strange world together.

"Where were you?" I finally asked. I didn't know how many minutes had passed with me lost in thought, but the road looked a little different. The highway had opened up, and there were more and more trees and fewer buildings. Maybe it was just my eyes, but the colors on Earth never seemed fully there. The world's colors had been mixed with too much water before the Creator took Her brush to paint the canvas of Earth. On clear, sunny days, especially winter days, when the sky tried its best to be a more honest hue of blue, I missed Trellis enough to break my heart again.

"What do you mean?" he asked.

"Where were you? How did I spend over five hundred years here and never find you?"

"You didn't look for me," Sherwin said. His voice was calm, always irritatingly calm. He gripped the steering wheel, another pale brownish thing in the mass of pale brownness that was his car. The outer paint was an attempt at blue, but the interior was just tan. Another dull color, but purposeful this time. That somehow made it worse than a color trying its best.

"I would have." I put as much strength into the words as I could. I didn't want it to sound like a command, but just the truth. I would have turned over mountains if I knew that Sherwin had been here.

"I know, Deign, I know. I tried to find you, but every time I caught wind of a possible lead, it wasn't real, or you had moved on. I thought I saw you once in Argentina." Sherwin always sounded so sure, so confident in his words and thoughts that when I caught the tremble in his tone, white-hot shame shot through me.

"It's possible. I spent a lot of time in South America. Europe was too cold and strange for me. I left in the mid-1600s. I don't remember the year."

"I was in Asia then," he said, scratching at his face. His human face didn't have a beard, unlike mine. My beard grew quickly, but the hair was different from how it felt in Trellis, and I didn't like it because it irritated my skin. I was overjoyed when clean-shaven men became a fashion style. The permanent five-o'clock shadow was as close to clean-shaven as I ever got, but I'd take it over a true beard any day. Sherwin's soft chin made him more youthful and emphasized the kindness in his eyes. I saw why people flocked to him wherever he was; that much had not changed from Trellis.

"Is this market far away?"

"It'll take a bit to get there. Do you want to rest? You look beat, Deign."

"Sherwin, I discarded that name a long time ago. I'm just Diego here."

Sherwin chuckled. He said that I was always too serious, and every time he chuckled it reminded me how much of a *mossy stone* that I was.

"Well then *Diego*, rest. We've got a good forty-five minutes before we get there."

My eyes were closing before he finished speaking, sleep tugging at me as the car lulled me to sleep.

I dreamt of Jack.

I said a prayer to her, hoping that she would hear me, that the heart link would pull our souls back together.

Her hands came first, outlined in stars, glittering like cut diamonds. The heart link shone pure gold, the charms jingling in my ears. The stars slowly weaved and knitted together the shape of her body. When the curve of her lips formed in the stars, my heart stopped again. She smiled at me. I ran my thumb over her star-laden lips. She felt so real.

"Diego Ortiz, I have an inkling that you want to kiss me," her voice whispered. Her breath on my ears sent a shiver through me. It wasn't just a kiss that I wanted; I wanted Jack to walk next to me through the Rainbow Forest of my home. I wanted her to see what real stars looked like, and how the suns would set in Trellis. I wanted her to see the moons standing on the balcony of my room, where the trees would dance in the moonlight. I wanted her to see what life would be like with me when I could be alive with her.

"Is that so terrible?"

"Only because you're not here." The star lights knitted together until she glowed like a night-blooming flower. The lights dimmed and brightened to match the emotions in her voice, and I tangled our fingers together. She was warm.

"I'll find a way," I said. A bump startled me awake.

"Find a way for what?" Sherwin asked.

"Oh. Um."

"Deign."

"It's nothing."

Sherwin stayed quiet for a minute, counting on his fingers, and I felt myself start to sweat. This was his tactic—he would do this *every time* I even thought of keeping a secret. I remembered when I smuggled a turtle into the castle and kept him under my bed. I lasted three hours before Sherwin broke me. He insisted that we name him Mel.

He held up one finger, and I bit my lip.

Then a second. I turned away.

Then a third—

"Okay fine," I huffed. Sherwin cackled. "I... I found out that I can connect with Jack through the heart links."

"Heart links! You gave her a heart link!"

"She gave it to me, actually."

Sherwin shut off the radio—I didn't even notice it was on until the sound was missing—and sighed. He pinched the bridge of his nose.

"Does she know what they mean?"

"She does now," I said. Sherwin laughed then, short and full of fondness. He gently punched my arm, and I beamed at him. Things would be okay between us one day. I could wait. I was good at waiting.

"So you can talk to her. You knew she was in Obius before we even got to the hotel room, didn't you?" I nodded. "And you didn't want to mention that *because*?"

"Peony—"

"—would lose it, got it." Sherwin shook his head but didn't look away from the road. "Glad to see not much has changed in all these years. We're nearly there."

Sherwin pulled off the road, past the shoulder, and parked in a grassy area. I didn't know the interstates well, and they felt disorienting to me. The roads stretched out seemingly forever, the same gray blandness of the road, with bright green signs to tell me which exit to take. I didn't know the names of these places, or where their exits would take me. It didn't matter though; much of this country was the same. The same stretches of stores and restaurants and people, just arranged slightly differently. The monotony of the modern human world was never ending. Sherwin waved for me to follow him into the trees.

He picked various leaves, smelling each one before deciding its usefulness. This was his gift: Sherwin could sense the magic and the strength of plants. He had a knack for gardening, cooking, and flower arranging. He was skilled with other forms of alchemy, but his heart was that of a gardener. He spent countless hours in the gardens of Trellis Castle, curating them to my mother's taste, the seasons, the holidays, even Snapdragon's requests a few times. But he wasn't crafting something beautiful today. Sherwin's magic flowed around him as he blended the basic leaves together until they melted. They were mushy and molten. Sherwin formed them into a key and whispered a spell to harden it.

He showed me his creation, dark green and brown, with the teeth of the key forming the crest of Trellis. It was exquisite; the details of the crest were all there, the outline of it serving as the ridges of the key. The two standing trees, the hourglass symbol of the Seer in between them, curved horns coming from the sides of each tree trunk, with a fan of feathers around the base of the trees. He handed me the key, and it was a little longer than my hand.

"A key? I see no door?" I asked.

"Follow me. It's here, but the trees are keeping it safe. Only Fae with a key can get in," he said.

"It has my crest on it."

"Yes. You have to declare where you came from for the trees to allow you to enter. Trellis is our home. Any nation's crest would open it."

"Where is the door?"

"There isn't one. Just watch."

Sherwin placed the key on the ground, in front of a large oak tree. It was a normal tree, not like one from the rainbow forest. The heart link tingled against my wrist, and I felt Jack's presence in my mind. She wasn't here, not like when we were communicating, but I felt her heartbeat and could smell a hint of jasmine and eucalyptus. *Hello, my Blossom.*

The trees shook a little, moving their roots and branches, and allowing us to see a new path. They didn't truly move but shifted as much as they could. The key burned itself up where Sherwin had placed it, and I watched as the crest of Trellis slowly faded. Everything was grainy, like a heat mirage, but Sherwin picked up the hot key and sliced through the air. The trees sighed, light wind brushing against us, Sherwin grabbed my hand and pulled me through to the other side. The trees brushed against my face, and I heard them calling my name.

The Lost King.

Trellis' Forgotten King.

The Shatterer.

King Deign.

We stood on a cobblestone street, and my knees nearly buckled. It was a replica of the city center in Treis, the only city in Trellis. Our cities were not like the human ones, full of buildings and cars and lights. They were the heart of the countries, where people came to trade and congregate. Treis was where Trellis Castle sat. The city center was about a morning's walk from the gates to the center where a statue of my mother stood. Orainia, Queen of Grace, stood coyly looking over her shoulder with the sweet smile she was known for. The artisans that created the statue had worked on it for nearly fifteen years, and their work was perfect. The folds of her dress and the emotion in her eyes—love, charm, hints of mischief—captured the essence of her spirit. The replica of the statue here wasn't nearly as grand, but it was lovely. It was just the center of the market area though; the huts and tables and little stands were surrounded by trees, instead of the stone paths out to the pixie groves or the forests or the wildflower patches that the sprites lived in. The details were amazing; the flags from each of the people who set up their stalls. A fruit vendor, with fruit from Obius! Arrow fruit, Trellian berries, Goddess hands. A king would never *charge* up to a stall, but I wasn't a king anymore.

"How much for the arrow fruit and the Trellian berries?" I asked into the air. No one was here, I realized. It was just Sherwin and I.

"Things here don't cost anything. You trade, just like in Obius."

"What do we have to trade?"

"I've brought lots of things I've crafted. Get some fruit. These are real, I know the guy that grows them. Catfolk from Chilijan. Nice guy, little twitchy."

"I don't think I'll ever be able to thank you for this, Sherwin."

"For what? The fruit? Your Majesty, there's hardly any thanks needed for that."

"For rebuilding Treis here on Earth. The statue…"

"Yeah, it's pretty great. In the 1700s, after all of us had been here for about a couple hundred years, we decided that we needed a refuge. Fae had been on the Earth for a while, coming and going before the links were gone. That's how the markets started, you know. Fae looking to keep themselves afloat. When one of us was murdered by a human when they found out she was a pixie, we built this. It's like another plane. We decided to use Treis as the model, since most of us were from Trellis. I don't totally get the magical logistics behind it, but I'm no engineer. I just helped with the design. I made sure there was a garden like in your courtyard. It's near the ba ck."

"How many of you are there?"

"There were six, but only four are left."

Sherwin picked some of the Trellian berries and handed them to me. They were small and red, but a little spiky, similar to cherries but a little more tart. I loved them. My favorite wine was made from Trellian berries. He left me to my snacking and wandered through the square. It was like looking at a memory; I remembered this place, but I couldn't tell you the details, like the colors the flags should be, or what shops were there, or who manned the tables. Those details had been erased with time, and watching Sherwin walk through this empty square filled me with sadness.

"Yvnes and Persi have died. Yvnes was the one that was murdered. She was from Trellis too, and she had the illusion magic that built the foundation of this place. Persi was from Labren, and he was a griffin. Persi built the key system and taught the others how to make their own keys. Now we teach other Fae that we meet, so they can find this place too. It's Fae Rules here–fair trade only. No human currency, no humans allowed or human objects to be left here."

"And the others?"

"They're still here. We meet up now and again, but they are settled in the human world and happy, I think. So they say. You know it's hard for the Fae to admit their sadness."

I turned away from him, looking for anything else to stare at instead of him. Perhaps things would have been different if I had ever really told him how dire Snapdragon's visions were. Maybe he could have seen how terrified I was.

"What were their names?" This was important–I knew the name of every person I met in Trellis, and I made it a point to remember. I was their king, not a tyrant. I ruled with the people, not over them. The corners of Sherwin's lips turned up; he remembered.

"Cassia and Lockwood, they're tree nymphs. Yvnes was a pixie. Arban is Catfolk. Tanner is a sprite. And Persi was a griffin like I mentioned. More beard though. He was really proud of it. Personally, I never liked it. He looked too griffin, not enough human, and I think that's what got him killed. The otherness about him stank up a room, and the humans could sense it, even though they didn't know what *it* was."

Cassia. Lockwood. Arban. Tanner. Yvnes. Persi. I repeated their names in my mind. I wouldn't forget the names of the friends that kept Sherwin alive and safe. One day I would honor them.

"I owe them a lot," I said, looking around again at the square. The fabrics were human made, not Fae crafted. I felt the varying textiles on the stalls, too blended and too manufactured, and I wondered how hard it would be to source some Trellian silks. There was magic in the fabrics made in Obius. The weavers and tailors would craft gorgeous linens and dresses and suits made from flowers, leaves, and wool. The table coverings were still nice, but like the details of my memories, a little off.

The sky was obscured, and what was visible was opaque and hazy; there was a dome around the square, protecting it from the outside world, with the trees standing guard around us. Trees in this little forest were greener than the ones by the highway; I felt the otherness about them and saw the Obius magic in them. They didn't glitter like they should, but I felt blessedly small in their presence.

"I think this is what we're looking for," Sherwin said. He ducked behind one of the stalls with the Trellian crest painted on it and came up holding a small box.

There was a sunstone in a carved box. I knew this box. I'd seen it a thousand times or more, growing up and running into my parents' room. My father, Lionus, the Prince Below, died when I was young. I remembered him and loved him, but the bond with my mother would always be different, stronger. The box was made for my mother–her personal jewelry box. A small Trellian rose was carved in the center with the feathers of my family circling it, the paint chipped and faded. The blue of the feathers was mostly gone, just little tips and tinges of blue. The rose had fully faded from its once soft, lush pink. Sherwin popped it open, the hinges now just a decoration, and there sat a sunstone.

Sherwin grinned wide, excited for me to see it.

I did my best to hide my disappointment–it wasn't a piece of my heart. It was strong, beautifully formed, it just wasn't a piece of *my* heart.

It was my father's.

"What?" he said. As always, there was no hiding anything from Sherwin.

"It's a lovely heart piece, it's just not my heart. This is my father's. When he passed, my mother had a lot of his magic transferred to a sunstone. I get my affinity for them from him. She always kept it in her jewelry box, next to her bedside." My throat closed up thinking that they were both gone now. I prayed that their souls were resting together in Sanctum.

"I know. But it's your bloodline. I figured it might help."

My father's magic was heady; the smell of honeysuckle lingered around the sunstone. Prince Lionus was a pixie. I inherited his hair and eyes and apparently his temperament, but not much else. I looked like my mother, with horns and feathers. My father had iridescent blue wings, curly black hair, and gold eyes. He was thin boned and frail in appearance but a force with magic. His death nearly killed my mother. He died suddenly, and she never spoke of what happened.

The magic stirred when I held the sunstone. It was larger than the pieces of my heart combined. My father didn't have royal blood; the binding and shattering magic came from my mother. My father's magic was airy, stormy. He commanded the winds and the seasons.

Energy crackled through my fingers. A small wind current rustled around us, shifting the flags and the cloths of the tables. I focused on the wind, and then I could see the outlines of each current. A little more energy, a little more power.

The wind picked up.

I wasn't controlling it. Dread roiled through me, and I tried to cast a peace spell to calm my mind. I imagined the music from the Bloom Festivals, the gentle rise and fall of the beats, and steadied myself. The wind only grew more savage, more chaotic.

"Sherwin–"

It turned violent, knocking the tables over and snapping the delicate branches of the trees within the market square. My mother's fountain cracked; her hand pouring water snapping off and the water cascading down too harshly. It splashed in the fountain below, the water soaking both of us.

"Release the spell, Deign!"

"I'm not commanding it!"

Another gust, this one was stronger. Another table was knocked over, spilling the Obius fruits on the ground. The bowls rolled away, rippling against the barrier of Sherwin's hidden oasis.

Sherwin ran his hands down his forearms, summoning magic from within. When his hands clasped together, a ball of energy formed between them.

Vacuum.

He shaped the energy into a small, black thing until the winds and everything else were sucked into it. His control was impeccable, even all of these years later. This dimensional magic was bestowed on him by my mother. Sigils were powerful things when inscribed on the flesh. He wore the small sigil on his shoulder blade as a reminder to always watch my back.

The winds ripped through the square, directly into the vacuum he created. He blocked everything else out, taking only the errant winds. The incessant sucking and ripping from the vacuum made my heart skip a beat and the two newly joined pieces were not in sync. Heaviness settled in my limbs, and I forced myself to keep breathing. Vacuum wasn't taking the air from my lungs, just the winds. Jack's face flashed in my mind, terrified and reaching for me, and then she was gone.

"That did not go how I was expecting," he mumbled. He squeezed the vacuum in his palms until it collapsed in on itself, tearing itself apart.

"You can still use Vacuum?"

"It's not easy here, but I've had to do it a couple times. I couldn't think of anything else to do without the winds tearing through the barrier spells. This place has to remain intact, Deign. We aren't the only ones that need it."

"I'm sorry–"

"Apologies don't mean much if you shatter this too." He scratched at his bottom lip, his chest was heaving. The wall that I thought was coming down between us felt even thicker.

"Sherwin–"

"I haven't forgiven you for it, you know." Sherwin was so quiet I almost didn't hear him. I wish I hadn't.

"But I thought–"

"I can miss you *and* also be pissed. It'll take time."

"I don't know how much of that I have," I said. Sherwin faced me then, staring at my eyes. I wondered what color they were now? The lifeless brown or the magic-filled gold. They were gold in Obius. Muted on Earth, like everything else about this world. He was taller than me; had he always been taller than me? Sherwin spent so much time behind me that I couldn't be sure.

"Don't even start with that. I've known Jack a lot longer than you have. She's too damn stubborn to let you die, and so am I. I've been looking for your ass for like six hundred years. You don't get to just check out now."

"Sherwin, you're not my caretaker anymore."

"I swore an oath–"

"To a king," I said. I held his hands in mine. Our human hands, that seemed so delicate, even though they were sturdy and large. He stood there, still as stone. Sherwin could make a statue envious with his stillness.

"Deign, you'll always be a king."

I smiled. It was a warm thought, that there was still someone in any of the worlds that could still believe in me, but it was just a thought. A king without a castle. A king without a crown. A king without a queen.

A king that doomed his homeland.

"Here, I'm just me."

I didn't want to tell him that I preferred it that way too. Sherwin stood perfectly still, and I groaned.

"You aren't entitled to *every* thought in my head, you know."

He barked out a laugh and let go of my hands. "Fair enough. Should I just stop calling you Deign? Is that too painful?"

It was, really. It was the name I discarded, but I only nodded that everything was fine. Sherwin took in every detail of my face, looking for the lie. I smiled, and he let it drop.

"Help me clean this place up. I don't want anyone finding a mess and being afraid that the humans have somehow gotten in here."

Sherwin pointed to some of the tables and I set myself to work. It felt like I was straightening Jack's shop all over again; everywhere I went, destruction followed me. Except I would have to build her some tables before I could set them right again. The fire took every piece of evidence that Jack had made a home.

There was a small figurine laying in the dirt; it was small and green, with little bumps on the head of the creature. It could pass for a frog. I put it in my pocket; I wondered if she would beam and smile at me for the little figurine. It could be the start of a new collection for her. Sherwin hummed a familiar tune while he worked, and I let my mind drift. Daydreaming of

Jack's face passed the time until the sun threatened to set. Once the square wasn't a disaster, we packed up and headed back for his car.

CHAPTER SEVEN

ARTURO

Snapdragon infiltrated the castle in minutes. She moved fast, too damn fast for us to keep up with her. We followed a trail of bodies to her tower.

I knew she would come back. This castle was everything to her. Snapdragon didn't see a reason to ever leave the castle, so like a caged animal, she came back to where she felt safest. Everything in her rooms felt overdramatic; the deep, emerald green curtains and bed linens. The canopy bed with hand carved posts and details. The rosettes on the walls, the paintings of the Goddesses hanging above her bed. The room felt grander than it should be, which suited Snapdragon perfectly. At some point, she'd forgotten that her role was to guide the King's eyes, not entrap him to her bedchambers.

The guard led me to her tower, and we stopped at her old rooms. The rooms were dusty and mold-laden. She forbade anyone from entering these rooms. As always, the wishes of the Emerald Priestess were followed without questions. I hated that I followed them too. She left them several years after the Shattering and hadn't returned to my knowledge.

A trail of dusty and bloody footprints lead us to her old vanity.

Her jewelry box was left open, and I dumped the jewels on the table. Nothing stood out to me. I wasn't an expert on the jewels she wore, and these I hadn't seen in centuries. She was searching for something in here, but I didn't have the faintest idea on what it was.

"Captain?" Bitterroot said.

"Hm?"

"More mage-hounds are back. They... found something." Bitterroot stood at the threshold of Sanpdragon's bedroom, still refusing to enter.

"Snapdragon isn't a part of this court any longer. Her rules don't apply. Get in here."

"Oh. Sorry." Bitterroot left the door and hurried through the room like something might jump out at him. Knowing Snapdragon, I couldn't fault him. He didn't want to meet my eyes. Bitterroot stared wide-eyed at the jewels on the table. So many pieces with Deign's personal crests on them. It was obscene.

"What did you find?" I tossed the jewels back in the box and closed the lid. Deign made this for her; I remember him carving it. *Forever my Queen* was inscribed on the lid. I shoved the box to the edge of the vanity, and Bitterroot jumped.

"Arturo," he said. His fist was closed, but he extended it to me, and I cupped my hands. He dropped a couple pale blue feathers in my hands and my heart stopped.

"Where did you find these?"

"Mage-hounds brought them back. Edge of Trellis. There's a little cottage there."

"Send them back. I want whoever owns those feathers brought back to the castle *immediately*."

"There's more, Arturo."

"More?"

"Humans. There's two of them. I looked at the images from Smokey again, and I think it's Seer magic."

"You think the Seer is back?"

"Not exactly." Bitterroot tucked the feathers back in his satchel. His spear leaned against the small vanity, slowly creeping down the floor. He was the most talented and lazy spearman I'd ever known. I waited for him to continue; sometimes Bitterroot needed a minute to gather his courage before the words would flow from his mouth. They live abundantly in his mind, but Bitterroot would rather have a limb amputated than have to share his inner thoughts.

He chewed his bottom lip before beginning, "It's Seer magic. The kind only a Priestess can cast."

"But it was a human," I protested.

"Yeah, she's been blessed by the Seer. There's a human Priestess in Trellis." Bitterroot's spear clanged on the floor, jarring both of us and my heart leapt into my throat.

A new Priestess. Praise to the Goddess.

"What about the feathers?" he asked.

"We have to know where those came from and if... if they're alive. We'll deal with that when the time comes. For now, send the mage-hounds back out. I want them brought back to the castle immediately."

JACK

Harold guided us through the ruins of the rainbow forest. The landscape went from bleak to bleaker; the tree stumps were smaller and crumbling. More ash, more charred rubble. I let my fingers just barely graze the charred stumps. The color of the forest was muted—so different from the visions I was used to. I missed the colors that seemed oversaturated and the density of each ray of light. I wanted to feel the color soaking into my skin, but all I felt was smoke.

As we approached the castle, there were more rocks to climb over, less of a path. Night had fully fallen, and the only light we had to guide us was my staff. We needed to find a place to stop for the night soon.

My staff jerked to the left, and Falcon grabbed my arm before I took another tumble. This rocky ground had ruined my leafy shoes, and my feet were bruised and tender.

"I can carry you if you want," Falcon said.

"Let's not make this any worse than it already is," I huffed. I was hitting my limits; sore, cold, and crawling through a tree graveyard. The souls of the trees were restless, and my hands itched to *do* something.

The staff stopped, waiting for us to catch up. Once I did, I held it and magic welled up in my chest. It snaked around my heart, like the roots of the trees were climbing up through me. Magic always felt green and full of life, but now I felt each of the colors that threaded through the trees. The reds of their treetops, and the oranges and yellows that ran down through their trunks. The blues and purples of each individual leaf. The souls were viridian green and luminescent. I had to do something for them—

Priessstessss, Priessstessss, Priessstessss

You're home

Welcome home

Welcome, welcome

How we've missssed you

"You can hear that, right?" I said. Harold's light changed from a soft white light to a forest green. Seer magic. It gave me goosebumps, and I grinned despite myself. Stepping into who you're meant to be revives the parts that you didn't know were dying. Each pulse of my heart, each breath was laced with the magic, and it settled deeper and deeper into me.

"Yep. Loud and clear. No likey. Bad vibes, Lefty."

"You missed me?" A zing of joy shot through me, and Harold pulled me away from the rubble into a small clearing. There were still some trees standing! How did we miss them? I trailed my fingers on their trunks, like I was touching a memory.

We came to sssee you, Priessstessss

The words were caught in the wind, a slight breeze carried the words around us, and I saw the silvery trails of magic. The trees tried to move closer, roots shifting underground and making the ground rumble under my feet.

"Baaad vibes," Falcon said again. He held his knife with the blade up and parallel to his arm. *Swashbuckler*, I thought to myself, and a little note of hysteria bubbled up in me. *The trees knew me.*

Yeeeeeeeeeeeeeeessssssss

There was a collective hiss from the trees, the wind rustling through what was left of their leaves. The anger for the forest hit me again, and my staff that had been hovering close floated into my grip. I held their rage in my hands, and I grieved for them.

Our time hasss passsssed, Priessstessss

Pleassse

It is time to ressst

The wind picked up again, and small pleas of *yesss, ressst, pleassse, ressst* echoed through the small clearing. Falcon had edged closer to me, ready to pounce, but I put my hand on his to lower the knife, and calmed the storm in him.

Magic blossomed through me, the heart link warming and responding to me, and my staff glittered. Chill bumps ran up and down my arms. Tugging off my makeshift shoes, I gestured to my staff, and it started drawing out sigils. I knew them, I thought, but they were buried too deep in my memory to recall their names.

Thank you, Priessstessss

"Lefty, what're you doing?" Falcon stepped out of the circle and the sigils that the staff drew in the dirt; the lines lit up with every connection point. It was the Goddess' Trinity, and I stood at the center.

"Sending them to rest," I said. Rightness flowed through me. I held my palms up, near my heart, and the magic came. My staff twirled and spun with me as I danced. My body knew these moves, deep in its core, to the trunk of my being. It remembered. So I gave in and let the magic flow.

I'd performed this spell before, with Diego, when we laid some souls to rest. He wasn't here this time, but I felt his presence with the heart link. It hadn't worked the second time I tried the spell, but he wasn't there then. It will work this time–it has to.

"Rest, be at peace. Return to Sanctum to be born again," I chanted as little orbs floated up from the ground, varying sizes and colors, all shining with life. The spell gripped all of the souls, and they all came together, growing in size and glowing brighter and brighter. They hovered in front above my hands, now the size of a watermelon, and the staff stopped spinning.

This was different–last time, they just floated up and up, like they were leaving the atmosphere. Now they just stayed with me. My staff was right behind them, and I waited.

We are ready, Priessstessss

"I don't understand–"

The souls broke into a thousand separate orbs again and flung themselves straight into the crystal ball on my staff.

"No!"

Priessstessss, thisss isss our gift to you

Welcome home

You will need our ssstrength

"But you're trapped in there! That isn't going to *rest!*" I rubbed the crystal ball and the trees' souls stirred. They came to the edge of the ball, trying to touch my fingers. I was crying now, and I couldn't stop the tears. The heart link pulsed gently on my wrist, a small hug from Diego, and the souls kept feeding themselves into my staff. The crystal took them all greedily, and I felt like I didn't know it anymore. Harold was my most precious artifact, and it sucked down the souls as fast as they could offer themselves. I clutched it to my chest, and said a prayer that they would be okay.

Peaccce, Priessstessss Jack, everything will be alright

Let our magic keep you sssafe

We've waited ssso long to meet you

Now we will alwaysss be near

I couldn't stop them. I tried. I dropped the spell and put myself between the flow of them, trying to block the crystal, but they moved around me. The orbs that brushed against my face and arms were featherlight kisses, and as the last of the souls nestled themselves into the staff, one last one stayed behind.

Use our power to protect the Trellisss bloodline. They need you, Priessstessss. The King hassss been waiting so very long

The last soul didn't go to the staff. It rose to eye level and merged itself into me. I felt the power unravel itself; magic burying itself into me, into each nerve and bone and cell. The tree's memories unfolded in my mind; I saw it as a little seed, then a sapling, and watched it grow. I saw the suns setting and rising as it grew to greet each day.

The last whispered words played in my mind, *Now you have the magic of Obiusss in your veinsss, no one can deny you. Goodbye Priessstessss, be well.*

The spell dissipated quickly. Falcon boldly stepped into the circles my staff had drawn, and he grabbed my shoulders to examine me. His magic prodded at me, scanning and looking for damage, but I wasn't damaged. I felt the centuries that Diego had waited for me; the heart link resonated differently now. It was deeper, connecting to the part of me that was

Obius-bound and speaking joyously to it. The Seer's Blessing *felt* like a blessing instead of a title. There was so much magic in me, I needed the staff to hold my reserves. I heard the call of every soul still lingering in the forests, the ones that had died from the fire and the ones that were trapped here from the Shattering, and I did my best not to cry.

The trunks of the trees stuck up straight in the air like rigid, lifeless flagpoles. The leaves had been stripped from the fire, and the branches crunched easily under our feet. The ground still felt warm to me, even though the fire was clearly gone. Life drained fully, finally, from the trees as the souls collected in my staff, and I wondered if this was the same depth of sorrow that Diego felt when I first met him. There were so many souls still here. A sense of duty rested on my shoulders as I leaned against my staff. I pretended that Diego was here and was satisfied that I wanted to help them.

"Jack?" Falcon placed his feet carefully, not stepping on any lines of the sigils, even though the spell was dissipating.

"Falcon, I can't just *leave* them here like this. There's still so many souls–"

"One step at a time, Lefty. Let's figure out how to get to the castle first."

"Yeah."

I said a silent promise to every soul I passed that it would be laid to rest. Rightness. That was the feeling; everything was right as it should be. The Blessing of the Seer. The magic hummed in my veins, and I reached again for Diego. I wanted to tell him what happened. I wanted him to see that I would protect his home, as best as I could. I picked at the heart link, touching each of the little charms, and I hoped that he saw how the Blessing was settling into me.

The ground shook again, but the trees weren't moving, only my knees were knocking. My heart link burned against my wrist, but there was no removing it. I tried to calm the magic, to calm Diego's heart, but he wasn't

hearing me. I couldn't hear myself think, much less the faint whispers from h
im.

Falcon covered his ears, pushing me out of the sigils that Harold had
drawn.

"Sky!" he shouted, and I realized then how *loud* the world was. My ears
ached too, the buzz in the air making me dizzy. My skin tingled, the hair
standing on end.

When I glanced up, the sky shone gold. The color of Diego's eyes, the
color of his magic before he was shattered. My staff hovered over my head,
trying to act like a shield. Watching the storm build overhead was like
glimpsing into the darkest parts of Diego's heart raging against itself. The
magic was chaotic and angry.

"Jack, that's not me—"

Winds danced across the sky; the currents were golden and wild. Falcon
and I took shelter in a small nook on the side of a mountain. It had been
so dark before that I didn't realize we were next to a mountain. The wind
shook rocks loose and they bounced off the ground as panic laced through
me.

"No!" I shouted, my staff spinning now to shelter us from the wind.
Then I felt the nuances of the magic that rained down around. The gentle,
golden way it touched my face. Everything smelled like sandalwood, and I
recognized Diego in the magic.

"Jack, it's not me! That's not my magic—" Diego's voice kept coming to me. His voice was higher, unsettled. His words wobbled, and I caught
a flash of him having a hard time standing. He leaned heavily on someone,
but I couldn't see who.

"Lefty, we need to take cover. This storm isn't letting up," Falcon said.

"It's not a storm, it's Diego but something's not right," I said.

"Please my Blossom, listen, it's not me!" His words clanged around through my mind, the heat of the heart link getting too hot, like it would sear my skin, leaving its own kind of brand.

"You know any water spells?" I asked. Falcon shook his head no, and I wished that Peony was here to move the seas again.

Lightning burst across the sky as the magic whipped itself into a frenzy, and I got another flash of Diego. This time he was collapsing, landing on his knees. ***"I'm okay, my Blossom,"*** his voice whispered in the back of my mind.

The magic dissipated as quickly as it came—no fire, just little embers that Falcon worked to stamp out. My staff hadn't stopped spinning, and barely slowed when I reached for it. Harold's crystal was still emerald green from sending the souls to rest.

I siphoned the magic from Harold and worked a healing spell. The land needed it, I needed it, and so did Diego and Falcon. I wrapped the spell around each of us, starting with myself. On Earth, I would imagine ribbons of light wrapping around my arms and legs and the trunk of my body, wrapping me tightly in a cocoon of energy. In Obius, the ribbons were real. They were a soft yellowish-white and tugged themselves over my body, then wrapped around Falcon. He *yipped* at the contact and then laughed. The ribbons moved quickly, dancing around him and feeding off the good vibe of his liveliness. His energy looked polished, like I had taken him to a shoe shine.

It was softer around Diego. I saw him clearly in my mind, sitting in a forest. I was glad to see him there; he needed to connect with the trees, even if they weren't the trees of Trellis. The ribbons weren't as visible, but I focused on them intently, and I prayed that the spell made it to him.

Then the land. Ribbons and ribbons of light wove themselves together as a blanket over the land. It stretched as far as I could see, which was pretty far even with the night upon us. The spell lit up the ground, lit up the world, and I pushed it farther and farther.

Just like when I had a vision and I struggled to find where my body started and my consciousness ended, I stretched and extended, like roots unfolding over the land. There wasn't much the spell could do, but I thought that maybe the souls that were still here felt a little lighter. For now it was enough.

"What the hell was that?" Falcon asked.

"Healing spell. It's a lot stronger here in Obius."

"I meant the lightning. It looked like Diego to me." Falcon tugged at the bandana on his arm, trying to cover the scales.

"I heard his voice; he said it wasn't him."

"Then–"

"Who else?" My words came out in a growl that Puddin would be proud of. Falcon held his hand up, telling me to stop. The magic from my healing spell seeped into the ground, leaving a soft glistening effect to the dirt and rubble.

"Did you hear that?" he asked.

"No?"

"Our hairy friend is back." I didn't see the thing that Falcon mentioned before, but now I couldn't miss it. It had some gnarly teeth, its fur was red, and I hoped my imagination was playing tricks on me, because I could have sworn the drool melted a stick next to it. The only light now came from the beast, and I was *freaking the hell out.*

It was still far off, but the smell of the beast's mouth was too close, too hot, and reeked like death.

"Please tell me you have some escape plan," I said.

"Not really. I think we're gonna have to fight it, I kinda doubt we're gonna outrun a fucking hellhound."

The marching seemed to come out of nowhere. Next to the hell-hound—whatever it was— there were soldiers. I'd seen them before: the crest, the weapons, the stance they took, all in a vision. I saw them when they tried to stop Snapdragon from burning the forest, but those soldiers all died. Their souls were in the ground here, mixed with the other creatures that died from the blaze. Little cries echoed in my mind, asking to be sent to rest.

"And we're gonna fight them too?" I asked. I shifted my weight back and forth because my feet ached like there was no tomorrow, trying to relieve the pain before something else made it worse.

"Of course there would be an army," he grumbled as he cracked his neck and flexed his hands.

My staff crossed itself in front of me. Battle mode. I was not a battle mode person. I was a psychic and a small business owner. The only thing I ever fought over was an online sale.

Falcon pressed his back to mine, keeping eyes in each direction, and putting himself out front. The forest tried to respond too, tried to add back some light to the now very dark forest. If Diego were here, he could call them off. They would listen to him. They'd obey their King.

Right?

As if summoned by thought—maybe he was—Diego's face came to mind, all smiles, the real, genuine smile he so rarely indulged. His face had a little more hair on it, more beard and less human. His horns curled lightly against his black, black hair. Ocean blue feathers appeared down his arms, the rest of his body coming to stand with me. I felt the hug of his magic wrap around me. Why did I ever think this man was only made of sorrow?

"Lefty," Falcon brought me back. Diego was still holding on to me, an embrace from across the worlds, and I leaned into that magic. The crystal ball in my staff lit up gold, just like the color of his eyes and of his magic. The

green of the Seer had faded, and I chose to believe this was Diego protecting me
.

The swarm of soldiers hit fast after that.

Grabbing the staff from its crossed, defensive position, I rolled the shaft between my fingers, spinning it in place. The magic crackled in the crystal like the electricity that danced across the sky. I swung the staff low, Falcon ducking just in time for me to make a Full Circle–the spell Mari and I could cast in our sleep, protecting and fortifying us. A golden sheen settled on Falcon's skin as he exploded away from me, knocking two men down that charged at us with huge blades.

They surrounded us from every direction–satyrs, centaurs, Fae men and women, some were more humanoid than others, but all of them were dressed in green armor with vines and flowers sewn into their clothes and stitched onto their weapons.

Falcon didn't stop; his magic was feral, sending gusts of air at anyone that got too close to me, taking swings at anyone that got too close to him. It was artful and terrifying–Falcon's tightly wound coil had sprung, and he was beating the hell out of anyone and everyone within arm's or magic's reach. My Full Circle was a stable, protected barrier around me.

"Something is wrong with my magic, Jack. Those are Trellian Guards, they won't hurt you!"

"You can see them?"

"I'm seeing through your eyes, we're connected. Something is wrong with my magic, though. I'm not controlling it–"

Diego's voice cut out, but I felt the link still. He did feel off–out of control, lost. A lot like Falcon, really. Falcon threw off three soldiers and was already back up, fists raised.

"Falcon!" I shouted, trying to get his attention. Someone was approaching from behind him. I lost my focus, and the circle fell. It didn't feel as important as helping Falcon.

Someone had gotten the better of him from above, the hilt of a long-ax jammed against his throat as he helplessly pawed at it, trying to break free. He shot his wind magic at anyone else that came close, but the lithe Fae man that had him pinned pulled the hilt tighter.

"Falcon!"

"–hind you" he choked.

I turned just in time to catch the edge of a sword to the temple. My world faded fast, faster than any vision, and I went down, down, down.

CHAPTER EIGHT

MARI

Listening to a cat spout off directions and commands was not how I wanted to spend my day. Any day. Ever. This damn cat. She sat in my lap and meowed orders at Peony. They fussed at each other, two mother hens fighting for dominance. I was getting an eye twitch. My living room wasn't large and it felt claustrophobic when Peony was here; her energy took up a room, and it did so quickly. Adding a pissy cat to the mix, made the atmosphere unbearable.

"Y'all."

"We're not using a blood spell," Peony said as she cleaned her glasses. She had been cleaning her glasses for the last twenty minutes. Puddin hopped down so she could get eye to eye with Peony. I paced around until I settled by the window. So close to freedom, yet so far.

"You think a locating light will find your mother? She's *in hiding*," Puddin spat.

"Y'all."

"And whose blood are we using, then? Hmm? Do you happen to have a vial of it just lying around?" Peony's voice ratcheted up an octave. Goddess, give me strength. A car turned into the parking lot while I zoned out, eyes glued to the window. Puddin settled on my shoulder like a deranged parrot, too angry to engage with Peony anymore.

"Yours! You have the same blood! Come here, I'll get the sample myself!" Puddin's claws were out, digging into my shoulder, and I bopped her on the head.

"*Y'all,*" I hissed, and they finally stopped.

"What!" they said in unison, angry that I interrupted their tiff. I buried my face in one of my throw pillows when I heard the elevator ding.

"Boys are back. Diego looks like a kicked puppy. Sherwin's got puppy kicker vibes. Something's happened." Peony turned immediately at Sherwin's name, and I said another prayer to the Goddesses that this was something that would work for her. She needed someone to take care of her and hopefully get her to chill out. She straightened her slouchy knit sweater and waited by the door. Then backed up, then switched sides, then smoothed her sweater again, and when a knock on the door came seconds later, she jumped.

"Sherwin?"

"My lead was a bust," he said. Diego didn't meet our eyes. He didn't even look at Sherwin, his bro from a lifetime ago.

Peony and Puddin interrogated Sherwin, getting every scrap of information from him while Diego hovered by the door of my apartment. He didn't allow himself to be a part of the group, and I couldn't figure out *why*. He'd been on the outside of life for centuries, and now he had a chance at life again—that's what Jack would give him, if he'd open what little heart he had.

Everyone's tension made the flame burning in my stomach grow, and my fingers ached with magic. I shoved them in my pockets. My balled fists stretched the back pockets of my jeans, but this pair was on the way out anyway–perfect for accidental fires and popping stitches.

"You okay?" I asked Diego. It took a second for him to realize that he was being addressed, and the magic that flashed in his eyes startled me. My heart leapt up to my throat, the fire constantly eating at me now dying to dance in front of his golden, vibrant magic.

"Not really," he laughed quietly. He was the smallest energy in the room when he kept his magic in check. *Always trying to be less*, I thought, just like Jack. I squeezed my fists tighter, forcing my nails to dig into my palms. *No more fires, Mari. Get it in check.*

"What happened to his lead?" I asked. The magic pinged around, through my body, and I fidgeted.

"Sherwin had a sunstone that he thought might be mine, but it wasn't. It was my father's, actually. After he passed, his heart was given to my mother."

"I hope you know how damn creepy that sounds," I said. Diego smiled, the golden magic lighting up through his eyes again, and I hoped I wouldn't light my pants on fire. Something about his essence was alluring for magic.

"Yes, Falcon explained it to me once. *'This is why you don't have friends, D. You can't go around saying shit like that.'* " Diego put his hands on his hips, mimicking Falcon perfectly, and I chuckled. Falcon was a problem for another day. I didn't know him, but my gut told me that he wouldn't just betray his best friend. I remembered how weak he was, half passed out in my parking garage. I thought about his bone-weary movements as he eased himself to rest on my couch, and how we ate pizza, and he seemed like the world was pressing down on his shoulders until he was bound to break.

"He's right," I said, playing with one of the gold bobbles in my hair.

"I don't know how I can ever forgive him," he said. Diego's voice reminded me of an echo; not because of the volume, but because it was the after effects of a voice instead of the real thing.

"You'll have to look in your heart for that one," I said. I patted his arm, unballing my fist and instantly regretting it. I left a little singe mark on his lovely, boring sweater.

"Mari, are *you* okay?" he asked, noticing the mark. There was no hiding the little trail of smoke that came from it.

"Peachy," I said.

"Fire magic is quite the beast. It takes a long time to master. How long have you been able to cast it?"

"How long have you been around now? Like what, less than a week? Somewhere in there."

Golden eyes again. "Well, that's worrisome," he said. I flashed a smile and felt the fire flicker in my chest.

"And you? What's going on with the eyes?"

"I wish I knew." He forced a serene smile on his face, and it was the epitome of serenity. He had to have practiced that in a mirror. It was kind but distant.

Regal.

"We have a plan!" Peony declared, breaking my attention from Diego's too calm face. Puddin floated over to me, landing on my shoulder like she would do to Jack, and I shrugged her off. I missed Jack too, but I refused to be anyone's stand-in.

PEONY

I hated this plan. Sherwin handed me my purse without me asking for it, and I grabbed my antacids. I hated them too. I took two and Mari passed me a glass of water. I hated that I was so predictable.

I hated everything about this day, but most of all, that Sherwin was lying and I knew it. He knew that I knew and he still said nothing.

"We're going to use a blood spell," Puddin announced. I also hated blood spells. Nothing good came from them. Blood magic played with fire, and we'd already burned down a damn house. I hated that the cat would be casting this spell.

I *really* hated that it required my blood too. Sherwin agreed with Puddin that a locating light would take too long, and time wasn't a commodity that we had. I grabbed the knife and inspected it briefly; it was inscribed with sigils that I didn't know or care to learn. Mari held my hand steady like I was a child that needed comfort, forcing eye contact that I *also* hated, and I slashed my palm with a knife. The knife was laser sharp and it *felt* like a fucking laser had gone through my hand. The blood welled up and the memory replayed of the blade slicing my hand made it tremble. I knew I hadn't cut it deep, but the wound was angry and red and white hot with pain. I dropped the damn thing because all I could focus on was my hand and *how much it fucking hurt.*

Mari held a crystal bowl under my hand, the blood dripping too fast and bright and too much until there was a red sheen of it in the bottom.

"Just a little more, Pea," Sherwin said. I hated that he was still so kind, tending to the wound. Mari and Puddin prepped the rest of the spell, while Sherwin stayed focused on me.

"Don't," I said, as he dabbed at the cut. Everything stung, and knowing that Sherwin was *lying* made the stinging worse.

"I can heal it," he said.

"I'm fine."

"Pea."

"Don't, okay. Just don't." I snatched the little bandage from his hand and went to the bathroom to run it under some water. Diego was there, hovering, like a ghoul.

"He really is an excellent healer," he said, leaning in a little to look at the cut. His fingers glowed golden for a second and he waved his hand near me.

"What're you—"

"There's no need for you to suffer," he said. The cut had fully healed—not even a scratch.

"How did—"

"Sherwin taught me." He stepped back, giving me space, allowing me to take up more space. His smile was sad, and I hated that too.

"I don't like you," I said bluntly.

"I haven't earned your trust," he said. Also bluntly, but with less venom. I hated it.

"What isn't Sherwin telling me?" Magic laced through my words, but nothing happened. His eyes changed for a second, from brown to gold, fast enough that I could have imagined it.

I didn't.

Diego held his hands up for a second—in surrender, not to cast—and then dug something out of his pocket. He handed it to me. A sunstone.

"This. It's not a piece of my heart, but it's powerful."

"Why would he lie about it?"

"Sometimes even those with the most courage don't like to admit that they were wrong," he said. He held his hand back out, waiting for the sunstone to be returned to him. I turned it over in my now healed hand, looking at the colors. It was like a sunrise had been captured inside it. The magic warmed, golden and joyful.

I hated that Diego was probably right, and that I was being cruel for no reason. I hated that I wanted Sherwin's allegiance to be mine.

"If I've learned anything over the years, it's that you should not keep your feelings silent. Especially the darkest ones. Those need to be dragged into the light," Diego said. He left the bathroom, and Sherwin was there, just standing, waiting. I hated how patient he was.

"Hi," he said. I felt the distance between us; it was me causing it, moving myself away from him. I saw the hope on his face and the otherness about him too. He was too charming, too attractive, too magnetic to be human. I hated that I didn't know that he was Fae.

"Hi."

"Am I still on the shit list?" he said. Sherwin pulled me into a hug and I let myself be moved, running his fingers down the side of my face. Even his fingers felt too good to be human.

"Yes," I said.

"Even after Deign gave you one of his sermons? That's impressive. Scary, too, but as always I'm in awe of you, Pea."

"I'm not looking for flattery," I said. Bluntly. My words were always too sharp, too pointed, and in the end they always hurt someone. Usually me.

"I know. I'll try to be an open book to you, but you have to remember that some parts of me aren't written in a language you know. I'll try to translate though." He ran his hands down my arms, and I felt my resistance melting away. *Please don't let this all just be magic. Please let him be real.* My throat was dry and my eyes were not. I pushed my face into his shoulder, hugging him.

"You promise?"

Sherwin kissed my forehead, the noise of the spell prep breaking the tenderness of this little moment. "Promise."

"Peony! Come get this damn cat!" Mari shouted.

"It's showtime," Sherwin said.

I groaned. I hated this.

DIEGO

The crew decided that they needed to call in more troops. Abuela-Nana was a bust, to no one's surprise. Mari was tight-lipped about what happened, and it wasn't my place to ask. Nothing about this little crew was my place. So I waited, watched, and stayed quiet. Most people thought that kings and queens were loud, boisterous folks, but really a true leader was a quiet one. Listening was the key to earning the right to speak intelligently, and especially kindly.

So I listened.

We wanted to complete this group—so we called for Jack and Peony's mother, Jazzy Hawthorne.

I'd only met the woman briefly, but I saw where Jack got her power and Peony got her intensity. She was beautiful, of course, like all humans. They were so strange; delicate, hairless mostly, hornless, wingless, featherless. The delicacy was what made them so attractive though. I loved the humans.

Puddin led the spell. No one objected, not even Peony. She was sullen but still went along with the spell. A blood spell. Blood magic was common in Obius; it didn't have the dark connotations that it did here on Earth. Puddin glided through the air, drawing out the sigils for clarity, precision, and a call to arms. The call to arms was typically only used for special events. War was a human thing, but in Obius the call to arms assembled a group quickly. We used it for parties.

Mari and Peony touched their palms together, anchoring the spell for Puddin. Spellwork performed better on Earth with more alchemists; the Earth's lack of magic worked against them, and having a coven of any size helped the strength of the spell. Falcon was the only human I'd seen work spells without ever needing the help of others, until I met these ladies. Their magic was magnetic, and I let myself get lost for a moment in the ceremony of their work.

With the spell secure, Sherwin came to stand next to me.

"Think it'll work?" he asked.

"I don't think even magic itself is brave enough to defy them," I said. He smirked, doing his best not to laugh and disrupt them.

"Good point. She's a force, isn't she?" Sherwin's eyes followed the curves of Peony's frame, and I nodded. Any woman that could capture Sherwin's heart was surely a force.

A circle formed around them with Puddin sitting in the center of it. Mari and Peony stepped back, their bare feet on the edges of the circle. Mari's small home felt even smaller, with all the furniture pushed against the walls. Once the spell was completed, I told myself that I would realign her home, so everything was back to where it was. That much I could do.

What looked like little stars materialized in the circle and I sucked in a breath; the star lights were the same as the connection with Jack but duller. Jack's star lights shone like glittering diamonds, but these had the soft glow of a quartz. I wanted to feel like I was looking at the sun, at the start of a galaxy, not the fading light of a hollow crystal. Slowly they knitted together the frame of a woman: Jazzy Hawthorne.

Peony's face was tight with anger. She seemed even more disdainful to her mother than me, which was a feat. Smoke trailed around Mari's head, and I wondered how much that fire magic hurt. I didn't even attempt fire magic in Obius; it was forbidden the same way that blood magic was here. Fire was reserved for the Creation Goddess, and though it may not seem like it, I didn't try to anger the Goddesses. She flicked her fingers when she thought no one was watching, and I saw the little sparks coming from them.

The spell was contained in the circle, and the floor glistened like the surface of a pond. The star lights floated out of it, and placed themselves to start looking like a person. Jazzy's eyes were fiercely green. Her eyes were the first thing to fully come through. The rest of her came in bits. Puddin danced through her spell–one I didn't recognize, oddly–and once Jazzy was here, she crashed into Peony, hugging her tightly to her chest. Peony stood limply, not returning the embrace. When Jazzy broke the hug, she ran her fingers over Peony's face. A mother's touch. It was universal in all realms; my mother did the same to me.

She turned to Mari and hugged her too, but Mari hugged her back. She flicked more sparks, trying to get them to stop. The hug seemed limp to me; Mari tried more to get the fires to calm than she focused on Jazzy's return.

Then Jazzy scanned the room, taking in where she was, and more of what wasn't here. Namely, her other daughter, Jack.

"What's happened?" she asked, sharp and biting, just like her oldest child.

The girls kept quiet, and Puddin landed gently on the floor. She swished her tail, and I wondered how exhausted she was after that. Her spell was brilliant; more magic than I hoped to handle here on Earth.

"What's happened?" she asked again. Peony let go of Mari, and reached for her mother, but Jazzy squared her shoulders and gently shook Peony off of her.

Silence.

"Ja–" I started.

"Where's Jack? Someone answer me!" she thundered. Energy crackled around her, until her attention landed on me.

"She's in Obius. She opened a link," I said.

"Mama, we need help," Peony said. The venom I was expecting vanished from her tone and Jazzy took in the details of her daughter more. Peony leaned on her now, and Jazzy folded her into another hug. Peony's frame shook just a fragment, and I averted my eyes. This moment was not for me to see. Mari's home was in chaos, but nothing was broken. The couch cushions and pillows were on the floor, picture frames were tilted with a few on the furniture and floor, but there wasn't any broken glass or holes in the wall. The carpet had seen better days, but that wasn't a result of the magic.

"Jazzy," Puddin purred; her breathing was labored. She floated up to be eye level, and Jazzy nodded to her. "We're going to have to open a link too."

"And just how are you gonna do that?" Mari asked.

"I know the spell," Jazzy said. She jingled as she moved, just like Mari, except Mari picked at something on her sweater.

"You know the spell?" I asked, my attention snapping back to them.

"Let me clarify, I know *a* spell," she said, "I've never attempted it, but with the King of Trellis here, we might have enough magic to get the spell going."

"But I–"

"Deign," Sherwin said. I handed over the sunstone; I was still holding it. A King of Trellis was in his hands. The sunstone glittered. The magic stirred, ready for whatever they would ask of it.

He handed the sunstone to Jazzy, and silver ringed through her eyes.

"That's my father's heart. His magic is there, but it's my mother's that you need to hone in on. She carries the Trellian bloodline."

"Thank you," she said.

"Maybe we should talk this through–" Mari started.

"There's nothing to talk through, Marigold. I'm going to open the link. The links were shattered, we know this, but they weren't severed completely. There's still threads to grab onto. So we're going to find a thread, energize it with royal magic, and you'll go through."

"Me!" Mari said.

"The four of you. Puddin is going to stay here with me, anchoring the spell." Puddin blinked slowly, nodding.

"Mama," Peony said.

"No tears, darling."

"How are we going to get back?" she asked. Peony started picking up pillows and righting the knick-knacks in Mari's home. She needed to be busy; the nervous energy around her clouding around her.

"The same way you came. I will be here, waiting and listening for your call," Jazzy said. She held Peony's face and kissed her forehead. She kissed Mari too, and glowered at Sherwin and I.

"I'll be sure they get back safely," I said, bowing my head.

"*All* of them," Jazzy said. I knelt before her, praying that she felt the weight of my words. Puddin hovered near my face, her fuzzy paws tapping the sides of my cheeks.

"Bring my girl home," Puddin said. Her words were muffled, either from the fur or her magic, I couldn't tell. She held my eyes until I was the first to look away. Catfolk needed to win eye contact contests; losing meant acceptance, and I wanted her to know that I wouldn't fail.

The wildness that I knew only from Obius flashed on Jazzy's face. My heart raced; this felt like a bad idea now. She was human, not Obius-made. Opening the link would be too much for her–

But the spell had started. She wasted no time pulling the magic from the sunstone. I watched the color fade, growing darker and darker as it swirled around her. The otherness intensified and all at once, I realized what Jazzy Hawthorne was.

A caladrius; skilled healers that could bend life energy.

Puddin spoke the words, the language of the sigils, of Obius. The magic worked. The apartment shook, Peony's quick work to restore the order in Mari's home was gone as the decorations and pictures shook themselves loose again, with a steady stream of curses to go with them.

My memories came surging back to me–the holy ground between the worlds where the Goddesses dwelled, the triangular patch of land that the mirrors and doorways stood between Earth, Sanctum, and Obius. The rope-like tethers that braided the three spaces together, then using my family's magic to destroy it all. I couldn't breathe, could they see this too? Were they seeing how the worlds fell apart?

"Deign, let's go, the link is open," Sherwin touched my arm, and the memory faded. Jazzy's twisted face, ghoulish and ancient, watching as I was guided through the links.

I was going back to Obius.

"Bring her home," Jazzy said. Puddin kept chanting, her feline voice perfectly suited for the old language. She winked at me, and the doorway was closing. The heaviness of gravity shifting and the universe yielding to allow us passage contorted around them. Sherwin yanked me toward him, and the stars shifted. I saw the outline of Jack's face written in the stars, and I watched as the link shattered behind me.

Chapter Nine

FALCON

I had to break free. Jack was gone. She took a fucking halberd to the temple. I prayed to the Judge, *please please please don't let her die.* I'd spent so much energy trying not to pass out that I didn't have the magic to actually help her.

So I pulled the very last trick out of my hat: I grabbed this asshole's hair, wrenched it down, planted a kiss right on his too-pretty lips. He dropped the damn lance long enough for me to shove him off. The guy stumbled back. He was about a head taller than me and had something like gills, but he was drop-dead gorgeous. As he studied me, I sucked in as much oxygen as my lungs would allow and put my fists back up. I'd been in worse fights before.

Jack's staff had rolled itself away from her unconscious form and into the bushes–it was a stretch to call it a bush still, but the shape was still recognizable. Good. Last thing I needed was some idiot playing with fire.

Unless the idiot was me.

Backing myself up, step by step, the soldiers tried to gain on me. Classic surrounding technique. No one was gonna get the drop on me this time. I knitted my Cube around myself; let them try to break through *that*. It was harder to keep the spell subtle, so I didn't even try. My whole body felt like a bruise and letting the enemy know I wasn't some rando could be to my advantage. The Cube was ancient magic–*their* magic–and watching a human cast the spell had to be unnerving. I hoped.

They lunged. I leapt backwards like I was trying to do a backstroke through the air, twisting just before I hit the dirt and rolled away into the bushes with Jack's staff in hand. It was lighter than I expected, but the heft came from the crystal. She would never forgive me–again–if I broke it, so instead I tried to cast any spell I could with it.

The magic summoned itself immediately. It lashed out inside the crystal like an electric storm. Lightning of all colors flashed and crashed inside it. The magic wanted someone to cast, to pull it from the crystal, but the staff made my hands itch. It didn't belong to me, and I was well aware of it.

However it did work well at goon-dispelling. I pointed it crystal out and everyone stilled. They didn't want to approach it, so they changed focus.

Jack.

A chick with wings and a small guy that gave off strong garden gnome vibes went for her. Wings lifted her up and Gnome held two pointed knives, one pointed at me, one pointed at her.

This was not part of the plan.

The beautiful gilled Fae said something in a language he knew I wouldn't understand. His voice was deeper than I expected and more nasally. The hoard of Fae soldiers all pointed their weapons at me, backing away from me and the staff. Wings and Gnome had captured Jack. She was limp in her arms, and I said another prayer for her to be alive.

"Don't think I'm gonna just let y'all walk off with my new BFF!" I was stalling. This wasn't part of the plan because I hadn't *made* a plan for kidnapping. Breathing out to calm my mind, I summoned my wind magic. It was weaker than it should have been, and none of the soldiers seemed impressed. A human in Obius casting anything at all should have gotten me at least a *wow*, but they still didn't see me as a threat. The gusts left as quickly as they came. I was depleted; I'd never been so down before. The brand on my arm burned like it was being freshened up. It took everything in me not to scratch at it.

"Bff?" Gills said, more like *bu-ffh* instead of the letters. The staff floated on its own, yanking itself free from me.

"Let her go," I said. I tried to be predatory. Diego told me I was downright scary when I wanted to be, and I really wanted to be scary now. The gilled man didn't seem phased. He didn't notice the threat in my tone, or he didn't care.

"She belongs to Obius," Wings said.

"Gonna have to disagree. She's human. She belongs on Earth." The staff crossed itself in front of me, still directed at the small army. I felt motion behind me and I spun in time to dodge some more little gnome guys. They moved silently, and I nearly took a knife to the back. The staff had all it would stand—float?—for, and magic erupted from it.

Lightning.

The electric storm brought the color back to the forest, lighting it up, and the Fae creatures scattered. The lightning was brutal, slashing at the ground, at the creatures, at everything other than Jack and me. Wings dropped Jack and she was still unconscious, a heap on the dirt forest floor, as the staff kept going.

She was going to get trampled.

Everyone scattered, desperately trying to dodge the lightning strikes. The ground was burnt, just like the rest of the ruined forest. Jack would be wrecked if she woke up to that, knowing it was her magic that did it. The air was charged with electricity; my clothes clung to my skin, the sweat in my hair tingled. I wasn't a hairy dude, but every hair on me was at attention. The next strike would be worse.

The staff was perfectly vertical now, hovering about three or four feet over my head, playing the part of a lightning rod. The strikes grew more violent; larger booms and larger sparks. My stomach dropped. The crystal glowed white, yellow, with flecks of orange.

It wouldn't be long before another fire broke out.

Bravery and stupidity were often–typically–two sides of the same coin. Jack was the brave one, which just left me with being the stupid one.

"Fuck me," I groaned as I jumped up and grabbed the bottom of the staff. Pain bloomed in my hands; it was a slow and fucking wicked pain. Heat seared through my nerves, and I was shaking. So damn *stupid*.

I held on, and the lightning started to die down–just like me, honestly–until I crashed with the staff hugged close to my chest.

"Nice time to find out you're semi-sentient," I groaned at the staff. The soldiers took that as the chance to leave. When I looked around after I could see again, they were gone. There was minimal damage to the trees, and only a dozen or so real scorch marks.

Not minimal damage to me.

My fingers were too numb to move. I didn't want to look. Everything was too sensitive, too fleshy, too *wet*. None of those things were good, and I didn't want to look at my hands and discover half of my fingers were gone. My arms ached, and my chest ached, and my throat, back, ass, *everything*.

I stayed flat on my back for several beats, not even having the energy to breathe, let alone get up. This was, without a doubt, the worst fight I'd been in; worse than Rio. Nothing had been worse than Rio. Bracing myself for maximum impact, I sucked in a couple deep breaths. That hurt, but not like how my hands throbbed. I gave myself another couple of beats before I looked at the ruin that my hands would be now.

Blood red lines crossed all over my skin. They looked like the veins of a leaf, unfurling down my arm. My scale tattoo had been severely damaged; a large, angry tendril went right through the center of the base of it, smaller veins blotted out the scales.

I had all ten fingers, and I nearly cried with relief. The backs of my hands were mostly okay; a few thin scorch marks, but nothing crazy. My palms though. They were a mess of veins stained an angry, wet red. I doubted I still had fingerprints. All of the little loops and whorls had been replaced with another brand.

The other brand, the original one on my arm, didn't burn anymore but I couldn't tell if that was because it *stopped* hurting or because everything *else* hurt *more*. The staff floated over to me, the crystal still glowing but without the rage from the lightning storm. The glow came from within, soft and golden.

A healing spell wrapped around my hands and arms. The relief was immediate, like someone had wrapped each frayed nerve in salve and gauze. I cried. The lack of pain almost hurt as much as the lightning. My body was in overdrive from the adrenaline and shock, that taking it away caused more shock. I choked out heavy sobs, crying harder than I ever remember crying.

The spell was a true healing: it accelerated how the body would heal naturally. I stretched and wiggled my fingers to make sure I didn't lose any motion as the spell took effect. Magic worked its way through the sinew of muscle and through the nerves and into the bones of my hands. The color had faded out. The scarring now was just another scar, lighter and raised on my skin. I was covered in scars, so it seemed like the color of my skin was lighter than it actually was. My skin color was considered *olive*, and I'd always hated that. I sounded like I belonged on a charcuterie board instead of in a crowd. The scars were light olive; they stood out but it could have been worse. My nerves still tingled, but I hoped that wasn't going to be permanent. I checked the brand on my arm from Abuela, but it was still red and raw, like it was fresh again.

"The hell just happened." I blew out a sigh and laid myself back down in the dirt. To take stock of things, I'd lost a fight, a friend, half or more of my magic, and gained a bunch of scars in mere minutes. Where the hell did they even take her?

Impressive Falcon, even for you. The staff laid itself down next to me, and I swore I could hear it whispering. I brought it closer, and it *was*.

Jack, Jack, Jack, help her, Jack, Jack–

At least I had a plan now once I could move again: rescue Lefty.

SNAPDRAGON

Mage-hounds were back on my trail–I could smell them. The sunstone was wrapped in silk and tucked into my small travel bag. I grabbed it from my chambers as I was leaving. It was simple, nothing royal about it. I stitched it one day before I became a Priestess, when I was a child. I didn't keep much from my days before my calling, but I kept this. It was small, useful, and worthless. No one would care that it was in my possession so I hid it from the prying eyes of the world; once the priestess accepted the Blessing, she would lose everything. Either voluntarily walking away, or by the Goddesses taking it. I walked away from the forests and the trees. I carried only this small bag with me as a travel sack.

The weight of the sunstone was practically nothing; it was lighter than the bag, and I kept checking to see that it was still there.

I needed the magic from the sunstone. My staff held so much of my magic that my body has forgotten what the essence of magic even felt like these days. I needed this for me, not for my staff to hold.

The spell would take time, and I didn't have that now. The mage-hound would pick up my scent easily, and getting dragged back to the castle in its teeth was not part of my agenda.

So for now, I hid. The trees concealed me, even though they weren't happy about it. The few of them that remained, anyway.

The gem of my staff turned red, and I flinched. It wanted so much magic, constantly looking for a new source of energy. Sometimes, when I let my mind wander into madness, I imagined that it wanted *me*.

It has only turned red once before: when Deign shattered the links.

I was still too close to the castle, outside the town square. There were soldiers everywhere, magic flying like it was still flowing freely here, and then I saw her. The human. Jack. She was being carried away by some Trellian Guards, unconscious and limp in their arms. Humans were the most fragile creatures that the Creator ever breathed life into. Her head flopped around aimlessly, and I wondered briefly if they had already snapped her neck, or if humans were truly that flimsy.

The red glow intensified in my staff. A memory nagged at me, but I couldn't remember the details anymore. I should have remembered everything with my magic, but the details faded as the magic faded from Obius. I tried to work out all of the pieces of Deign shattering the links, but it was laced with so much sorrow that finding threads of truth and emotion were hard.

Then the land rumbled. I slipped from my tree limb perch, falling gracelessly on the ground. My staff didn't slow the descent or even try to help—the red glow shone bright enough that it was almost too much to look at. It was blinding, and I had to shield my eyes.

"No," I whispered, watching the sky.

The clouds parted. The suns had gone down, but the sky was full of light. I saw no stars, no moons, just the opening of the heavens. A funnel came down, twisting and raging and unstable. My feet tried to root into the dirt, and I shook them free. I needed to be able to run.

I only recall being truly afraid twice in my life: the first time was when I saw my own death, and the second was now. I saw no visions of this day, no signs of the sky opening, or the raging funnel descending. Why were my eyes blind to this?

The heavens roared, thunder clapping around me, lightning raging and flashing. I covered my ears, kneeling beneath a tree canopy.

My staff stayed red. The color was sickening, and I didn't reach for it. I stayed as hidden as I could. The Trellian Guards that held Jack shielded her, and rage bubbled in my chest. They shielded her from whatever fell from the sky, but I hid in the underbrush like a common thief. The guards hurried–one of the guards with wings cradled her like an infant in her arms, and they hurried back to the castle walls. Arturo sent the guards after her instead of me.

The funnel in the clouds darkened.

Four falling lights, one brilliantly, perfectly gold light.

No. It couldn't be.

My staff reflected the golden color now, and the sunstone in my bag was hot enough that my leaves would be singed if I didn't move it.

No, no, no.

What little life there still was around me, sighed and chatted and whispered joyfully. *The King! The King! The King!*

The lights hit the ground with a thud, and for a second another flicker of Deign's magic flashed in the sky, lighting me up inside. The others with him were vibrant with magic. Judge's magic. Creator's magic. Some Obius-being. They sparkled like they had all been blessed.

He's back, he's really back! The King! It has to be him, right? Yes, yes, yeesss. Fae creatures that survived Wildfire came out in droves. Most of these creatures didn't even know that Deign had been a king, but they all turned their faces toward his magic, like flowers to the sun.

He was the sun; when the worlds shattered, Obius was left in the cold and darkness. A knot formed in the bark of my throat.

Why had my future sight disappeared so thoroughly? Surely, the return of a Trellian King would be something worthy to reveal to a priestess? My staff laid itself across my lap, no longer glowing. The captured souls in the gem barely stirred and I slammed it against the ground. These souls were *mine*, and king or no king, their magic would bend to my will.

I held the sunstone to my heart, feeling the heat stirring in it. It was responding to Deign's call too. Everything in this realm responded to him. Even me.

The spell.

I needed to cast the spell.

I needed a circle and space. I needed to clear my mind.

There was only one place that would provide the peace that I needed.

Emerald Lake.

JACK

I dreamt of Diego.

He told me stories of his memories, and I listened with peace settling into me. Flashes of his childhood when his horns were little nubs on his head and his feathers were still more fluff than plumes came to me in waves. Diego played with a host of other children–some covered in vines, some with wings and beaks, some with horns. I saw him as a young man, still a prince, standing awkwardly in a court with everyone bowing and smiling at him. He pulled on his sleeves, tugged at the scarf around his throat, itched at his cheeks and ears and nose. Anything to keep his hands busy; it reminded me of Falcon. There was energy around him, constantly buzzing. A man with fine bones and finer features hovered near a woman on a throne. She had curled horns, like Diego, and I saw their resemblance. I saw the grace from the fine featured man in the Diego I knew now. His parents.

I reached for Diego again. It was so easy with the heart link. The magic stirred and flowed effortlessly. The star lights came to me, and I held a hand up in my mind's eye. The lights touched each of my fingers until I felt the warmth of his hand seep into me. I saw his outline, his true outline with his horns and feathers, even through the dim lights of the stars. The magic draped around me, and I cuddled into it like a blanket.

"I'm coming, Jack, hang on." Star soft fingers brushed my cheek, the breath of his words warm against my ears.

"Coming where?"

"To Trellis."

When the dreams faded, and his voice felt far away again, I realized how much my head ached. Ached wasn't the right word. Pulsed. Throbbed. Something made me fall. Something hit me. I remember getting hit, but not much else. I didn't want to open my eyes or try to examine the shiner I knew was growing by the second. I didn't have my staff. Falcon was either silent or missing. Missing seemed more likely; even if we were prisoners, Falcon would have something to say about it.

I sat up slowly, taking stock of where I was. My immediate conclusion was a dungeon. Mold and age were in the air and my lungs rejected it. Trying to keep the panic down, I counted my breaths, but it made my chest ache and the magic burned bright, wanting attention in this dank place. I counted each of my fingers, and rubbed my hands together, down the fabric of my old t-shirt, taking in the textures to center my mind. Magic snaked through every nerve in my body and I felt myself leaning into it instead of away.

Once I knew the hysteria was in check, I let my eyes get adjusted and scanned the room.

Small. Stone. Damp. There were several chains attached to a wall, with one unlucky shackle around my ankle. I tugged at it. Locked. Stuck. There was a small bowl of water. The bowl was probably white at one point. There wasn't a lot of light, but enough for me to see that I was alone. My staff was definitely missing. Someone had left a change of clothes for me by the door, along with some bread. *Door* was being optimistic; it was a prison. It was made of metal bars, and they were spaced just enough for me to stick my arms out if I wanted. I didn't.

The clothes were simple, but finely made. A dark blue, short dress. It looked like it would come to the tops of my knees. The skirt was sort of pleated; it had more fabric to make the garment move. There was a blue and green pattern sewn into it. Sigils for the Seer. The main one dominated the front of it, sitting in the center of my chest. It laced up the back, with laces long enough for me to manage it myself. I wouldn't call it a beautiful dress, but it was clean, more my size than my nightgown/t-shirt, and a lot less tattered. The shirt was one that Mari leant me; it was one of the shirts she wore whenever she painted or did housework, old and soft, covered in stains from over the years. I couldn't remember what the words were now that they were too faded to read.

I got changed and slipped on the boots that came with it. They were brown, the soles made from thinly braided roots, and wrapped up my legs with thin vines.

These were Snapdragon's clothes.

I instantly hated them. I hated them *more* that they fit me.

"Ah, you're awake." A man's voice carried through the cells, and I realized then there were more cells than just mine. Maybe Falcon was still here!

"Yep." I stepped back away from the door, putting as much space between me and the voice as possible. This would have been a great time for Falcon to chime in with some wise-ass remark.

Silence.

A satyr-like Fae came up to the cell door. He had straight horns, short, and close to the top of his skull. Sandy blonde hair–fur? There were small yellow flowers that I didn't know the name of, braided in his beard. He didn't smile, and he didn't try to hide the scowl that covered his features. His blue eyes were sterile, and looking at him made me want to shove myself out of the tiny window. His face felt familiar, but the voice I was sure I knew. *Arturo.*

"Priestess?" His words were gentle, but there was no concern in his voice. This man had the body of a satyr but the mind of a snake. The dislike was mutual.

"Yep," I said again.

"Are you injured?"

That was a good question; I hadn't seen my face yet, but everything else was just sore. I shook my head *no*, and his scowl deepened for just a second. I tried to probe at his thoughts, tried pushing my magic out a little, just to get my bearings.

"Your magic will not work on me. Where is Snapdragon?" he asked.

"Snapdragon?"

"Your predecessor."

"I know who–"

He slapped at the cage and I flinched, but I stood my ground. I met his eyes and stepped closer to the door. I wouldn't let this asshole see me afraid. I willed my feet to stand strong, stable. My fight or flight instincts were choosing *fight* a helluva lot more than I ever imagined they would.

"Where is she?"

"How the hell would I know?"

The light hit his armor, and it shone gold. There was the Trellian crest of the forest on his chest. Writing I couldn't read was embroidered around the crest, and the soft white cape that hung from his shoulders was dirty. He scratched at his forehead, running a hand between his horns, and huffed.

"I don't have time for games," he said quietly. Deadly.

"Tell me your name."

"No," he said.

"I just wanted confirmation. I know your name." His eyes were cruel. My heart beat painfully fast in my chest. *Give nothing away, girl. Stand your ground.* I smiled–my damn lips better not be trembling–and said, "It's Arturo, isn't it?"

He stopped the scowl-smirk then and stared at me with anger and understanding. This wasn't his first Priestess rodeo; Snapdragon must have used her magic on them constantly. Constantly trying to prevent the dog fight because someone else was bored.

"What did you say?" he demanded. He was back to the cell door again, trying to press himself closer, taller.

"Your name. I said your name. Arturo."

"How–"

"I'm a Priestess." I remember what Falcon had told me about fighting. Lean in. Lean into your strengths and whatever advantages that you had. So I leaned *way* in. "How *dare* you lock a Priestess in a dungeon."

"Never seen a human Priestess before."

"Never seen a goat-man get so uppity about a human."

"*Goat–*"

"Open this door and let me out of here," I demanded. I commanded. I puffed myself up, holding as much eye contact with him as I could without throwing up. My toes were shaking so I gripped them tight in the boots.

"Why would I let my caged Priestess fly away? In here you're safe. For now at least." He turned away, his cape billowing like a commercial for laundry soap, and I reached through the cell and grabbed it.

Stupid, stupid, stupid! Bravery stops being brave if the bravado falls!

He yanked it hard, ripping it from my hands and pulling me to the cell door. I bumped my head again, and I winced. I couldn't keep it in.

"Deign said that you would help me." Arturo truly stopped then. He rushed back to the cell door and grabbed it with both hands. His nails were long–remember that, Jack, long enough to take a couple chunks of skin off if he wanted to.

"Deign is gone."

"No, he's on Earth. He was with me."

He huffed again. This time there was a laugh that made my skin crawl, and I stepped further away, close to the window again. Shoving myself through the tiny, tiny bars seemed more and more appealing. The smell of moss was overwhelming, and my lungs felt like they were filled with mold. Magic surged in the heart link; the panic in me had surged, and Diego's magic came in like a tidal wave. It wrapped around my arm and sailed up through my chest, fortifying me. It felt so close, like he was here instead of just connected through the heart link.

The man's lip curled up and for the first time I realized that his teeth were pointed. Not so much like vampire fangs, but like the teeth of a predator. The growl that escaped as he stared at me was rage-filled, and I wondered *again* why everyone in Obius hated me so much.

"Lies."

"Why would I lie?" I held up the heart link and he ducked a little, anticipating a blow. "Look at this. It's a heart link. We both have them."

"Now I know you're lying. Deign was so loyal to Snapdragon he tore the fabric of our worlds apart to protect that snake."

"But I'm the one that put his heart back together." Emotion threaded through me, and my eyes teared up. I wasn't afraid anymore; I was proud. This man was clearly going to kill me, but I wasn't afraid. Much. Diego was with me because I stitched him back together with–

"So you're saying Deign, King of Trellis, is alive and in love with a human?"

"A Priestess." I puffed myself out. *Rightness.* Hearing the words out loud–*Diego was in love with me*–made everything in me twist with joy. I knew I was grinning and probably looking a little manic. The heart link practically sang in my ears, finally happy that I was figuring out what all of the warmth it brought to me meant. Warmth. Happiness.

Love.

Diego was in love with me. Please let that be the truth.

"I used a binding spell and bound the fragments of his heart together."

"Enough with–"

"His heart is made of sunstones. They shattered, but he kept a piece with him, in the locket that he made for Snapdragon." The man charged the prison cell again. This time I didn't flinch. The magic made me bold, and I leaned into it even more. I whispered to Diego in my mind, and his golden magic lit me up–he felt *so* close. "I said, release me, Arturo."

"Stop saying my name," he growled.

I didn't need my staff for magic. I didn't. I had my necklace, I had the heart link, I had Obius and Diego's love in my veins. Elemental magic always eluded me; Mari and Peony could summon fires and dance through water, but all I could do was peer into people's minds. Arturo's was an iron box, but years of doing psychic readings taught me enough body language to know he was running out of plays here–he couldn't kill me, he couldn't just *leave* me here, and he didn't want to let me out. I rubbed my wrist with the heart link and let the feel of the bracelet spark the magic to life in my hands. The citrine warmed and glittered.

I sent a little prayer, a thought, to Diego. *"I hope you can hear me."*

"I'm listening, my Blossom. I'm always here. Be brave and get out of the castle. Get away from Arturo."

I was going to bust out of this damn cell.

Calling to the forest, I danced through the sigils I knew best: life, the Seer, and love. The forest listened. It heard me, just as the flowers and the bushes and the rest of the flora. Roots and leaves and vines and thorny branches burst through the small cell window. I moved aside, the small flowers curling around my arms, decorating me in their protective beauty. Flowers that looked suspiciously like Jack-in-the-pulpits rested squarely on my chest, the roots and stems of them embedding themselves in the dress, overtaking the Seer's crest. Three flowers. Always three.

The plants were ruthless; they tore through the window, breaking through the meager bars like they were small twigs, ready to be snapped.

Open the doors! I asked. The forest listened.

"Yesss, Priessstessss," echoed through me. The branches and roots ripped at the bars of the cell door, more roots and leaves forcing their way through, until finally, finally, finally the door was destroyed.

They didn't stop. They rushed past the door, seizing Arturo with blinding speed, and squeezed him. He struggled and tried to push the roots away, but they were too strong, came on too fast. His hands were bound. His legs were bound. His cape was probably ripped, and I took extra pleasure in that. Arturo struggled hard but the vines only tightened around him. Leaves covered his mouth, silencing him, which only made his rage larger.

"My name is Jack, Priestess of Trellis, and you will not keep me here." My voice was thunderous–it had to be Diego's magic to amplify it–and Arturo held my eyes. The plants did not let him go, but he shook his head *no* and bit at the leaves.

"Yes, I will!" he spat out, and the plants fully encased him. They covered his face, his entire body, until not even his horns were visible.

Flee, Priessstessss, pleassse, the forest whispered. They worked so hard to help me; I hated leaving them. The roots and leaves were singed from Wildfire, but they were *alive*, and I was so grateful they chose to help me.

I listened to the forest just as it listened to me. "Thank you," I said, lightly rubbing the petals of the Jack-in-the-pulpits.

And then I ran.

Chapter Ten

DIEGO

We fell through the sky.

Rainbows of light soared around us, too fast for me to see any one color clearly. The fall pushed my insides together, and I was weightless and hurtling toward the ground at blinding speed.

I felt sick.

Sherwin had wrapped his arms around Peony, his back to the ground, Peony on top of him. She clung to him, terror plain on her face. Mari was to my left, grinning wide. Fire flowed from her hands, and she looked *free*. Mari soared through the tunnel of light, burning bright, creating her own light as she felt the air on her face. There was no terror or freedom for me.

I felt *sick*.

My body ached—not my heart, but my body. I was used to the ache stemming from my heart, but this was different. My bones felt like they were snapping and bending. I glanced over at Sherwin again, and saw the nubs of his horns forming, purple feathers sprouting from his arms.

I grabbed at my head, as best as I could–I flailed around trying to get my limbs to work the right way, but thinking about my head made me realize that I could *feel* my horns. My arms were blue. The feathers that lined my forearms were coming back. Was I grinning or was I crying? My heart pounded harder and harder, threatening to shatter again.

The ground was getting closer and closer. We needed a way to *slow down* before we collided with the forest floor.

"Mari!" I screamed.

She stopped swimming in the air to look at me, then look at the ground. She grinned again, forcing herself vertically in the air, falling even faster. The neon green of the Cube burst forth from her and she *laughed*. Her magic was wild, responding to every whim, and I'd never seen her so happy. She spun in the air, the sigils for protection lighting up around each of us as she pointed her fingers in our directions. Flames sat at the tips of each finger, and she hugged herself together, then exploded out. Fire danced across the rainbow sky, a circle of fire around each cube–protection of a different kind: a weapon.

"No! No fire, please!" I begged. Mari either didn't hear me or didn't care. The fire blazed as she tumbled faster and I shouted again, "No fire!" The trees were there, the forest, I couldn't stand to see it go up in flames–

The ground was getting closer and closer.

"Deign!" Sherwin shouted, and I saw him still cradling Peony. She was still terrified, but her eyes were fixed on Mari. Peony yelled for Mari to hear her, but she didn't. Mari ignored my screams too.

The ground was getting closer and closer.

I readied the only basic healing spells I knew; healing was not my strong suit, and with depleted magic, there wasn't much I could to do to really help–

Peony pushed away from Sherwin grabbing for magic. Water formed in her hands, and she rubbed it up her arms, across Sherwin's face and chest, shooting it directly at me–it hit me in the face–and wrapping around Mari. It was another healing spell.

"Brace!" Sherwin yelled.

The ground was here.

We smashed into it, crashing loudly. Sherwin and Peony made their own little crater; the light of the Cube still stitched around them. Mari landed softly on her feet, cackling with joy and energy practically igniting against her. Her laughter echoed across the land.

I had no cushion, nothing to break the fall other than myself. The speed picked up, hurtling me faster toward the forest floor. Adrenaline pumped through me, and I hit the ground last–too hard, too fast–and rolled into some bushes. It was probably just seconds, but it felt like ages before my body stopped tumbling. I rolled and rolled, collapsing against a prickly shrub. My eyes stung and when I lifted my arm to wipe them away, I saw my feathers fully. Cerulean, kings' blue. They were silky and the smell of down tickled my nose like I was a child again. A memory of my mother's face flashed and then the tears came faster.

I sat up, noting that nothing was broken, and let out a shaky breath. I couldn't stop looking at my feathers. They were real, connected. I plucked one and winced, noting the drop of blood that formed in its place. They itched like all new plumage. A sob lodged itself in my throat; I was *me* again, but I didn't want to be. Not here, not now, not when Jack would see this face and see the monster that I had been. Flexing my hands, I cracked my knuckles, looking at how even my hands seemed wrong here. This was how I felt when I got to Earth too: wrong, monstrous, alone.

When I shattered the links between the realms, the Goddesses tossed me to the Earth, and the fall was much the same. Except I broke a *lot* of bones then and lost most of my heart. Sherwin was already at my side, helping me up and he smiled so wide I thought he might burst. If he didn't, I would. I forced the smile to my face, and that was all the encouragement he needed.

"We're *home*!" he shouted, hooting and whooping with joy. He hoisted Peony in the air, spinning her around. When she was back on the ground, he quickly ripped his shoes off, feeling the ground beneath his feet.

I did the same.

I sank back to my knees, feeling the grass and dirt and flora of my homeland.

But something was different–everything was darker, coarser. Was grass on Earth just that much softer? No, that wasn't it–

"Deign," Sherwin said. His voice cracked, and I turned to see what he was looking at. I wish I hadn't.

We were at the beginning of the Rainbow Forest; we had to be, because I knew the shape of the horizon and the shapes of the mountains around us. Through the trees would lead us to the Trellis Markets, and beyond that, the castle. The three towers of Trellis Castle loomed in the distance. I saw them too clearly and my pulse picked up, the disjointed pieces of my heart not wanting to cooperate and beat together. There should have been trees *here*, blocking the view.

There were no trees.

There were no trees *anywhere*.

"What–" I started. Then I remembered Jack's words, her warnings and her sorrow. The fire. Wildfire. It was real. It happened.

"No..." Sherwin trailed off.

"Oh god," Peony said, gasping, covering her face. The joy from Mari dried up immediately when she saw the forest too.

"This..." Mari said.

"Wildfire," I said. The words dried up in my throat. I had nothing to say. What was there to say? I ran my fingers through the ashen dirt. The smell of fire and burnt wood filled my lungs and I bit back a scream. I touched some charred wood next to me, next to the obviously burned bush I landed in. I touched the branches as tenderly as I could. They had to be in agony.

Time stopped as I looked around. Wave after wave of grief hit, knocking the wind out of me. This can't be real. This can't be Trellis. It just can't be. *Please, Goddess, please–*

"*The King! The King! It's him! The King!*" Sherwin and I looked around, looking for the tree that spoke to us.

A small sapling made it through the fire and I crawled over to it. I stroked its leaves; they were so small, one was broken, the other singed. The petals were still soft, still covered in the tiny hair-like fuzz of infancy, and I absently rubbed at the base of my feathers.

"*You're alive!*"

Fully on the ground now, I combed my fingers through the dirt. It felt like dirt on Earth: lifeless, magicless, existing but not breathing. I didn't need future sight to see what happened here. I felt more dead now than ever. A sob escaped and I scrubbed my face, trying to will the tears back down.

"*Please, my king! Don't cry! You're here! The King has returned!*"

I cried harder just so my mouth wouldn't be cruel and yell. The sapling tried to curl its leaves around my finger, embracing me, and it couldn't. The leaves were too fragile. How did this tree child know who I was? It wasn't alive when I was here last. Magic welled in my chest, hot and angry, demanding I *do* something for this child. A tear plopped on the dirt, and I watched the little ringlet of water soak into the scorched field. The forest wasn't even a forest anymore; it was a *field*, because there weren't enough trees to even call this a woodland now.

But I wasn't a healer, I was two-ninths of myself, and all I could do was send a little energy to the seedling. Focusing on the threads of my magic running down my arms, I funneled tiny bits through to my hands and fingers. I rubbed the leaves as carefully as I could–too hard and the leaves could tear or crumble. It shivered from the magic, growing steadily from the charred forest floor. When it was about two feet high, I stopped the flow of magic. Its leaves had unfurled even more, dark red and black striped flowers curling over themselves, with larger green leaves wrapping around them like a royal cape.

They were Jack-in-the-pulpits.

"There's a new Priestess! She shines so brightly! Maybe she can heal the forest, my King. Please don't be sad."

The sapling danced around in the sunlight, preening and showing off its budding but dazzling flowers. It would grow into a strong, lovely tree nymph one day. The nymphs were made from the trees, covered in various flowers, and bloomed with the seasons. I prayed that this little one would grow with the seasons too. She should be growing in a forest with her mothers and grandmothers, not alone in this wasteland. I swallowed again; my throat was too dry, too acrid. Kings don't break down in front of the world, and I sure as hell wouldn't allow myself any more comfort.

"Have you seen her, little one?" I asked, forcing my tone to be gentle. This sapling had enough grief without trying to ease my own.

"No, but her magic is so green."

"And... have you seen the other Priestess?"

"No, not since—you know."

Sherwin stood at my shoulder, just off to the side, falling naturally back into old habits. I shifted away from him; this wasn't my world anymore. I wasn't a King, just a castoff. The forest was blackened and scarred. The sky was too open. The castle was too far. Everything was worse than before, worse than it ever had been, and I was not entitled to claim even one blade of grass as home.

This wasn't my home anymore.

"Grow strong, build roots, little one." I rubbed the petals of the flowers once more. They were silky soft, with the barest hint of fuzz on the petals.

"Are you okay?" he asked me, and I shook my head no. There was nothing okay about this. Mari put a light hand on my shoulder too but it was awkward; she pressed too hard for it to be an attempt to console, and she didn't grip to pull me up. She sat her hand on me like it was too much trouble to hold it up, and I shrugged her off too.

"Can you feel Jack here?" Peony asked. She coughed from the remnants of the smoke. The fire had come and gone, leaving this mess in its wake, but the smell should have dissipated by now. It was like the forest wouldn't let go of the smoke as proof of what happened. I sucked in a deep breath, letting its murky, hazy truth burn my lungs.

None of this would have happened if I hadn't broken the links.

"Diego?" Peony said again. I was being rude, ignoring her and I didn't care.

"Stop," Sherwin said. My feet moved on their own, and I was already heading toward the castle. Where else could I go? I remembered the path even though the path had been burned away. This place was a memory I'd never forget.

"Deign–"

"*Stop* using that name," I spat back. The anger I'd suppressed and ig-nored for centuries burned through me, like someone had set Wildfire upon me instead of the trees. I would have preferred that; anything that would have saved these trees. My hands tingled. The nerves were on fire, aching and aching like only my heart had ever ached before. I cracked my knuckles again, magic flicking from me with each snap. This had to be the only moment where I was thankful for my lack of magic. I stuttered out a humorless laugh; finally, I wasn't screwing up anymore with my magic. Sherwin reached for me again–he was always so tactile, needing touch to connect to the world around him. "Stop acting like it means a damn thing!" I shouted, throwing his arm off of me. The sapling closed a few of its flowers, and I wanted to scream again. Everything around me was shattered.

The Shatterer.

Shattered King.

Shattered realms.

"Diego," Jack's voice was not even a whisper in my mind. Blackness overtook my senses; Peony and Mari and Sherwin's faces all faded out, the hellscape of the forest disappeared, and all I was left with was the starry outline of Jack. Her presence had changed. She was more commanding, more alive. The magic had fed her soul, and she was blooming.

"My Blossom," I said. My words echoed in my mind, and I didn't know if they were real. I felt her hands on my face. Silky, just like the petals of the flower. The star lights were blinding in this blackness but I kept my focus on her. She was more real than the death surrounding me in the forest. How could that have happened?

"I got away. From Arturo. I saw the falling stars." Her words were hurried; she spoke fast, and I reached for her to slow her down.

"Falling stars?"

"It was you, wasn't it?"

"I fell, but I'm no star, Jack."

"You light up the world for me," she whispered and I smiled. I felt the press of lips to my forehead, and I let out a breath. She wasn't here, this wasn't real, but it felt real. The heart link warmed and soothed the pain in my arms. I had forgotten about it until I realized that it was gone.

"Where are you?" I cried again, my words shaking more than my body at this point.

"I don't know really, I just ran from the castle."

"I'll find you," I said. The stars faded but I reached and jumped and grabbed for them. "No," I pleaded, "don't leave yet."

"I have to keep moving. You'll find me, I know you will."

"Tell me what you see–"

Jack was gone. Everything faded out, the light from the suns coming back, and everyone hovering over me like a wounded child. I saw Peony's face first and the likeness to her sister knocked the wind out of me. Her pink hair bounced in light curls around her face with her oversized glasses sliding down her nose. She had a healing spell at the ready; it twisted and twined around her arm like a snake writhing. The spell was aimed at me, and instead of a splash, the water seeped into my pores, into my skin. My hands stopped tingling.

"Are you with us? Where did you go?" she asked.

"I was talking to Jack," I said.

"No, we got that much. Sorry for eavesdropping. Sorta," Mari said. A breeze swept across us and Mari's various charms all jingled. She would have been an excellent dancer here—strong and graceful, with music that followed her everywhere.

"Her magic overwhelms me sometimes, and I just meet her in my mind? She builds the setting. I'm just along for the ride."

"Did she tell you where she is? Like, where do we even go? Is there anything left to go to–" Mari bit down on her lips, sucking the words back in.

"I really hope there's something left," I said.

"We should head for the castle. Makes the most sense," Sherwin said, standing further away than he ever had before. He stood next to Peony, and even though it was mere steps, the distance felt like a canyon between us. He tugged on Peony's hand, pulling her toward the path to the castle. Mari fell into step with them, and I stayed sitting on the ground. The buzz from the heart link lingered in my head, and each time it got harder to disconnect from her. The little sapling had closed up, soaking in the sunlight.

"Are you coming, Diego?" he said. My chosen name sounded foreign in his mouth. I brushed the dirt out of my feathers, taking an extra second or two to feel them. I had feathers again. My outer forearms were covered in the deep, cerulean feathers my family was known for. They were a little too fuzzy, like a child that just got their plumage. Sherwin's arms were the same, except his feathers weren't blue. They were the color of lilacs, and they set off Peony's hair perfectly. Sherwin had stopped at the edge of the path. We had fallen in what should have been a field of trees and flowers, but was just ash.

I kissed the top of the sapling, on one of its closed flowers and stood up.

The path would lead us straight to the castle but would take a good day's worth of walking.

"Alright! Road trip without the car or the tunes! This won't be boring as hell at all," Mari said. She bumped her shoulder against me once I caught up, and I bumped her back.

We're coming, Jack.

Chapter Eleven

FALCON

Operation: Rescue Lefty was in flight. The staff and I had a mutual dislike of each other but had come to an agreement. It would try not to kill me again as long as I rescued Jack. The staff didn't actually *talk* but we understood each other. It also wasn't alive or anything–that I could tell–so there was that too. After the fight and the lightning, I was wiped out. The suns had set, and I needed to rest. I couldn't get over watching two different suns set, one in the east, then another smaller sun trailing after it. The smaller sun was a brighter orange with the flames more visible. I'd heard tales about the Creator's love of fire and how She set the sky ablaze, but I thought it was just a story.

It wasn't. The sky looked like it would burn away into nothing, but it didn't. Color in Obius was truer. Everything was sharper, crisper, brighter. The sky was red and orange as it faded into blue and purple. Clouds passed through the sky, tinted by whatever patch of color they glided through.

I saw four lights flash across the sky, like falling stars. Two were clustered together, two more spread out. One of the stars sparkled too brightly, like it was a chunk of pure gold falling from the sky. For a second, I thought that I felt the impact of them hitting the ground, but that had to be the exhaustion talking.

I'd found a small, intact house not too far from the clearing. The house was too small for my frame; I had to duck quite a bit to fit through the door, and I couldn't stand up fully. My stomach growled at the sight of food. There were some types of fruits and bread left on the little kitchen table. The rooms were all shades of brown, light wood on the walls, dark wood for the furniture. The couch and chairs were stuffed with leaves, and there were sigils hanging up on the walls. Life. Blessings. One for each of the Goddesses. The bread had a stale feeling to it; too hard and crumbly to feel fresh.

I hated being a thief, but I dug in. The bread was harder than I initially thought and struggled to chew through it. It was savory and dense and would probably be delightful when freshly made. I judged the state of the fruits as on the stale end too, but beggars can't complain and neither can thieves. The bundle of small, spiky red fruits smelled like sugary cherries. The oversized plantains were greener than I was used to, but tasted similar. A small pitcher of honeyed water sat by the small window. I drank it down in one sip and the liquid reminded my body just how dehydrated it was. I'd lived rough for a while–not enough food, not enough water, too many hours in the sun, too many nights without a roof to keep the chill out my bones–but the damage from the lightning had worn me down more than all of those years combined. My everything hurt.

My insides were hollowed out and shriveled, but I'd already downed the last of the water in this little home. I found a little bed, and I was comically large for it. My feet and half of my calves hung over the end, but I passed out before I could talk myself out of it. The staff planted itself in front of me, a–thankfully–silent guard.

I was alone when I woke up from a dreamless sleep. The suns had come back up, and I'd missed them rising. My stomach growled again, but I'd cleaned out the kitchen last night. After finding some more food, I'd head to the castle. Those goons had too much armor and too much pride to be average citizens. Dudes like that always had something to prove, some point to defend. They were soldiers through and through, and I'd tangled with enough of them over the years to know what kind of fight I was in for.

Pain still buzzed in my hands, and I tried not to give it too much attention. The scars were settled now, thanks to the staff doing whatever healing spell it could. I was marked by the lightning, and there was no hiding that. I'd lost my bandana that usually covered the tattoo in the fight. It looked ridiculous, and I knew it, but it was something my mom gave me and one of the only things I had of hers. As much I wanted the comfort literally tied around me, I didn't think I deserved it. Losing the piece of her felt like a penance.

But the Judge's scales tattoo had been destroyed, and part of me felt *lighter*. No master to serve, no voice screaming in my head. The lightning had burned away whatever connection there was and for the first time in a long, long time, the only thoughts I cared about were my own.

What was left of the forest was bathed in light this morning. The entire rainbow was on display, and the trees seemed to delight in the colors as much as I did. My chest tightened thinking about how dull and lifeless the Earth must have felt to Diego after living in this world. How did he survive living in such a drab world? The Creator was playing favorites when she designed Obius, that much I was sure of.

Grabbing the staff, I headed back out. Jack had to be somewhere in that castle, and I'd storm every tower they had to find her. As if reading my mind–who am I kidding, it probably *could*–the staff glowed.

"Let's rock and roll," I said to myself. I moved too fast and nerve pain radiated through me, another penance.

JACK

I ran all night, until I'd gotten as far from the castle as I could. Diego's voice replayed in my head, *I'm no star, Jack*, and I wondered where he was now. The connection was quick–I tapped into him and out again within just a minute. As much as I wanted to be there for him, I had to run. Arturo would be hot on my heels, and I needed to put distance between us. I was alone–no Falcon or staff in sight, and Arturo had the advantage of knowing the land. I knew nothing. Diego's emotions were too chaotic for me to dig through his memories to find a path.

My feet moved on their own, autopilot fully activated, and I was beat. I found a small lake and I could sense how many souls were floating around, lost and aimless. They called to me, tugged at me, and I forced myself to stop until daybreak. I fell asleep on a flat rock, and the trees around me wrapped their branches around me in a protective cocoon.

Ressst, Priessstessss. You're sssafe. The trees whispered comfort in my ears, and I let myself sleep.

I dreamt of Snapdragon.

She was hiding in a tree, her legs swinging under a branch. She looked worse for wear, her dress was torn, dirt smudged on her face, and her bare feet were a mess of broken twigs and mud. A little thrill of joy shot through me–she always looked so beautiful, in all of the visions I had of her. But she was smudged and overgrown, swinging her legs back and forth like she hadn't committed the crime of the century. The world was still green around her; was that just my mind making the forest alive, or did she find a pocket of life? I didn't know which I wanted it to be more.

Snapdragon held a small stone in her hands, golden like the sun, and my heart skipped a beat. She cradled it to her face, the gold intensifying and reflecting against her cheek.

"Once upon a time, this would have broken my heart," she mumbled. A spell twisted through her fingers, the magic a dull green instead of the emerald color of her title. The Emerald Priestess was more like an Olive Priestess now. Her magic even felt weak in the dream; the color around her was muted, like I was watching her underwater. When did this moment happen? Time became more flexible as my magic strengthened. I moved through it easily, forwards and back, seeing the future and memories alike. But this dream felt like I was watching a stop-motion picture. Snapdragon felt so far away and so close that it made my perception dizzy. Staying grounded in the present was getting harder and harder. Staying grounded in my body was important, I knew that, but when I was dreaming I couldn't remember *why*.

The stone in her hands was really shining now. I'd lost focus on her for a minute, and then the dream snapped back so everything was crystal clear. Her eyes were greedy–the pupils were too wide, her eyelids too narrow, too intense. She caressed that stone like it was a lover.

"I'm sorry, Deign," she said.

Deign?

It was a sunstone. I felt Diego's essence then, like a memory of him reached through the sunstone to stroke her.

Snapdragon pulled the magic from the stone, the power radiating like she held a star in her hands. I shielded my eyes. Everything was too bright with spots floating in front of my eyes like how my visions started.

"I'm no star, Jack." Diego's hushed words were almost an apology replaying through me.

Oh, but Diego, you truly are.

The sunstone pulsated with energy. She was extracting it. She pulled the magic out in streams, lassoing them around her fingers, up her arms, around her neck, until they wound down her chest, seeping close to her heart.

Her eyes lit up green. Emerald green.

"No!" I screamed. Could she even hear me? I doubted it; she seemed so far away. She shuddered, the power flowing into her in steady streams. The sunstone seemed to respond to me, like it was the one that heard my voice. It blinked out, the perfect shine that came from it fading fast.

"Nooooo!" Snapdragon howled. She lost her grip on the spell, the magic trail falling off of her like limp strings. She grabbed at it, her hands passing through until she lost her footing in the tree. She slipped but her vines caught her, and she landed easily on the ground. The tree cradled her and the anger about the fire boiled over in my dream.

She felt it.

Snapdragon's eyes scanned and searched, looking for something. Her arms were held out in front of her, like was readying some spell to unleash. Her feet rooted themselves in the dirt, until they had disappeared completely. Snapdragon bared her teeth. They were pointed.

She looked feral.

When her eyes locked onto me, seeing me through the dream, the vision, whatever this was, I yelped.

She hissed. Fire formed in her hands, her emerald green eyes turning black, and shot the flames at me. I flinched, my body twitching against its will–

I woke up screaming.

"You're fine, you're fine," I said to myself. No flames. Nothing burning. Nothing on fire. I hugged myself inside the little cocoon the forest had given me.

You're sssafe, Priessstessss. I hugged my knees into my chest a little tighter.

"Not really feeling safe," I said. A small vine snaked through the cocoon, and I jumped at it. I fought the urge to stamp it out–it looked just like Snapdragon's vines–and tucked my hands into my knees. A small white flower bloomed at the edge of the vine.

Sssafe, the trees sighed.

"How do I know when things are real?" I asked the trees. I wasn't expecting an answer, but I wanted someone to talk to. The days stretched out longer and longer in my mind until they felt like weeks or months. Minutes were so distorted here when I connected to the Seer's Blessing. I could knit myself together in the stars of any universe, but I couldn't tell you if it was still the same day. The visions and memories happened so frequently now. Where did I draw the line? Could I even get a handle on the magic enough to draw a line? I tried to catalog the grooves of the trees that wrapped themselves around me, bringing my spirit back to my body.

I really wished that I had my staff.

Or that I wasn't alone.

Not alone, the trees said.

I ran my fingers around the edges of the little white flower, and the flower twitched. "Ticklish?" I laughed. The flower didn't respond but that was fine. I wasn't actually alone.

"Jack? My Blossom? Answer me," Diego called. His voice hugged me and I smiled; I felt the warmth of his words like he was lying next to me. The heart link glowed with energy, brightening up my little cocoon.

"I'm here," I said.

"So am I," he said with a confidence I wasn't used to from him. I knew Diego was a confident man when he was in Obius, but his years on Earth made him humble and quiet. His voice was loud, assertive. Sure of himself. It was potent; warming me through.

"Where?"

"In Obius. Trellis. I'm heading for the castle."

"Don't! Arturo is–"

"Arturo won't defy me." The tone of his voice had changed; the tenderness that I always heard in his words was gone. This was his royal voice, his commander's tone. The cadence of it made his memories flood through me; when he was being crowned, when he ran drills with his soldiers, commanding the energy of a ballroom to make announcements. Alive, alive, alive.

"Yes, he will. He's not the same person that you knew," my words trailed off. My attention shifted from Diego's voice in my head to the knocking on the cocoon. The trees closed the roots and vines even more, keeping me safe.

I stayed silent.

The knocking continued.

Then the smell hit. Like death and sulfur. Hot breath seeped through the cocoon. Another beast. I clapped my hands over my mouth, forcing down any sounds I made. It pawed at the cocoon, huffing and sniffing at it. It knew I was there.

My heart pounded. Sweat formed at my hairline and it made my scalp itch. I was aware of my human body, not adrift in the stars, and it made the fear tangible.

It pawed at the cocoon a little harder.

Magic pooled in the pendant around my neck. The citrine sparkled in the darkness of the cocoon, and I pretended that I was brave again. I trailed my hands over the cocoon walls, trying to speak to the trees without saying the words out loud.

No Priessstessss, ssstay, we'll keep you sssafe.

But I couldn't stay here–the beast would rip the cocoon apart, rip another tree apart. They'd already lost too many.

Emerald green magic flooded the cocoon, and the tree released its hold on me. The cocoon unknitted itself and the beast sat heavily on its furry rear, tongue lolling out, watching the scene.

For a second, it reminded me of a puppy. A harmless puppy that didn't know how to handle its oversized body.

But then I saw the teeth.

"Easy," I said, the magic gathering in my hands. I had no elemental magic, just whatever perks came from the Seer's Blessing. Some offensive magic would have been *peachy* right now, but I focused on looking brave more than anything. If the beast saw me shaking, I'd be done for.

It wagged its tails. All of them. There were at least three; I didn't look too closely, trying to keep track of where its eyes and teeth were.

"Flame, heel."

I knew that voice–

My feet were already moving, turning and running toward the voice. It couldn't be. It couldn't be *real*. I didn't trust my eyes. I broke into a sprint and launched myself at him; not a starlit version but–

Diego.

"Jack," he said. His voice trembled, and his thoughts were so loud that I wasn't sure if he said them or not. *Please be real, my Blossom, I'm here.* He held his arms out wide and I landed easily in them. I fit so easily against him, cradled in his arms like I was made to fit. Safety washed over me like a tidal wave and I clung to him, digging my fingers into his shoulders. Diego pulled me closer, hugging me to his chest. The scent of sandalwood cleansed the smell of the beast from my senses. He leaned his forehead in, pressing us together, with his breath brushing against my lips. He was breathing, this wasn't a vision or memory or a dream. Diego ran his fingers through my hair, hooking them at the back of my head, massaging at my scalp before they moved to my cheeks, my neck, my shoulders.

"You're real," I said. Were the words out loud? The heart links hummed with magic, intense and glittering. He fingered each charm on the heart link, lighting it up with more energy and light. Feathers brushed against my sides as he wound his arms around my waist and squeezed.

When I finally looked up enough to really take in his face, the air left my lungs. He had freckles across his nose, one dimple that made the years fade from him. I didn't need my magic to feel the nervousness in his eyes, so I cupped his face, felt my pulse rise again.

He was beautiful. He was full of life. Even the trees seemed happy that he was here. The wind had picked up a little–their doing, I was certain–to make him more windswept and lovely. The rustling leaves their soft applause for his return, maybe even for us both. My chest ached like my heart was breaking. He was *here*.

Diego's dark pink lips were full and smiling wide, and I touched them. Just the barest hint of a touch, where his skin felt so silky that I could have imagined it. Like in the visions. His slightly crooked nose crinkled with mischief. His eyes were pure gold, shining with vitality. He was alive. His black, black hair was just as playfully messy as it always was. I ruffled his hair, my fingers brushing against his curled dark brown horns. Diego had two curled horns on his head that rested against his skull, his curly hair filling in all the space around them. It was the missing piece of him that I couldn't see on Earth.

He studied me, his hands roaming my back, my face, my hair. The feathers on his forearms tickled as they brushed against me. Diego smiled like the sun and my heart skipped a couple of beats. Diego bowed his head, lending me a better view of the horns; I'd seen him do this in visions, bowing in greeting, in politeness. It struck me as royal, graceful. He finally settled on holding my hands, kissing the backs of each one. Heat flooded through my cheeks, settling low in my belly, and a slow, deep smile formed on his lips.

"I'm real," he said, turning my hands over and kissing the pulse points. His teeth grazed my wrist softly as he placed kiss after kiss on my hands until I pulled him up to see his face once again. He was real.

"Took you long enough," I said, tugging on a curl. A playful little growl escaped as he stood to his full height, even taller than I remembered on Earth, and he bowed.

"Apologies, my Blossom. I won't be tardy again," he said with a raised eyebrow and a smirk tugging at the corners of his mouth.

He scooped me up again fast, crushing me to his chest. The beast nuzzled at his hands, wagging its tails happily. It still reeked of death but at least it wasn't *trying* to kill me anymore. Diego snapped his fingers and the beast flopped over, exposing its belly.

"What is that thing and why does it listen to you?"

"A mage-hound. He listens because I raised him since he was a pup." Diego whistled, the mage-hound sat up at attention, sucking its tongue back in, still wagging its tails fast enough to shake its butt. If I squinted, it was sorta cute. Sorta. The fiery red and orange fur made it menacing, but the tail wagging less so.

"There's no way in *hell* I'm touching that thing," another voice said. No, she couldn't be here too?

Diego grinned—who was this man that *grinned* all willy-nilly now?—and covered my eyes with his hands. He leaned me against his chest, steadying and comforting me, his heart beating stronger and more unified than ever.

"I have a couple of surprises for you," he said, swinging behind me and then he removed his hands. Mari, Peony, and Sherwin were there. They hung back a bit, giving us some privacy, and I was suddenly *mortified* that my sister watched me snuggle Diego. They jogged over to us, and I held my arms out. Mari and Peony enveloped me in a hug and then I couldn't hold the tears back any longer. They felt like home, and holding onto my family made me realize how terrified I was that I'd never hug them again. Peony wiped my tears away. Mari bumped my shoulder. Energy flowed between the three of us like we had opened a Full Circle spell. Magic ran wild in Obius, and we were tied together.

"How–"

"Mama. Puddin helped find her, and they opened a link," Peony said.

"Mama?"

"Yeah, she's okay, she's back. She's holding the link so we can come home," Mari said.

I let go of them, stepping back. Go home. Is that still what I wanted? I had so much work to do here–the souls of the dead called to me constantly, and I needed to set them to rest. I needed to find Snapdragon. I needed to find Falcon and my staff too.

"Jack?" Mari saw the emotions playing out on my face; I couldn't hide anything from her, even if I wanted to. Relief. Joy. Concern. Mari held my face, our foreheads practically touching and our spirits connected. Magic for magic like we were casting in time with each other again.

"I can't leave yet," I said. Diego was still behind me, and I reached for him. He came immediately. "There's too much to do here."

"That's not your problem, Jack," Peony said. Her brows were intense, and her glasses slid down her nose. Peony was ready for a fight, but I had no fight in me for her.

"It is, actually. Literally *no one* else can help–"

"Snapdragon should have been helping," Sherwin said. He had horns too. And feathers. Purple ones. *He* was from Obius? The aura around him was the same color as his feathers; on Earth, anyone with magic had green energy, but in Obius, the colors had shifted. Sherwin was all shades of purple, and some I couldn't name.

"Shoulda been yeah, but she–"

"Will pay for this," Diego said. The finality of his voice made me shiver. He had snaked his arm back around my waist, resting on my hip and pulling me closer to him.

"Won't it be kinda... awkward to see your ex being all... psycho?" Mari asked.

"Probably," I said. My hands needed something to do; I folded my arms, unfolded them, played with my necklace, my hair. *Awkward* was the understatement of the millennia for them.

"Definitely," Peony and Sherwin chimed in. Diego sighed, pinching the bridge of his nose. He had every intonation of an annoyed school teacher that I found endearing.

"I'm not looking forward to it, if that's what you're asking." The pain he felt traveled through my body, starting at my feet and nearly suffocating me when it hit my lungs. His body angled to me, tender and gentle, with his magic stirring in my chest. I felt his words before he spoke, knew the words that would tumble from him likely before he did.

"You don't have to see her," I said.

"Yes, I really do." Diego kissed the top of my head. His feathers tickled my arm, and I twitched a little. It would take some time to get used to the feathers. "Is this too much for you?" he asked. His eyes shot up to the horns and he gestured to the feathers. I rubbed his arm, going with the grain of his feathers. The skin where the feathers started was a little rough, but not unpleasantly so. I scratched it with my nails just a bit and the feathers fanned out some.

"Blue is a good color on you," I said. I scratched again at his feathers, and I heard his voice in my head, a low growl in his throat.

"Keep doing that and I won't be fit for polite company, my Blossom." My cheeks heated up, Diego's golden eyes turned molten, and he nuzzled my hair. I made a mental note to do *exactly* that when we weren't with polite company.

"So what now? We just wander until we find that overgrown pile of crazy?" Mari asked. Her aura was always intense but here in Obius she had a glow that hovered just off of her skin, bright enough for everyone to see. I saw a fire lit inside her, and it was gorgeous. Mari had the glow of someone that was jumping gleefully off a cliff. The crackle of the flames surrounded her, a faint sound like knuckles cracking.

Peony looked like she had been thrown off a cliff. Her hair and clothes were disheveled, messier in a way that I had never seen her before. For the first time probably ever, I saw how fragile Peony was, how small she actually stood.

"I think we need to find Falcon first," I said.

Diego's mood darkened, his grip around my hip tightened, and I stepped away. I held my hands up, everyone was already ready to throw *him* off the cliff, so I had to intervene. The warm greeting changed to fiery anger, and I saw it written on their faces. Except for Mari; I saw the worry tugging at her.

"Look, I know he's not perfect, but I don't think–"

"Jack, he *literally* tossed you into another realm and you're *defending* him?" Peony spat. She was livid and making no attempt to hide it. That was bad. Peony didn't like emoting, especially any emotion that could cause a wrinkle, and her brows were positively furrowed. Her aura had darkened to a navy blue, the color of a warring ocean. She fussed at her hair, ripping out the hair tie and redoing the bun.

"He didn't know–"

"Ignorance isn't an excuse," Diego said. Everything in him shifted so quickly to being cold and distant. The pointedness I expected from Peony paled in comparison to the depth of anger that simmered in Diego's golden eyes.

"You should know, right?" Sherwin chimed in. He smiled, bitter and angry, and I wondered what the dynamic was there. I probed at his thoughts, digging a little, and saw Diego yelling at him, flashes of when they were young.

They knew each other. They were in Obius together before the Shattering.

"How do you fit in here, Sherwin? I knew you were trying to date my sister, but like, you're clearly Fae," I said. He had similar horns to Diego, but shorter and straight. Purple feathers and a beard.

"Yup. I served Deign before the shit hit the fan. When the Shattering happened, I hopped through the links before they were torn apart. I've been on Earth ever since. Never actually thought I'd make it back here," he said. Everything about Sherwin was different from when I worked with him; he was an herbalist on Earth, and he supplied a lot of the ingredients I used for lighter alchemy. His herbs were potent, but safe for people without magic. We had a good business relationship, and mostly I thought he was a stoner. I got none of those vibes from him now. He was aloof and serious, hovering around Peony like a moth to a lightbulb.

"So you just wanted to go home? Came along for the ride?" I asked.

"Sorta," he said with an easy, tight lipped smile. It was weird. It was nothing like the guy that I knew, or the one I pictured Peony falling for. And she was falling for him–I could read that even without my magic.

"I think we need to go to the castle," Diego said.

"I'm not itching to see Arturo again," I said. Arturo scared the crap out of me, and my bravado had run out. Now that they were here, my safety net, I felt like I couldn't be everything that I wanted; a Priestess, someone to stand at Diego's side, and walk through the remnants of the forest. The thing about safety nets was that it was easy to get tangled up in them. I felt myself shrinking a little, wanting to be quieter, calmer, *less*.

A vision tickled the edges of my eyes, and I leaned back into Diego. Breathing him in, I let it unfold because here in his arms, I knew nothing would happen. I was safe. It wouldn't overwhelm me like it did on Earth;

I was getting better with controlling it, but feeling blind made me uneasy nonetheless.

Falcon. His skin was blurred, like I was watching a censored TV show, but his face wasn't. He had dirt on his forehead. My staff hovered next to him, and he kept trying and failing to put some distance between them. He stalked around the castle, looking for a way in. I felt the groan more than I heard it, before he started scaling a wall. For a guy named after a bird, he certainly climbed like a cat. His hand slipped, I heard the string of curses, and felt a sharp pain shoot down my arm.

Diego's toasty hands sat firmly on my hips, and having something to ground me in the present made the vision clearer that this *was* the present. Falcon was at the castle now.

And he wasn't alone: Arturo was there, loads and loads of soldiers, and my intuition said that Snapdragon wasn't far off either.

Something wet and sticky nuzzled at my side and I jumped. The vision disappeared too quickly, leaving me dizzy. The mage-hound rubbed its head against me, and I cringed. Its fur was like sandpaper and burrs.

"Flame, down," Diego said and the creature flopped down, like a pancake.

"You named it Flame?" Mari deadpanned.

"Err, yes? All of them have fire-based names, because of their fur," Diego said.

"How creative," Mari said, stifling a laugh. She held her breath and a little flame ignited on her fingers. Mari blew it out and giggles took over. My throat closed up a little; I missed hearing her laugh. I missed seeing Mari stand without a shadow hounding her face, casting doubt on her confidence.

"I hate everything about this, but we need to go back to the castle. I'm pretty sure Falcon is there, and he's gonna be walking into a firing squad," I said.

"What?" Mari's voice ratcheted up an octave, fires burning in her eyes and again in her hands. Her energy was explosive, reactive–like a bomb ready to blow.

Peony had been too quiet, but I didn't want to poke the bear. I didn't want her to hover. A tiny part of me hated that she was *here*. Obius would amplify her truth-seeking magic, and I knew she'd smell a lie from my lips immediately.

"I can lead the way," Diego said.

"I can help too," Sherwin hadn't moved from Peony's side this whole time; his arm was wrapped around her shoulders, like he alone could shield her from the world.

"I hate this, but let's go," I whined, and Diego threaded his fingers through mine.

He whispered with the heart links, ***"You've nothing to fear, my Blossom."*** I gave his hand another squeeze. Sherwin, Peony, and Mari had already started heading out of the clearing, but Diego wouldn't move until he felt the tension ease from my shoulders.

"I'm good."

"You're brilliant," he said, sending butterflies cascading through me.

Chapter Twelve

ARTURO

That damn Priestess destroyed the dungeon when she broke out. I had enough of her blood to track her though; her feet were a mess of cuts and her human blood made the stone floor look muddy. The mage-hounds were restless; they had the scent of *two* Priestesses and neither within their sights. Snapdragon had broken into the castle and left just as quickly as Priestess Jack. They both slipped through my fingers so easily, like sand through an hourglass and I hissed as I pounded my fist on the desk in my small office. This was the space that Deign had given me–it was my post, and I had little desire to leave it. My office was the only part of the castle that wasn't in ruins. I maintained every crevice just the same as the day it was bequeathed to me.

Except for now; Priestess Jack's blood was on my floor. My hands itched to scrub it away, to erase the stench of her humanness in my space. Something caught my eye and I glanced out the small window, watching the sunsets light up the sky too brightly. Four falling stars hit the land. This happened more and more these days; stars fell, magic crumbled in the most fundamental of places, and I stayed in this small room, waiting for the end of days.

Today could be the end, I thought grimly. Would that really be so bad, though? There wasn't much left of Obius worth saving.

The mage-hounds brayed and growled in their courtyard and I remembered Deign holding them as young pups. They stank and cried, but Deign would force Sherwin and I into their cages to bond with them. I never did—not like Deign and Sherwin, but there was always so much love in Deign's eyes that I felt guilty not trying to.

Their howls were incessant. The courtyard was clear across the castle grounds but you could hear them throughout the entirety of the towers. They were anxious for the hunt, but I was torn on which one to send them after. A coordinated attack would be smarter—pool the resources to bring one back to Trellis Castle, and then go after the other.

Priestess Jack was closer; a human couldn't get far.

"General?" A soldier that I didn't know entered my small office. His words were stilted, and I wasn't a General. Something about his face was off, strange. I studied him a second and then realized—

Another human?

He had the Priestess' staff—Jack's, not Snapdragon's—and he swung it like a club. It bounced against my horn, and he stumbled back a little. I leapt to my feet; he has the advantage of surprise, but that would be his *only* advantage. My body ached for a target, for something to *do*, anything to snap myself out of this constant stasis, and this human was just the thing.

"Well fuck," he muttered.

My sword was in my hand before I even had to think about it. War was a game we played, but didn't practice. The soldiers of our countries were more for protection and enforcement of the King's words, not to kill. But still. The habit, the training—it never left you, and I lived for it. War was the only thing that made me jealous of the humans.

This human clearly wasn't a soldier but he was a brawler; I'd seen the type before, looking for the joy of throwing a punch more than a fight itself. He took a step back, eyes assessing, and I did the same. A grin played at the corners of his lips. He reminded me of Deign, and I shook the memory away. There were too many ghosts in this castle.

I'd misjudged him. Miscalculated. The human cracked his neck, loosening his bones, and tension rooted me in place.

I noticed how he planted his feet, one forward and the back up on his toes. The way he held his fists, guarding his face and chest told me everything I needed to know about him: if he bested me and took my sword, I would lose quickly. The scars that wound their way up from his hands were a tangled mess of torn up flesh. What the hell had he grabbed willingly and with *both* hands? The scarring was visible on every patch of skin on his arms and I shuddered.

His eyes darted across my face, around the room, and back very quickly. Whatever he saw or decided upon, I didn't like. The glint in his eyes went from panicked to cocky. The human lowered his shoulder, shifting himself so he was more angled. None of these were good things for me. I was never a brawler; I rose through the ranks with my skill with a sword or a scythe, never my fists. What good was throwing a punch when I could use my weapon to keep any foe at arm's length?

"Where is she?" he asked. Priestess Jack's staff hovered behind me, another threat. It thundered with a deep green fury; storm clouds colliding inside the perfectly round orb. It had the same fury that was etched on Priestess Jack's face when she was here.

My office was small for one person, but with both of us and the staff, it was comically small. The man took up most of the doorway, and what little room he left there, the staff occupied. My desk was in disarray from the first attack, but I had the advantage of stature. I was nearly a head taller than the human—were they all so small?—and that seemed to worry him so I straightened my back more, raising to my fullest height.

"Who?" I asked back.

"The Priestess!"

"Which one?" I kept my voice calm. Emotion was his weakness; the more he panicked, the jumpier he became. His eyes tracked around the room, over me, moving at an alarming speed.

"Fuck, is Snapdragon here too?" He bounced on his toes, needing some release from his energy without giving away his position of power. The door was blocked from the size of his body. I was too large to fit through my tiny window. The staff radiated anger, and there was no escape. The unending conversations with the King played through my head—him insisting that I take a larger space even though he had picked this room out for me when he was child, you're a large fellow, you need the space, a Fae of your station surely deserves at least a proper window—

I regretted not taking him up on the offer of a larger window.

"Snapdragon is no longer here," I said carefully. He groaned, and I didn't know what to make of that noise. Humans were so expressive, but in the oddest ways. Their faces always looked confused or frustrated, so trying to parse anything else from them felt nigh impossible.

"What about Jack? The human one? Where's she?"

"She's not here either."

He laughed. It didn't appear like he was amused—why did he laugh? "Where is she then?"

"Gone."

That was a poor word choice—he lunged at me and I barely dodged the blow. Part of his hand connected with a tiny sliver of my face and I recoiled. The staff swung itself, directly at my throat this time, not my horns.

"Bro, I'm a reasonable dude. I just want information. We can dance around this little office until I beat the shit out of you, *or* you can just tell me where she went and I'll leave. Trust me, this place isn't where we're trying to set up shop."

"She left quickly. She wasn't in a chatty mood."

He groaned again, and this time the frustration on his face was clearly written on his features. "My hands are still aching from the lightning fiasco, my dude."

Lightning! I thought wildly. He grabbed lightning magic and *lived?* I held my sword defensively, crossing the blade diagonally across my chest, freeing one hand. I needed to cast something to get him out of the castle, but my magic was all but gone these days.

"Right, hard way it is, then." The staff listened to our conversation, and it hovered in front of him. He didn't take it—so he wasn't completely stupid—but he started to cast something. His magic was full and powerful; being in a land of magic was doing him a boon, unlike the rest of its inhabitants.

I recognized the sigil work immediately. The Judge. He was invoking the Judge. Not just a scion of Hers, but the Goddess of Justice Herself. I steeled myself, locking my knees and tightening the muscles of my thighs to hold myself steady. Certainly he couldn't possibly–

"What are you–"

"I got friends in high places," he said as he worked the spell to call Her for help.

"I've told you everything," I said. I hadn't seen this level of magic in an age, and I did not want to be here when he woke the Judge for a simple question. My locked knees worked against me now, my body struggling to keep its focus and not give way to his magic. These damn humans didn't know what the Goddesses were like, what Their power and rage could be, how easily invoked. They didn't *know* anything! My throat was dry and my hands started to shake. No, no, no, no, no–

"Tell me where she is." His voice went deeper, ragged, and magic-heavy.

"The Rainbow Forest, west of the castle gates," the words tumbled from my mouth automatically, freely and I was glad of it. Anything to avoid the spell he worked.

Magic swirled in his eyes, and I realized that he wasn't calling for the Judge to make an appearance; he was invoking Her will. The truth. There were so many things that needed to be said, and I pressed my lips together: there were things that humans simply had no need to know.

"Don't hold back now, my guy. Let it *all* out."

"I should have killed her too," I said and his eyes turned murderous. The magic that lit them up turned black, and everything about him was dark, dark, dark.

The staff crackled with lightning, and the fire started almost without anyone noticing. Little sparks catching on the papers and the little plants that had invaded the office. The staff spun in place, building the fire up faster and faster.

"You need to think about your priorities if murder is your go-to. The Judge wouldn't be too happy about that shit."

He waved at me–his fleshy, human fingers wriggling like worms–and the staff let him pass, and stones from the castle walls crumbled down, blocking me in the tiny room.

FALCON

Destroying part of D's old place was not part of my plan, but I found more and more that my plans tended to go to shit. That goat-looking asshole was *huge*. He seemed terrified of me, which *haha* I'm *not the giant goat man*, but okay. Jack's staff was getting more bold, and acting more and more on its own. It blocked him in as the stones started to crumble and the fire picked up. I don't fuck around with fire magic. One, I'm bad at it and I know this. Two, it's hard to control and entirely too easy to screw up.

The staff didn't seem to care. It lit the papers and other little knickknacks on fire in the man's office. I wasn't sure that it was capable of *empathy* but it was certainly capable of fire. And lightning, let's not forget that party trick.

About an hour after we left the castle to burn itself out, the staff started glowing. It leaned forward, tilting itself instead of bobbing straight up and down. And it just went. It was completely okay with leaving me in the dust, but I wasn't about to let it just up and disappear on me. Jack would want this staff back–and I was going to make sure that I brought it back to her.

I picked up the pace, having to jog to keep up with the staff. Soon the castle was behind me, and I ran through the trees. It was good–the running. The latent part of my brain was coming alive. This was what humans were made for. My feet connected with the ground, the fallen leaves crunching underneath my boots. The air was crisp and clean and filled my lungs in a way that the air on Earth never had. I pumped my arms, running faster and faster, and now the staff was struggling to keep up with me. Darting through the trees, I moved effortlessly. *Yes.*

This was a runner's high on steroids–everything in Obius was like that. It explained Diego too. He was polite and gracious but so extra about it. It always felt like an act, who could be that damn humble and honest, but it wasn't. It was the essence of Obius in him. Everything was purer, brighter. The joy of running. The smell of the air. The kindness in my best friend's heart.

Goddess Almighty, I loved it here.

The staff detoured and I had to pivot to follow it. I nearly crashed into a tree, but I missed it, the tree bending its trunk to accommodate me. I yelled a thank you, and felt the barest hint of magic brush against my cheek. A greeting. The trees finally saw me and decided I was one of the good guys, even though I was only human.

The Rainbow Forest was completely undamaged here. Wildfire didn't make it out this way and I was so relieved. The trees were painted in every color, with the suns rising and changing them as they moved across the sky. The leaves were iridescent, the trunks were stained like painted glass, and branches twisted in colors I'd never seen before. Reds and oranges, blues and purples. Truer colors. It made me tear up.

The staff led me to what looked like a market. I pictured the fairy tales I grew up reading with Nana again–the pictures in the books looked just like this place. The dirt gave way to stones and cobblestones. There were stalls set up with pennants and flags flying over them. I couldn't read the signs, but I imagined they were little advertisements.

I stopped to catch my breath, sucking in that gloriously crisp air, when something struck me as *off*.

It looked like a place of life. Well worn stones. Stalls and stalls packed in tight, wares still on the countertops. The flags and pennants were bright, but not *Obius-bright*. They looked like standard, run of the mill cloth from Earth.

And it was empty.

Where was everyone? The staff had left me. I scanned the area fast, looking for the floating and bobbing hunk of wood. Nothing. Where could it have gone in just a couple of seconds–

"You realize that anyone could have heard you hooting and hollering all over the place right? Someone other than me, I mean. Pretty amateur move, I'd say."

I jumped at the sound of Jack's voice. She was perched up on the top of one of the stalls, at the edge of the market area. She swung her legs back and forth, smiling. She had some actual clothes on now, and I felt a rush of relief from that. The amount of guilt I carried for tossing her over here in her PJs was ridiculous. She had shoes too. The staff rested across her lap, and contented energy poured from it, from Jack.

"Oh my god, what happened to your arms!" Jack jumped down and came rushing over to me, examining my hands and arms. They were still tender, when I thought about it or paid them too much attention. I'd given my long sleeve shirt to Jack before we separated, and I felt naked in front of her. I didn't want her to look at the scars, to examine my stupidity up close. I didn't want her to notice that the scales had been burned away and how much I missed their grounding presence on my arm.

"Talk to your walking stick," I muttered.

"What did it do to you?"

"Electrocuted me. With good reason, but yeah, it'll be a fun story one day, once all the tissue grows back."

"Your scales," she said, tracing over the destroyed scales.

"Yeah, those are gone. Just an excuse to get some new ink, right?" Her eyes welled up with tears and she hugged me tight around the waist. Jack was a lot smaller than me, but most people were. I was a solid six-foot-five and had nearly a foot on her.

"Hey Lefty, no tears, I'm alive. It's all good. This isn't even the worst scar I've got–"

"I'm so glad you're alive," she said.

"Jack, it's gonna take more than a little lightning storm to take me out. Like seriously–"

"Oh shut up. Diego is gonna be happy to know that you're okay too." She nudged at my arm, accidentally bumping one of the deeper scars and I winced a little. They were healed, the staff made sure I wasn't going to die, but everything was raw. My nerve endings tingled a bit too much when I thought about the pain, so I did my best not to.

"Somehow I don't think D is gonna be *happy*–"

"Damn right I'm not," Diego said.

By the time I was turning to find his voice, I found his fist. He decked me square in the nose and I crumbled. I could take a punch, even a gut punch didn't take me out, but the nose? Done. Toast. Finished. Hopefully he hit it at the right angle to straighten it back out. My hands were in the dirt, again, and I felt blood drip down my lips. I spat blood and gritted my teeth. Great, now my face would be swollen. It was really the only thing I had left going for me at the moment.

"No, that's fair, I deserved that," I coughed out.

"Diego! What the hell!" Mari shouted and she skidded to the ground next to me. Mari's hands were on my face, pulling me up to inspect the damage. Mari wasn't great at *gentle* and I winced. My fucking face *hurt*, and Mari grabbed handfuls of me, twisting me back and forth to look at my ever-swelling nose.

"He really did deserve that," Peony chimed in. Ah, lovely. The whole crew was here.

"Does he need some healing spells?" a dude asked. He had horns. Feathers. Cool. It was a look, that's for sure. When I finally looked up and saw Diego, I noticed that he did too. Curled horns. Blue feathers. His arms were crossed but he finally looked like someone that enjoyed breathing instead of an action figure. I pushed myself up on my feet and Diego refused to look at me.

I hugged him.

"I'm sorry."

"It's going to take time for me to forgive," he said, but I could tell the walls were already dropping. He couldn't stay mad at me. I played up the nose and let my eyes well up a little more than I normally would. He'd forgive me. One day.

I could wait for that.

"Where were you? After we got separated?" Jack asked.

"After you went down, I got mobbed by the rest of the goon squad. They moved too fast for me to get to you before they took off. I had my hands full after that." I gave them the play by play of the fight, including what happened at the castle, and she winced and nodded right along.

"Arturo is a jackass," she said.

"Agreed, but he seemed kinda scared of me. His magic wasn't working right, and then your staff sorta went rogue." It glowed at the compliment and I kept my distance. I know it probably didn't mean to nearly kill me, but I was the forgive-not-forget type.

"Is the castle alright?" Diego asked.

"I think the damage was minor, really. It's still standing."

"In one of my visions, I remember Snapdragon talking about the magic of keeping the towers standing tall. I wonder if the lack of magic here is making the castle weaker," Jack said.

"I was wondering what caused the stones to come down. It was a little fire, nothing too crazy. Nothing like–"

"Wildfire," she said. The staff glowed at the word, and I flinched again. I was too jumpy and Diego noticed. His assessing eyes took in every inch of me, looking me over head to toe. His eyes lingered on my scarred up arms. I wished for a jacket. My nerves were on fire, aching with every breath, every gust of wind, or movement.

"Yeah."

The mention of Wildfire made my chest tight. Jack was right all along. I glanced down at the ruined scales on my arm, and my chest got tighter. The Judge never spoke to me; I was never favored, never noticed, like Nana had always told me. I was guided by my own conscience, and I mistook my good judgements as words from a Goddess. The magic that caused the scales to tip was probably just another illusion.

"I really am sorry, Jack," I said. I was no good at apologies–they rarely did anything other than lip service, but this time was different. Jack didn't need to see my face to feel the weight of my words; her magic, her actually blessed magic, would be able to spot a lie miles away.

"Don't be. Snapdragon was manipulating you. I'm not sure what her goal truly was though."

"Isn't it obvious what her goal is?" Purple feathers said. He had been silent since I saw him, but I noticed the way he hovered around Peony–like she was suddenly about to start shitting gold nuggets and he had to be ready to catch them. He weirded me out, but he seemed harmless enough.

"I can't see what she hoped to gain from all of this," Diego said. He was a stone wall talking. His features stilled. His mouth was a flat line. His normally warm eyes were arctic and I was again grateful that things wouldn't stay that frosty between us. His energy reminded me of the rage in Jack's staff and my hands twitched. I wasn't looking to repeat my stunt with the lightning ever again.

"Deign–Diego, sorry, even before the Shattering... Snapdragon had her eyes on the throne. She wanted to be the Queen of Trellis. She'd always wanted that," Purple feathers said.

"Sorry, hi, I'm Falcon. I didn't catch your name."

"Sherwin."

"And you know D how?"

"We grew up together. Here. In Trellis. I was part of his vanguard."

A pang of jealousy lobbed through my chest, and I sucked on my teeth to keep me from saying something petty. Like *this isn't a contest, shithead, and even if it was, D was my bestie.* Besides, where was he when D was barely able to stand upright? Where was he when I held D up when his energy was totally depleted? Diego seemed to sense the tension and he rolled his eyes; a human mannerism he'd never embraced before. Being in Obius made him more *aware.* Something like this would have gone right over his head on Earth, but then again maybe he was just too depleted to even register body language. Can't say that would be high on my essentials list if I was struggling to stay upright and breathing.

Obius looked right on Diego. The horns and feathers were kinda weird, but not really. His eyes were brighter and the magic that radiated off him from his emotions was a thousand times stronger.

"Have you found any more of your heart?" I asked Diego.

"No, why?"

"Just curious. So *Sheeerr*, why exactly did Snapdragon have her beady little eyes on the throne?"

"Why else? Power. We Fae folk aren't so different from humans, you know," Sherwin flashed a million dollar smile. He snaked his arm around Peony and she leaned into him.

If I had met this dude on the street—on Earth—I'd consider his face to be *punchable*. He had the skater-bro, surfer-bro vibe that I hated. The kind that assumed they could hide themselves around the persona of being too stoned to care about anything. Everything about this guy was sharp, alert.

He tried to take a page out of my playbook and I didn't like it.

"I can't believe that everything was a lie," Diego said weakly.

"I'm sure it wasn't, D, but people do change. Something changed for her, and that's not on you." I clapped him on the shoulder, something we had done for years at this point, and he seemed comforted a little. *Things will be okay*, I told myself.

Mari, who had been essentially silent, finally tapped my arm to get my attention and I flinched in pain. My head stopped spinning and I saw all of the fire that danced around her. She was practically igniting herself. Mari was stunning in the evening light. The setting suns highlighted her dark brown skin and the breeze picked at the beads in her hair to make them jingle. She sounded like a good luck charm, and I desperately needed some of that in my life. I patted her hand, and her eyes met mine.

"Don't look so worried, girl. I still owe you some pizza. I'm not gonna be checking out until I repay my debts." I winked at her. If we were alone, I'd consider kissing her, but not here, not in front of everyone. One day, maybe, if I was ever brave enough.

"Easy there, Falcon," Jack's voice rattled around in my brain and I scratched at my pony tail. It was a tangled mess.

"Is there somewhere we can stop for the night?" Peony asked.

"The square would be our best bet, I think," I added. Diego nodded, and so did Sherwin.

"D, there's some of the forest that wasn't hit by the fire over there. You have to walk a little out of the market center, but it's there. In case you needed to see it."

Diego grinned at me. This was why everyone was so drawn to him; Diego's energy felt like sunlight. If he was fully powered up, whole heart beating in his chest, I might end up licking his boots if he smiled like that. He had charisma coming out of his ears and it was utterly bizarre.

"I need to see it," Jack said.

"Maybe you two can check it out? We can start building a base camp. Maybe find some food," I said. Jack and Diego stood hand in hand and I hated myself for ever trying to break that up. The bond between them was so evident that I felt pathetic for being blind to it.

"I can help on the food front," Sherwin said.

"I'll help too," Peony added. They took off in the opposite direction of the forest. Jack and Diego headed into the trees, and I was alone with Mari. I saw fires in her eyes and heat radiated from her.

"Did you really stab Diego?" she asked.

"*Stabbed* is a bit exaggerated. I hit him with a syringe full of some hardcore la-la juice. I knew it wouldn't kill him. It was just supposed to knock him on his ass for a bit-"

The fire had taken over her irises.

"It was bad," she said. "Diego looked *bad*. I thought he was gonna die. And then Jack was missing. You were *gone*–" I tilted her chin, forcing her eyes to look at me and tried to bring her back from the brink of igniting.

"Marigold Groves, were you *worried* about me?" The smile crept up before I had a chance to stamp it down. The fire hadn't lessened, but the color darkened. The heat sizzled between us and I didn't think it was her magic. I hoped it wasn't.

She was the kind of electric I liked. Intense. Brilliant. Terrifying. Not-skin melting.

"What if I was?" It was the quietest I'd heard her speak; not bold, not brazen, but maybe a tad shy.

This wasn't the time or place for me to try to put the moves on this woman.

Timing, among other things, was not my strong suit.

I tilted Mari's face up with the faintest touch of her chin. She allowed it, but turned her head so she presented a cheek instead of her lips, and cut those gorgeous eyes at me. She was all hard edges, and I wanted to learn what caused each ridge.

I kissed her cheek, first pressing my nose to her skin, allowing myself an extra second to be close to her. It was a chaste kiss; my lips brushed against her, right on the apple of her cheek. Mari's skin was cold despite the obvious amount of fire magic simmering just under the surface.

"Thanks for caring enough to worry," I said, my words way more husky than I intended.

Mari was already on the move, waving me away. I saw the smile and the sparkle–literally–around her and let her go. "Come help me find somewhere to sleep. We're all beat," she said.

"Aye, aye captain." She laughed at my mock salute, and the knots in my stomach started to unclench. My face hurt, my everything hurt if I was being really honest, but I hadn't fucked up bad enough to lose my family.

My friends. Blinking away the irrational tear that formed, I trotted after Mari.

I wouldn't fuck up and lose them again. I promised myself.

Chapter Thirteen

JACK

Falcon pointed us to a small path leading away from the markets. They had been mostly spared from the flames, and I took an extra few moments to soak in the atmosphere. It reminded me of the crystal markets, but without the plastic tables. The stalls were made of wood and stone, cobbled together with clay and magic. I could smell the magic from them, like moss and joy, made in happier times. I caught glimpses of the past, with the square full of people, dancing and drinking. There were still some flower banners hanging from the light posts; the flowers were dried and hung limply like someone had forgotten they were even there. The posts themselves were forgotten too. The glass globes on top had burnt out wicks and cracks all through them. If I touched one, the glass would have shattered.

Some of the stalls still had goods on their counters: small jars of some type of elixir, flower petals in baskets, moldy looking bread and mottled fruits. The market was desolate in a way that the fire couldn't have done. It was lifeless from exile, not lifeless from flames. There were stalls meant to sell crystals and jewelry, but the sign hung from one hook, and all that was left was some twine. One day, this square would be restored and the festivals and light would return. That day just wasn't today.

Diego said their official name was the Trellian Market Square, but it had many names: markets, market square, town square, and so on. He called the city center, Treis, and explained it was the closest thing to a city that existed in Obius. Diego held my hand as he led the way. I stepped faster to keep up with his larger strides and just to be a little closer to Diego. Tucking my hand in the crook of his arm, I leaned in.

Sandalwood. He always smelled like sandalwood, and the forest.

Once the town square was behind us, I saw the trees. They were massive; how could I have missed them? They stood like they had been there since time started ticking, and could tell many stories of the Fae that had come and gone.

"Thank the Goddesses," Diego said. His voice was worshipful, and I thought he might get to his knees to pray. I squeezed his arm, bringing him back.

"Diego, are you okay?"

"I... I just never thought I'd see these trees again." He wandered away from me and into the forest. The trees sighed and their happiness was contagious. Of course they had missed him. The trees reminded me of Giant Sequoias; the trunks were massive, larger than any tree I've seen before. They were heavily knotted, the branches and limbs were high in the sky as if they were part of the clouds.

And then the colors.

The trunks were reds, oranges, yellows, and pinks. The leaves were all cooler shades; blues, greens, and purples. There was magic laced through them as well, little streams of magic running up and down the trunks in thin lines like lace.

"I didn't see these at all when I left the castle," I said.

"I'm not surprised. These trees are the sentinel guards of Trellis. They move and hide as needed. When I was a child, Sherwin and Arturo and several others would hide in these forests. We'd make a game out of who could stay hidden from the guards the longest," his voice was hoarse. He cleared his throat, and some vines snaked down to caress his face.

Your Majesssty, the trees sang. Their words floated on the wind and Diego held a hand out for a small wind current to spiral there. He held a tiny cyclone in his hand, little leafy bits spinning with the current.

"I'm so–" Diego's voice broke and he rested his face against them.

We missssed you. The cyclone sped up, unfurled itself and wrapped around Diego like an embrace. The colors of the trees shifted again. They rippled through them like they were doing The Wave. It reminded me of the aurora borealis but in the trees. Awestruck, my eyes swept through the sea of trees. Emotion welled up in my chest, hard and painful, around my heart.

Homesick. I missed my home, my ruined life on Earth, and yet standing here in the forest, home felt nearer. I pulled off the pretty boots and socks, standing barefoot in the dirt and my magic hummed through me. My staff was in my hands before I realized I had called for it.

This was right, this was my place.

I moved without thinking, dancing my way through the steps of a spell I couldn't name. The Priestess' Call. Its name came to me quickly, and Diego watched as I danced. The staff spun in my hands with ribbons of magic flashing against the dusky sky. Joy broadcasted across his face.

The visions wrapped themselves around me and I watched as my body glided through the spell.

It was just Diego, smiling. He stood on a balcony, thousands and thousands of Fae were below him, cheering. He roared with magic, the sky exploding in light, and the crowd erupted. I saw Sherwin and Arturo behind him, playful and smirking. Diego had a long, white cloak that shimmered around his shoulders. A large golden and green jeweled crown sat on his head covering his horns. It was his coronation.

Then he unbuttoned the cloak, turned to his friends briefly, eyes wild with mischief, and leapt off the balcony. Sherwin and Arturo laughed, reaching for him, but he was gone. Diego somersaulted through the air, landing heavy on his feet. The jump had to be several stories, at least four, and he landed without a care in the world. The crowd roared again.

As the vision faded, Diego stood in front of me. The spell wound down, my body still dancing through it, and when I stopped, I was directly in front of him. His chest was heaving and a sparkle glinted in his eyes.

"You're magnificent," he said.

I chewed on my bottom lip, trying to keep the grin down. The heart link was weightless on my arm. It changed depending on how far away he was from me, but now with Diego holding my face in his hands, it was weightless. I was weightless. Diego's lips were so close to mine. The heat of his breath brushed against me, making me shiver. I licked my lips, waiting for his kiss, and he rubbed his thumb over my bottom lip.

And then he ran away, into the trees, laughing. His laugh shook through the trees, through me. All of the walls and guards and blank faces he hid behind on Earth had fallen away completely. Happiness poured out of him like he was only made from sunny days.

"Ohhh, you are *awful!*" I yelled back, chasing after him. He had disappeared in the forest, the trees no doubt helping to hide him.

"Can you find me?" he said.

I couldn't tell where it was coming from, but then I remembered the first visions I had of him, when he was just dark, black energy. How I could feel him anywhere in the forests of the vision, so I stopped and closed my eyes. Focused. Felt around until I recognized his energy, and turned toward him. His energy now was so different, so joyful. The weight he'd carried for centuries seemed to be lifting, enough for him to *smile* so freely. That homesick lump formed in my throat but I kept walking toward him. Like a homing beacon, his energy flashed in my mind, and before I knew it, I was running too.

Straight into his arms.

Diego stepped out from behind a tree and scooped me up, mid jump. He was waiting for me, waiting for me to find him.

"I see you," I said, hoping he understood. I saw his joy, his peace. I saw the way he melded into nature, like he had never left. I saw the unity in his heart and how being in Trellis awakened the parts of him that had long fallen asleep.

"Hmm, it's hard to hide from a Priestess," he said between breaths. He was breathing hard, and every breath that grazed me felt like a gift.

"No more hiding from me," I said. My tone was more serious than I meant, and Diego caught the edge of it. Of course he did.

"Jack? What's wrong?" Diego rubbed his thumb between my eyebrows, soothing away the wrinkled up skin, soothing away the gnawing feeling that everything was going to change again.

"Nothing? I'm not even sure, I'm just a little homesick, I think." Diego looped his arms around my waist, his hands steady on my hips.

"Do you think this could ever be your home?" he asked. He kept the words light, soft, but he couldn't hide the question in his mind, the hope that I would just immediately say yes.

I *wanted* to say yes, I wanted to agree with him. Part of me wanted to agree to anything he asked, ever, but the truth was that I didn't know. My own future was never part of my visions, even after the magic boost from being in Obius. Forwards or back, my life was always a mystery.

"Maybe," I said. The calm, stoic Diego that I knew from Earth had all but faded, but I saw the pensive face he permanently made creep in. It wasn't a bad face. Just thoughtful, chewing on his words carefully.

"Jack, my Blossom, you know that I will follow wherever you go, right? If you stay in Trellis, then so shall I. If you travel the entire realm of Obius, then I'll walk beside you. If you walk into the afterlife of Sanctum, I'll be holding your hand." He held up our joined hands, squeezing as if to show me that he wouldn't be letting go.

He tightened his grip on my hip, holding me firm. I didn't move, I just watched him as he spoke slowly, letting the weight of his words really sink in. I swallowed hard, "And if I want to go back to Earth? To my life, my shop?"

"Then I'll follow you there, too. You can teach me how to garden." He lifted me like I weighed nothing and held me against a tree trunk gently. Diego had one arm under my rear, and the other cradling my neck. He trailed kisses over my throat, my collarbones, up my neck to my ear. His voice was husky again, and I shivered. "We are linked together, my Blossom. You were destined to be in my path, and I in yours. That means nothing will keep me from you."

I wrapped my arms around his neck and hugged his face to my chest. His horns were a little rough against my face, but this was him. This was Diego. This was the former King of Trellis and he was here, holding me like I was the only anchor that could keep him steady. The feathers on his arms rubbed against mine and I dragged my nails at the base of them again.

"Can I kiss you now? Properly?" I nodded, and then his lips met mine.

Diego kissed me slowly, taking his time before deepening the kiss. He was warm and tasted like honey as our tongues just barely brushed together. His fractured heart thudded hard in his chest, so much so that I heard it–or was that mine? My hands were on his face, touching the stubble on his chin, another tactile reminder that this wasn't just a dream. He nipped at my lip, before he ran his free hand up my back. I arched into him, my skin tingling every place he touched, and I opened my mouth to him a little more. He growled, low in his throat, and I pressed myself to him.

"Don't let go of me," I said, the words tumbling out more needy than I'd ever heard myself be, and he lifted my chin so he could see my eyes. I got lost in the depths of his golden, radiant eyes.

"I won't, I promise," he whispered and I nodded quickly, a little embarrassed at how emotional I got from a kiss–the best kiss of my entire life. He left me breathless, and I clung to him. The trees had closed ranks around us, moving silently. We were hidden from view. I sighed happily against Diego's chest.

Priessstessss, King Deign, watch out.

We are not alone.

Diego straightened immediately. He dropped me softly on the ground, and stood in front me, trying to shield me from whatever the trees sensed.

Magic poured through the forest and Diego had his hands raised in front of him. Small, black orbs hovered in his hands. They felt like black holes, all consuming, the pressure forcing me closer to them.

"Stay behind me, my Blossom." My staff crossed itself in front of me again, and I gripped the shaft. My knuckles were white. Panic bubbled up in my chest, and I tried to breathe it out. I tried to picture this just as a movie; Diego standing battle ready, magic coursing through him, ready to greet whatever threat had his hackles raised and his feathers puffed out. But this wasn't a movie, and Diego's magic was suffocating.

"But what if I want her to come out to play?"

We froze. We knew her voice instantly. I started casting protection spells, lighting up a Full Circle to keep us safe. Snapdragon was in the branches of one of the trees. They tried to shake her out, but she leapt from branch to branch nimbly, until she finally landed soundlessly in front of us.

"Snapdragon," Diego hissed. The all-consuming feeling from his magic transferred to his voice, but she wasn't affected. I flinched. This was the side of him I knew existed, but never saw: dangerous, lethal, destroyer of worlds.

"Hello, my king."

She pulled something out of a small bag, and I recognized it from the vision. A sunstone. Diego dropped the magic he held and it bled into the dirt floor. The trees scooted away, the rumbling from their roots making my legs feel like jelly.

"How did you–" he started.

"Find this? Oh my beloved, I couldn't survive without a piece of you." Snapdragon's smile was wicked, cruel. She quickly closed the gap between us and my feet felt like they were rooted along with the trees. Her staff hovered straight up and down next to her. It looked more like a spear now instead of a staff; the crystal on the top was more pointed than I remembered from the visions, and the blue feathers that dangled from its top were gone. There were some remnants of the decorations that were once there, but now her staff looked battle worn and sinister. My eyes darted back to the pointy end.

Diego waited centuries to see Snapdragon again, and now that she was here, standing in front of him, there had never been more distance between them. They stood face to face but universes apart. Diego was a ball of black rage that Snapdragon wanted to play with. The heart link around my wrist felt barbed, and my wrist ached. It was Diego's heart breaking all over again.

Snapdragon opened her hand and the sunstone floated up. It spun slowly, the magic in it winding up, like I had seen in the vision before. Except this time, she wasn't trying to pull the magic out of it.

She was shoving magic into it.

"What're you doing!" I shouted, but the spell was already unleashed. Diego shrieked in pain, grabbing at his chest, right at his heart. Where that sunstone should be. It darkened as Snapdragon worked the spell, and I tried pushing energy through the barbed heart link to him, to calm him.

He gurgled and then spat blood like he had been struck.

"Diego!"

Vines unfurled themselves from Snapdragon's arms, snaking along the ground over to us. They slithered on the forest floor, rustling the leaves in a sickly manner, like the vines were poisoning them. I stepped in front of Diego, standing between Snapdragon's incoming vines and him. My staff sizzled with lightning. The storm built inside of Harold's perfectly round self. *Help me*, I thought as I swung the staff. The air sparked around us. Diego was on his knees, choking, and I swung the staff again, right at Snapdragon's head.

She leapt back just in time to dodge the blow, laughing as she moved. She moved so much faster than I could, slipping in and out of view quickly enough that I struggled to keep up with her.

Diego was struggling to breathe.

"What are you doing to him?" I spat out. Rage simmered just under the surface and I struggled to keep it in. The staff shifted from lightning to healing–the spells were summoned on their own, reacting to my emotions as rapidly as they changed. Diego was doubled over on the ground.

She was going to kill him.

I leapt at her. I didn't think about it, I just went for it. I grabbed a handful of her dress and dragged her down. We hit the ground hard, rolling around, vying for dominance. I wasn't going to let her win again. I flipped her on her back and called for backup.

Roots and vines from the trees twined and twisted and zigzagged around us, trying to help me pin her down. Snapdragon tried to grab her staff before I did. Mine was pushing itself against her throat now. She clawed at it as much as she could with one hand pinned.

I immediately regretted it when I picked up her staff. It felt as poisonous as the vines she released, and my stomach churned. For a split second, I remembered the scars on Falcon's arms, and really hoped that I wasn't going to be matching him. My arms ached and burned, but I didn't let go.

The magic in it felt like darkness. Every ounce of the energy was full of rage and sadness. Snapdragon snarled at me, cursing while I held onto it.

I couldn't let her have it. I wouldn't.

The tree roots pried her hand open, trying to get to the sunstone, to break the link it had over Diego.

He was turning purple.

He was going to die.

I dropped her staff and helped the trees—the sunstone was more important, I had to get to it. Before she did anything else, before she killed him. The relief was instantaneous once I let go of it. The sunstone tumbled away, and I scrambled for it.

Snapdragon broke free from the vines and snatched her staff from the air. Our eyes locked, and she broke first, the glint of the sunstone distracting her.

"Stop!" Diego roared, his voice carrying through the forest, through the ground, through the sky. The hair on my arms stood up and I jumped. The magic of kings. He stayed on his hands and knees, his head hung low. I heard his thoughts but they were too muddled to understand; the undercurrent thrummed with sorrow that left me shaking.

There was more blood on the ground than I was comfortable with. I swallowed hard, my throat dry and aching. The tree sentinels were at the ready. Their magic was waiting for a command from their king.

Snapdragon leaned heavily on the staff, the skin of her ankle an awkward purple instead of its normal emerald green. She was panting with exertion, and I knew I should strike, but I couldn't break this moment for Diego. He needed to stand before her on opposing sides, making her answer for the destruction she had wrought. He needed to see what she had become.

He needed to let her go.

We both eyed the sunstone.

I went for it, and I pleaded silently with the trees for help. They covered the stone in roots, burying it deep in the ground. It was safe for the moment.

"Snapdragon, just stop, this is madness." I huffed the words out. My chest felt too tight and I couldn't breathe deeply enough. The heart link was working overtime, linking my feelings too deeply to Diego. The Full Circle spell was still going strong, but it did nothing to stop the onslaught of her magic.

"No, this is war," she said. Her voice was deadly calm, even though she was limping. Bad. Her ankle was getting more and more purple.

I felt more than saw the pained look on Diego's face. He wanted to help her, the conflict of wanting her to pay for her crimes against the forest and wanting to save her. He wanted to scoop her up and hold her in his arms, anything to make this right, and hated himself for even allowing the thought. Diego had shattered Obius and Earth alike for her, and he would do it again if he had to. I rubbed circles on his back, steadying him, forcing him to breathe slower. I searched Snapdragon's face, her aura, looking for any trace of the woman that Diego had once loved. All I saw was malice. He must have too, but the longer he stared at her, the more he fought back hi s tears.

But this wasn't the time for tears.

I helped Diego up, and he clung to me. He was much larger than me, larger still in Obius, but he held onto me like I could keep him from drowning. I'd never let go; I'd never let Diego fall back into the pits of desolation that I found him in. Even if he ended up running back to her, I refused to let go of him.

The heart links pulsed with energy, magic surging in my veins. I'd give him all of the magic in me, every last drop, if he needed it. Anything to keep him *alive.*

Snapdragon was already casting again. She limped through the spell, limped as she danced through it. Her staff bobbed along, perfectly in sync with her, and the gem glowed red.

Fire.

"Don't you *dare*!" I screeched.

But it was too late.

She was already calling for fire. Wildfire. I leaned Diego against one of the trees, and it was opening the trunk to tuck him safely inside. He pounded again it, demanding to be set free, and I begged the trees to trust me, to keep him there. Harold crossed in front of me and I pleaded with it or the Goddess or the trees–anyone that would listen–to teach me how to cast something that would stave off the flames.

Harold sparked.

She called for Wildfire.

I called for Lightning.

Activating in my blood, I felt the magic coming and working its way through me. I put my hands together at my heart like I was praying and when I pulled them apart again, Lightning broke between my hands, arcing in every direction. Shooting at Snapdragon. She flinched–she didn't expect *that*.

"My Blossom! Let me out of this tree, I can help–"

"No," I breathed out.

Snapdragon screamed. She was small, looking fragile–she was anything but. I was ready to cast another round of Lightning, when she floated up like Puddin. Staff in hand with a green orb of energy encasing her, Snapdragon fled.

Wildfire had been cast.

The flames were picking up, and she was simply leaving. I shouted at the sky as she floated away. There was nothing I could do to stop them, but I tried anyway. The trees were busy with Diego and trying not to get burned.

Snapdragon's laugh filtered through the sound of the fire, and I watched her.

Before she was out of view, she opened her hand showing off her victory. She had recovered the sunstone.

Chapter Fourteen

PEONY

Sherwin and I wound our way through the market square. It was the first place in Obius that looked like a *place*. There were stores and a fountain in the center of the square with a lovely woman carved from stone that was well worn but still nice. The stores were odd to me. There were no bricks or stones to make a building, but rather they were carved out of the sides of mountains, built within the trees, or simply laid out on finely woven fabrics. There were flags and wind chimes and what I guessed were some kind of instrument everywhere. The instruments were stringed, sort of gourd-shaped, with no necks like a guitar would have. A lute? The word eluded me; I wasn't sure there was a word for them.

I held Sherwin's hand, and it felt the same. He was still the same man as he was on Earth, but now he had feathers and horns and he smiled even more than before. Earth Sherwin was suave and sexy. Obius Sherwin was going to give me a hot flash just by catching my eyes. But neither of those versions felt like the whole truth, and I wasn't sure how much I cared. He said he would try, that he would include me in his worlds, and that was enough.

"This square is in the heart of Trellis. There's several other meeting places like this of course, but being so close to the castle and the King, people gravitate here. It's always buzzing. There's something new every day, and music fills the air. Deign would come here every chance he got to dance with the people. I'd dance here too. Everyone does, it's as normal as breathing." Sherwin twirled, his feet moving in step to a song I didn't know. He extended his hand, an invitation, and I took it. Sherwin spun me, catching me easily again in his arms, and the smile on his face was infectious. I was brighter in his presence and not so overbearing.

"Is that why you're always in motion when you're relaxing?"

"What do you mean?"

"When you're cooking, you dance. I just thought it was cute," I said.

"Ah, maybe. I never really thought about it." Sherwin kissed the back of my hand and spun me around again. "One day I'll teach you." He glided me through a few more steps, and I let myself be led.

"I'd like that."

Sherwin grinned and it gave me goosebumps. This man. There was something addictive about him, about his attention and affection. He let go so he could inspect some of the goods still left out on the tables. I used the word *table* lightly; they were tree stumps or pieces of bark cobbled together. I didn't know how they were standing, and didn't care to ask. Obius was the land of magic. I didn't need to peek behind the curtain to see how it all worked.

"What're you looking for?" I asked.

"Not really sure, honestly. Everything looks so normal, except... where is everyone?"

"Maybe they're hiding, because of the fire," I offered. I didn't want to say what I was really thinking. *Maybe they were all dead.*

"Maybe, yeah," he said softly. He picked up some berries, and handed one to me. They were small, red, and spiky. They looked like something I would purposely *avoid* on Earth.

"Umm–"

"Try one. Trellian berries. Kinda like cherries. They're what cherries are supposed to taste like." He popped one in his mouth and hummed happily. I did the same, but spiky outside kept me from really savoring the experience. I chewed it carefully, and he was right; they were like cherries' more prickly sisters.

"These are delicious! But thorny," I said.

"Kinda like you, huh, Pea?" He popped another in his mouth, crunching it, eyebrows waggling. The juice stained his lips a little, and he licked it off his fingers. I was having a flash and he chuckled. He fed me another berry, and rolled another around in his mouth.

"I'm not that prickly," I said. The flavor was growing on me.

"Easy there," he said. Sherwin continued digging through the goods. Mostly, the market reminded me of a thrift store, like the ones that Mari would frequent to find Abuela. The goods seemed random, and I couldn't tell what their purpose or value was. Bracelets and crystals, of course, but the bottles of liquids that screamed danger to me were normal for him. They all looked like poisons from a story book, but Sherwin examined each one, stuffing them in a bag he had found.

"Where do you think we can sleep tonight?" I asked.

"What do you mean?"

"Well, where can we sleep? I haven't really seen any place to stay–"

"Pea, we're going to sleep here, under the sky," Sherwin said slowly, watching my reaction. I fiddled with my glasses.

"This is probably not a great time to bring this up, but I'm not like, *great* with darkness. It's a whole thing, we don't really need to talk about it, but like *I don't want to stay outside all night long.*" I pushed my glasses up on my nose, but I pushed them too far and my eyelashes felt smooshed. I adjusted them again. Ugh, how did I even *see* out of them when they were this dirty? I cleaned them on my shirt, and why was he just staring at me.

"Peony. The nearest building is the castle. We aren't going to make it there by nightfall. We've only got maybe another hour of light left before it'll be dark." My stomach got acidy. I hadn't brought my antacids. I folded my arms and then dropped them. I didn't know what to do with myself.

"Oh."

"I'll keep you safe," he said, rubbing the top of my arms. I believed him. My magic was stronger than ever, and I felt the truth of his words. He couldn't predict the future–that was Jack's schtick–but the idea of waking up to some monster in my face made me want to vomit.

"So, blankets? Pjs? Am I being ridiculous?"

"Blankets I can find. Pjs probably not." He was smiling and I felt the tension ease. The suns–plural–were setting. The larger one was lower in the sky, and the smaller one trailed behind it. The sunset colors were killer. The reds were the same color as the Trellian berries, and the waning light made the market square feel alive. I could imagine how wonderful it would be to be here when everything was in full swing.

"Let's find the others. I think we can set up some barrier spells to put your mind to ease, and we can make some beds–"

I held my hand up to Sherwin's chest, quieting him. I could smell something. It was thick and ashy. Smoke.

"Do you smell that?" I asked, my eyes already searching for the source.

"Smoke," he echoed.

"Fire," we said together, and then we were running.

MARI

Falcon looked like shit. Hot shit, but shit. He was beat up. I'd seen people on the tail end of an ass whooping, but Falcon looked like he had been beaten within an inch of his life. I wasn't a healer, especially not now with all of this fire magic in me, but I did my best. I tried. I had to try. He looked just *awful*.

"Mari, look at this," he said, waving me off.

We were at the other end of the square. Peony and Sherwin were inspecting something, while we looked around too. Falcon mentioned building a base camp, but my camping skills were nonexistent. I didn't *rough it* out in nature. I communed with nature, casted my brilliant magic, and then took myself *inside* for a shower and a snack.

Falcon pointed at Peony and Sherwin. They were having a moment, and it felt intrusive to watch them. "Stop being a creeper, let them be."

"Do you trust him?" Falcon asked.

"Yes, why?"

"I dunno. Just something about him bugs me."

"Is it that he was Diego's BFF before you?" I asked. The hurt in Falcon's eyes was worse than any of the injuries on his face, which was impressive. He really looked terrible and I hated how little healing magic I knew.

"No, I don't think that's it," he said flatly. I laughed and then he did too, but quickly held his ribs.

"I'm sorry I'm not a good healer. It's never been my thing," I said. It was the truth; until very recently, the only thing I ever felt decent at was making artifacts. I knew I had skill at it, but I didn't love it. Enchanting stones and bracelets felt like the least magical thing I could be good at, and it was where I shined. Until the fire magic, anyway.

"Yo, what's going on over there?" he said. He straightened, obviously in pain but not giving in to it.

"Hmm?" I said, straining to see what he was pointing at. It was getting dark fast, and we needed to regroup with everyone.

"Ah fuck, do you smell that?" he asked. And then I did; I knew the scent well. I checked my hands and feet and felt along my arms and neck. It was fire, but it wasn't coming from me.

"Smoke," I said, and then realization hit me.

It was coming from the direction that Jack and Diego went. It was coming from the forest. I was so sick of running, but we were off, running again. Falcon didn't slow down for me, but the busted ribs slowed him down enough that I could mostly keep up.

"I am so fucking *sick* of this place trying to burn itself down," he muttered.

"I'm sick of pulling Jack out of the fire. You know she's right smack in the middle of it," I said. I was out of shape; this little jog was going to take me out.

"Oh for sure. D's prolly there too, all weepy and shit," his words were barbed but his tone was fond.

"What a pair," I added, and he winked at me, the building of this inside joke.

"Seriously."

The forest was familiar; Jack had grabbed me and we sorta walked through it once in her visions, when she was spirit walking. That felt like so long ago, but really it was just a few days. Life with Diego and Falcon in it seemed to stretch on forever, and it was hard to remember the days without them. Falcon's energy filled any room he entered, and it was exhilarating. I hated seeing people trying to shrink and be less of themselves. Falcon never seemed to have that problem. I wanted to match his energy, to sparkle and take up space with him.

When the trees shifted, I gasped and reached for Falcon. He felt safe. He was an asshole, no doubt about it, but he was safe. I'd be safe standing here with him as the trees uprooted themselves and ran from the fire.

The beauty of the trees struck me as they sailed past; I saw the swaths of colors and got little impressions of what their magic felt like as they moved, but I couldn't take it all in properly. My eyes were focused solely on the fire in front of us.

Wildfire, it whispered to me. The magic called, sang through my blood, and I felt like I was boiling alive. Flames burst from my fingers, trying to respond to the fire that I saw. My eyes glazed over. It was beautiful. Wild. Free. Chaotic.

I loved it.

Falcon was talking to me, I saw his mouth moving, but the words were lost to the crackle of the fire. I was lost to it. Wildfire was a dangerous spell—I'd seen what it had done—but it wasn't evil. Fire wasn't *evil*; it was the element of life. My hands itched to play with it. I breathed it in, the fire making me larger than myself, consumed. I didn't want to feel small ever again.

It's not like I could make it worse. Falcon cursed; I didn't need to hear the words to understand the look on his face, but I couldn't tear myself away from the energy bursting in front of me. He took off, heading straight into the thick of it. Falcon was going to kill himself.

Sucking in a deep breath, I took all of the heat and the smoke and let it course through me. I saw the sparks of the spell trying to unfurl itself in my mind, trying to teach me its secrets. I drew a circle around myself, centering and focusing on the flames. I needed to calm them. I needed them to understand that this wasn't the place for them to run free.

Here in Obius, I didn't need an artifact to cast. Magic came when I asked for it, flooding my senses and filling me until I thought I would burst, and all made of fire, always, always fire. I saw the sparks and let them dance across my skin, the scent of ash and char surrounding me. I pulled my shoes off and stood barefoot on the forest floor.

Sometimes the rhythm of spells felt like music. It moved me on its own, and I just flowed with it. My arms twirled and when I twisted my hands to bring them back to my heart, fire tracing the outline of my hands. It was blue and white, pure and breathtaking. I stilled, the dance of the magic slowing and just studied the flames. They felt joyful, seen, and so did I. I stared into the center of them, seeing the soul in them.

"Hi, I'm Mari," I said. I felt stupid, talking to the fire, but then it crackled and shimmered orange for a second. Unbridled joy pulsed through me. I wanted to burn this bright forever. Was that even possible? The fire made it feel like I could. I was alive, alive, alive.

The fire got too hot in my hands, and I set it down in my circle. It enveloped the circle almost instantly, but I was okay. I was safe. I knew that I was safe; the flames didn't want to burn me, so they played with my feet, licked at my legs, but didn't stay long enough to injure me. Little sparks twirled through my fingers, and I had never felt more in control of my magic.

"Oh fuck, Mari!" Falcon's voice broke the trance, and I saw his terrified eyes through the fire. He reached for the circle, reaching for me, but quickly pulled back. "Mari! Can you hear me? Fuck, Mari, come here, it's gonna be okay–"

Falcon's words fell away. The fire wrapped itself around me and I was blissful. I was burning bright. I was being consumed by the fire, and this was *right*. This was my purpose. I sucked in a deep breath. My lungs felt like they had expanded past my body as I breathed this glorious, divine magic in.

And I took it *all* in.

Wildfire filled my body; I breathed it in like I was swallowing soup. The magic filled my mouth, my throat, my belly. I burned and ached and was *so fucking free.*

Falcon watched in horror. The fear of me getting hurt had morphed into just a fear of *me*, and I felt lost. I wanted him to just see all of me, the extent that I could be, but I detached from him. A larger part of me didn't care–the part that was melding with the fire and becoming a part of it.

I breathed out, heat flooding my mouth. I exhaled out the flames, and then I cackled.

Wildfire had been put out.

The circle faded, and I saw Jack and Diego behind Falcon. He did it, he found them and saved them. He really was a hero. I winked at Falcon and he crashed into me, hugging me tight against his chest.

"You're burning up," he said.

"Well, I sorta swallowed a wildfire."

"What the hell were you thinking?" he shouted, examining me. I didn't expect him to be a fusser like Peony, but he was, inspecting my face and letting his eyes scan for obvious wounds. Falcon tucked some of my braids behind my ears, tilting my face here and there, trying to see if I was hiding anything.

"I'm fine," I said, and it was the truth. I was fine. I was more than fine. I danced with Wildfire and it didn't leave a scratch on me.

Jack wormed her way between me and Falcon and hugged me. She didn't have to ask what happened or how I was feeling; she just knew. Jack's magic allowed her to feel my emotions, whether I liked it or not, but this time I wanted her to see how happy I was. I wanted her to see the strength of the magic that boiled and lived inside me now. I wanted her to see that I was more than a trinket maker.

"Don't hold all of that magic too tightly," she said. "Wildfire was never meant to be contained."

"I know," I said. She was right. I needed a way to let go of the spell, but I didn't know how. My stomach wobbled like I had been trapped on an endless roller coaster. Up and down, up and down. My bones and muscles were hot, almost painfully so, but I savored it. I wanted it to settle into me fully.

"Mari, you cannot just keep Wildfire in... in *you*," Jack said. She held my hands like I needed to be talked out of jumping off a cliff. I was in control. More so than I ever had been on Earth. I was in tune with the fire, and I didn't want to let that go.

"It's not like I can just let it out either," I said. The conversation got cut short when Diego collapsed in front of us. He tried to keep himself upright, waving Falcon off of him, but about a minute after Falcon let go, he fell again. Falcon panicked–he was too beat up himself to be blowing through his energy reserves–but he was frantic, hands shaking and breathing too shallow not to be painful.

"What's going on?" Peony asked. She was slowing to a halt; her and Sherwin had followed the source of the fire too. At least that was one problem dealt with. Sherwin also knelt with Diego, and it felt too intimate to look at. He looked like he was dying, and I didn't feel like I had the right to watch that.

"He isn't dying!" Jack hissed at me.

"No one is dying!" Peony shouted. She was the best healer that we had unless Falcon or Sherwin could pull some tricks out of their hats. Falcon could do some basics, more like field medicine instead of surgery.

Sherwin was mashing stuff up; he had a small bag, and he began grindling leaves and berries on a larger leaf. The paste looked sickly green but he rubbed it on Diego's face, just under his nose. Then he reached for Falcon, but he backed up.

"What is that?" Falcon asked.

"Healing balm," Sherwin said, and he reached for him again.

"I can do it," Falcon swatted him away, and rubbed some over his lip. He looked like he had dried guacamole on his face. I stifled a laugh.

"What the hell happened?" Peony demanded, her magic lacing through her words and patience paper thin. She wove a few healing spells together to strengthen the effect and then started on Falcon. He was the worst of all of us. As the spell took hold, she turned her focus to Diego, who was finally sitting up.

"This is becoming a habit," she mumbled.

"My apologies," Diego said as he gritted through the pain.

"Bro, just say *sorry*," Falcon groaned as the spell worked on his ribs. He winced, touching them, and I had the sneaking suspicion that he had cracked at least a couple.

"So, what happened?" Sherwin asked. He offered the balm to Jack and Peony, who politely declined. I took a heap and rubbed it under my nose. I just swallowed divine magic. A little healing guac probably wasn't my worst idea.

"Snapdragon showed up. She has a piece of Diego's heart. And she... did something. I'm not sure what, but then Diego started coughing up blood, and then she–"

"Called Wildfire," Diego finished. His lips snarled, in what had to be the meanest expression I could imagine on him. Diego was serene and calm–or maybe too dead inside to emote–but right this second, he looked *hateful*. Curled lips, crinkled nose, deep set brows. His hair hung in his face too, sweat making his curls more intense, and the way they sat on his forehead made him look dangerous. He *was* dangerous; I had to keep reminding myself that. Diego on Earth was a chained dog. Diego in Obius was a dog unleashed. This was his world.

"*Again!*" Sherwin pounded his fist on the ground, knocking over his weird arrangement of stuff.

"She just doesn't care about Trellis anymore," Jack said as her words trailed off. "It's only going to get worse."

"Lefty, dammit, why would you say that?" Falcon scrubbed a heavy hand over his face.

"Say what?"

"*It's only going to get worse!* It's like you *want* the universe to fuck us over again-" Falcon chewed on his knuckles, clearly pissed. I wasn't superstitious, but then I heard something that sounded like thunder.

The sky was clear. Dark, but clear. Falcon threw his hands up in disgust. He pulled Diego up, and Diego rolled his neck, cracking it. They exchanged some silent bro code signals, standing back to back, ready for whatever came their way. Sherwin stood too, flexing his hands and making fists; he stayed off to the side of Diego, his eyes glancing between him and Peony. It was like watching some movie; I was detached and wrapped in fire and I was blissful in it. Little fires danced between my fingers, and in that moment my whole world made sense.

"Don't you think y'all are overreacting?" I asked. Jack took a few steps away from me, straining to hear.

"Can't you psychic some shit up for us? Just this once? Please?" Falcon asked. Her staff came soaring through the air and bobbed next to her. It crossed itself in front of her and my stomach did the floppy thing again.

Not good. None of that seemed good. Except my flames; they were perfect.

"It doesn't really work like that-" Jack started, but the words fell away. We all stared at the horizon, at the very bright green orb that floated through the sky. And the *thump thump thump* that came from that direction. The hum of the magic in the air sent shockwaves through me, and I let out a shaky breath, watching flames come with it.

"Anyone want to take a guess at what that means?" Peony asked. She was still casting healing spells, and frankly, looking a little ragged.

I wasn't sure what day it was anymore, but this day seemed to stretch on forever and it was taking a toll on all of us. I had Wildfire burning through me, and it singed away the exhaustion, making me want to burn even brighter.

"This fucking day getting worse would be my guess," Falcon grumbled.

And he was right.

The orb grew brighter and brighter, like a bright green sun, and beneath, the outline of figures started to appear. An army of them. I didn't need to be a psychic to figure out what they were. The familiar, creepy gait. The hanging gloom in the air. Snapdragon raised a bunch of dead shit again.

Chapter Fifteen

JACK

Falcon might be onto something with speaking things into existence. Things had, without a doubt, gotten worse. Magic and intention were so closely tied and here in Obius, everything was magnified.

Or, the timing was just coincidental.

Either way, we stood in a valley, looking up at a small hill that held Snapdragon's horde of soulless, lifeless beings. This magic—death magic—was vile, and I felt the depth of its repugnant nature, toxic and slimy, clinging to the air and filling my lungs. Waves of sorrow and rot rolled across the field, seeping into my pores. It was the moments these twisted souls remembered in life, possibly the moments of their deaths, and the pain of being woken from their restlessness.

The lightning storm in Harold's orb had returned with a vengeance. Falcon twitched every time the lightning flashed; he said nothing, but I heard the panic race through him at every spark.

Peony was concentrating her magic on Falcon now. Diego stood unaided and breathing normally. My heart unclenched a little. His golden eyes met mine. He positioned himself in front of all of us. He looked like a king just then with the width of his shoulders rising to his full height, the tilt of his chin. There was a challenge in the set of his jaw, and magic simmered across his skin. Diego always looked a bit golden from his skin tone, but now he seemed to glow. We lost the sunstone, but having it close by must have given him another spark of life.

"Stay close to me," he said, putting his arm out in front of me.

"Are those–" Sherwin's words fell away.

"Lost souls," I said. "Snapdragon can force them to obey her, I'm not sure how though. They're like the creatures she sent after me on Earth. I didn't expect her to use that kind of magic here." I reached for my citrine pendant, connecting to the magic I carried on Earth. Watching the souls writhe across the field toward us made my stomach knot up; their pain was deafening.

The tree sentinels formed a U-shape around us, Diego at the dead center of it.

"Please take shelter," he pleaded with them. "We don't know what she will do."

No, the trees answered, and the word reverberated around us. I rubbed the spongy bark of one of the trees. A small vine came down and curled around my fingers. The leaves were gold, just like Diego's eyes.

We ssstand with King Deign. We ssstand with the Priessstesss.

Mari coughed out more fire then, trying to hide it. Wildfire raged in her. What the hell was she thinking? She pointed to the right–the *opposite* direction that the lost souls were and we all froze. Another army stood at the edge of the markets. The Trellian banners flew high, and I heard Falcon cuss up a storm. The stench of the mage-hounds made Peony and Mari gag. Diego snarled at the banners, *his* banners, that flew in opposition to him.

We were standing on a battlefield. A real battlefield.

Things were getting worse.

"D, I think we need to a pull a–"

"Do not say Rio. We are not blowing anything up," Diego said.

"Hate to agree with him, but blowing shit up sounds like a great idea to me," Mari chimed in. We stood back to back with everyone in a small circle: Diego who faced Snapdragon's monsters, me to his left, Falcon to his right, Mari next to me, Sherwin beside Falcon, and Peony in the middle, never breaking the rhythm of her spellwork. Sweat formed on her brow, but she didn't stop. She wouldn't. Her thoughts came through loud and clear. *I'll keep y'all safe, I won't let anything happen, fucking* try *to stop these spells.*

"Deign, it's Arturo," Sherwin said.

"I know, I can smell him from here," he said.

"How long are nights here? We need some light," I said. It was entirely too dark; the only light we had came from the moons, Snapdragon's eerie glow, and Harold.

"I've got this," Mari said. She stepped away from our little circle, and my heart sank. Even just being three steps away made her seem so vulnerable with threats at every side, and I wanted her next to me. I wanted Mari's bravery to rub off on me because I was running out. Diego squeezed my hand; the heart links alerted him to my panic, and he stood a little taller.

"Nothing will happen to you, my Blossom. I will keep you safe." I wanted to ask him *how* but I wouldn't say that. He was still weak, functioning on just fragments of magic and fragments of his heart.

Mari pointed to the north, the south, the east, and west with fires lit at her fingers. She exhaled more fire, her eyes alive with energy and a grin like I'd never seen. She swayed to a beat the rest of us couldn't hear, the flames gently wrapping around her in small embraces. When she released the spell, four little suns rose into the sky, lighting up the horizon like it was high noon. She blew kisses to each of them, twirling with her arms out wide, and the suns sparkled and danced.

"Just like lighting a candle. Just, you know, bigger." She winked at me with sparks still in her eyes.

"Any chance we can talk our way out of this?" I asked. My words were shaky, my knees were shaky. I wasn't a fighter, and standing at the center of two armies really solidified that fact.

"So we're not pulling a Rio?" Falcon asked.

"Let's call that plan B," Diego said.

"What's plan A?" I asked.

"Still working on it," Diego said. The souls inched closer and closer. Arturo's army waited for him to take the field in earnest. Diego tensed, and I felt that black hole of his magic from earlier forming around him again.

"I think they made the choice for us. Put the Cube up! Full Circles! Peony, keep the spells going! Fuck," Falcon said.

The choice was made. Arturo's troops charged at us, the roar from the soldiers were deafening and I cringed. The lost souls moaned into the night, their sorrow filling me until I felt dizzy. They picked up the pace too, not wanting Arturo's soldiers to kill us before they got the chance themselves. I grabbed Diego's arm, and he pulled me into his chest, wrapping his arms around me. We were going to fight.

I love you, he said. His words were soft, tiny in my mind. I searched his face, looking for confirmation that I heard him really say it, but suddenly it felt like a goodbye. I felt the walls building up in his mind, keeping me at arm's distance instead of letting our souls stay touching. I pulled his hand to my heart with the words stuck in my throat and I prayed that the heart link could speak for me.

No, don't go, please.

I love you too.

"Diego–"

And then he rushed off, a battle cry on his lips now instead of the tenderness that he held for me. He ran straight toward the lost souls, toward Snapdragon. Falcon swore again, but took off after him still favoring his right leg as he ran. The scarred skin of his arms made him look like a blur as he moved, and I felt sick. Sherwin kept himself in front of the three of us. Mari danced through the Cube spell and it knitted around our bodies like a glove. She wove the spell easily, moving through it with confidence and grace.

Then she lit her hands on fire and took a place next to Sherwin. Mari was always a force, but she was finally standing in the spotlight she created with the fire burning inside of her. She was made for war.

And this was war.

Peony grabbed my hand, pulling me to her. We stood head to head, and she stared into my eyes, grounding me. I needed to summon the trees, to ask for their help. We needed them now more than ever. She nodded to me, a quick sign telling me it would be okay, and she was back to casting. Peony's healing spells wrapped around each of us, working into our muscles, fortifying and renewing our strength. Her hands were prayerful at her heart, fully focused, but completely exposed.

Releassse the Lightning, Priesstessss. The trees formed a protective wall behind Peony and I. They didn't seem concerned about Diego or Sherwin, or even Mari. But they huddled around us like we would fall without someone holding us up.

My staff spun wildly in wide, arcing circles.

"Could really use a spear or something right about now," Sherwin said.

Arturo's army would be on top of us in seconds and I pushed down the sudden anger I felt toward Diego. How could he just *charge* off? I watched as he broke through the throng of souls, gold and glittering, his magic a well of power like looking into an inferno. Falcon was at his back, keeping it clear so he could continue casting. I felt the connection between us pull taut like it could snap, and it pushed more anger toward him. He was leaving *again* because he thought he knew better.

Arturo hung back, the mage-hounds around him. He seemed bigger than when I saw him before. So did the mage-hounds. They stayed at the back of the force; we'd have to fight our way through to him.

I took stock of the surroundings, and my eyes wandered to the front of our battle lines. Sherwin bounced from foot to foot, a lightness to his body that I wasn't expecting. Mari didn't bounce–she was practically vibrating from all of the magic coursing through her.

Mari was made for war.

She threw her head back, fire exploding from her mouth and the troops slowed down. Sherwin took that as his cue to attack. Sherwin jumped up against a tree, using it as leverage to rocket himself forward. He landed hard on one of the soldiers out front who looked a little like him, but in shades of red instead of his soft purple. Sherwin punched the guy square in the nose and I saw the dazed look on his face before he fell. Sherwin scooped up his fallen weapons–two long, thin swords and tested them in his hands. It was effortless, like he was handling a pencil instead of a sword. He swung them around his wrists, really getting a feel for them before he swung in earnest. This was why he was the King's Shadow–no one would get through him to hurt Diego.

Mari's hands still burned with the energy of a falling star. She conjured fire between them, pulling and shaping it into small bursts of fireballs and flung them through the air. Some were aimless, some were aimed directly at soldiers that got too close. Where I was afraid, Mari was joyous. She moved through Wildfire like she was playing with matches.

"Give me your citrine," Peony croaked out. Her arms were shaking.

"What?"

"I need some more power, I can't focus and I can't let anyone die–" Sherwin took a hit to the back and Peony upped the speed of her spell, sending soothing healing spells at him with tears in her eyes. I stripped off the pendant and slipped it around her neck. *Be gentle to her,* I pleaded. The citrine couldn't hear me, but I hoped the intention was enough.

Releassse the Lightning, Priesstessss!

I stepped out of the protective bubble away from Peony. She shook her head *no*, but I had to. Harold was still cracking with lightning and I palmed the shaft of my staff. The frantic circles stopped and Lightning welled up in my chest. It wasn't elemental magic like Mari or Peony–Lightning was *light*. It was like a laser, with all the intensity of nature's rage. I swung the staff over my head, the force of the spell building until the staff couldn't contain it.

Releassse the Lightning, Priesstessss.

So I did.

Lightning bounced over the land, shooting straight through the soldiers as they closed in on us. Mari flung fireballs at anyone she didn't immediately recognize, no one daring to get too close. Her hands burned brighter and brighter, and every glimpse I caught from her was fierce. Untamable. I was so damn proud of her. Mari was made for war.

Sherwin slashed through the air, hacking away at anyone that got too close. A large soldier with a horse-like face barreled through the field, right at Peony. He took aim at her, and Sherwin leapt in front of him, trying to knock him off course. The horse-guy tackled Sherwin, and they rolled through the dirt, until he tossed Sherwin clear across the field like he was nothing.

He charged Peony.

"Trees! My sister!" I yelled, and they responded. Peony was wrapped in vines and lifted high into the air, up into the treetops of the giant sentinels. She was suspended in the air, freaking out, but safe. She lost her pace with her healing spells for a second, and Sherwin still hadn't gotten up. Mari kept her magic going, and I ran toward Sherwin. He wasn't *moving–*

The lightning still roved over the battlefield and started to lose some momentum as it got closer to Arturo.

A roar stopped everyone in their tracks. It was devastatingly loud. Feral. Frenzied. Full of sorrow. It sucked and pulled me apart, and I knew it instantly.

Diego.

The black hole in Diego's heart was coming out, the magic he teased and threatened earlier was bubbling up, and I felt myself coming undone. I felt the magic tearing me apart, and even though I was still angry that he would run off again, I couldn't walk away from that sorrow.

Mari held her own. Sherwin was finally, finally, *finally* moving. Peony's magic was stronger now that she was away from the danger and solely focused on keeping everyone alive. She had a silvery sheen to her from all the casting, just like a pearl.

Go Priestessss, they will not fall.

I trusted the trees. I did. I knew in my heart they would burn to ashes before they let anything happen to my friends, my family. I took one last look at them fighting and casting with everything they had, and a leaf floated down to me with the Seer's sigil on it.

They will not fall, Priessstessss.

So I raced across the field to Diego.

FALCON

I hated this fucking place. I tried. I tried to give it a chance, but no, Obius could go fuck itself.

This bitch was *insane*.

The lost souls—the few I had the displeasure to deal with on Earth and the gaggle of them that we dealt with at Jack's—were overgrown and even angrier. Bigger. Louder. Smellier. The whole place stank of death on a hot day, and my usually very strong stomach was getting queasy. She had pulled out her trump card, and she was laying her hand down on the table for us to see. Snapdragon could also *fly* apparently, because *of course she could fucking fly*. She soared over us, shrieking like a drunken banshee.

The smell was really getting to me. It was too close to the burning, sticky flesh smell from the lightning when it scorched me. My arms tingled but I didn't have time to think about that too much. The lightning didn't burn through the brand on my arm, and I was thankful. I didn't need anything else to summon magic.

I throat punched something that was probably tree-related at one point. There was a mushroom on it—at least I *assumed* it was a mushroom—and I punched it right under its cap. I had nothing but my fists and a few offensive spells to aid me. I was a scrapper; I fought dirty and felt no qualms about it. My best offensive spells were all earth based—rocks, dirt, boulders. I could get down with the wind too, but I needed something heavier. Substantial. Solid.

So I started a sandstorm; the rush of it came on fast, not giving them time to adjust. The lost souls moaned and howled as the sand buffeted against them. It was a nasty one, playing off my emotions. It flung larger rocks around too, stones and pebbles and hunks of earth flying everywhere.

Diego let out a roar that shook my insides. Everything felt too *gooey* in my belly, but I didn't stop moving. I swung at the next thing that got close. It was mostly a mouth. The rest of it had fallen away, disintegrated with time. Or because Snapdragon was forcing these poor bastards to move without their consent.

I slammed my fist into the mouth and sent it backwards. Something hovered behind me and I turned just in time to dodge before it snapped its jaws. It was vaguely piranha-like. This place was fucking weird. The sandstorm wasn't dying down. Magic took on a life of its own here, and the storm raged on.

The lost souls were relentless. They clung to my legs, pulling me down and wrapping themselves around anything breathing. Diego was covered in them too; he looked like a statue covered in moss. We had lost control quickly—not that we really ever had an upper hand, but the seed of failure sunk into me and I needed to stamp that shit out fast before I threw in the towel. Two dudes versus a thousand lost souls was still a battle we could win. Theoretically.

I caught a glimpse of Jack as she barreled toward us; the lightning caught my eye more than her, really. So much for staying put and letting Diego handle it. The roar probably summoned her; I wanted to go help too, but I was stuck at the center of the sandstorm. It would take me a minute to calm it enough to help anyone. Her hair whipped behind her as she ran unflinchingly through the storm, toward Diego. Jack's staff was bright enough that I could track her through the haze of the sand, which meant that Snapdragon could too.

Snapdragon hissed and whined as she started to cast, throwing a tantrum in her little green bubble. Jack wouldn't stop until she was with Diego, even if she was running straight through whatever Snapdragon was conjuring. I hated hitting women, but she was going to be the exception. I worked on lifting a boulder, pulling a chunk of rock from the ground to fire it at her. I strained as I lifted the boulder, my back and arms trembling with exertion. I felt something *snap* in my chest and pain ratcheted around that I did my best to ignore.

Her fingers glowed red.

That can't be good.

"Lefty! Hit the deck!" I shouted as loud as I could. The storm was slowing down finally, and I could see through it now. She turned, likely hearing my thoughts more than the words, our eyes locked for a second.

She understood. Jack jumped at Diego, trying to shove him down. He didn't budge an inch when she hit him, but with enough pleading, he knelt down, an arm around her shoulders covering her head.

The boulder was bigger than I thought it would be. The amount of magic I used was substantial but I didn't think it was *half a mountain* worth. I forced the energy to travel through my arms, spinning the boulder over my head to gain some momentum, and then I lobbed that thing right at Snapdragon.

A wall of fire came right at me. The boulder soared through it, but the fire didn't stop either. It headed straight for me, and my heart sank. There was no dodging that. I tucked into myself as best as I could and rolled into the now burning grass. Wildfire didn't give a shit what it burned or where it went. The lost souls cried out, burning up in the flames, and I just closed my eyes, casting the Cube as quickly as I could to have *something* between me and the fire.

"Sorry D..."

I prayed to the Judge to hear my plea to keep the Cube going as I blacked out.

MARI

Too hot, too hot, too hot.

Wildfire was wild, but I had it under control. My hands felt blackened, but my energy wasn't. This was the freedom I'd always craved, and it was blinding. Everything in me was charring and burning up, but I couldn't stop the magic and I didn't want to. I'd burn myself to ashes before I let go of Wildfire. I didn't know what I was searching for until Wildfire settled in my chest. It called me, pulling me toward the edge of the blaze. I saw colors I'd never even imagined before. It was *life*. I needed this fire to keep burning, for *me* to keep burning. Pulling the fire back in, I let it bounce around my body before another spectacular fireball burst from my hands.

The army slowed their descent towards me. They didn't wanna tangle with the flames, and I couldn't blame them.

I was *made* for this.

I was made for fire.

I danced through the magic and let it guide me. Wildfire hummed its spell in my mind, enchanting me as I moved through the steps to keep it alive. To keep us both alive.

The guy with the creepy dog-things hadn't moved. They watched as their friends and comrades came and perished in my flames. *My* flames. My fingers cracked a little, feeling a bit too charred, too *crunchy*, but not enough for me to drop the spell. Nothing would make me drop this spell.

I blew fire out like I was a dragon and heard myself cackling.

I was made for fire.

Sherwin sliced his way through the crowd, and I tried to cut a path for him without setting him on fire. He was light on his feet, and dodged quickly enough that it wasn't a *huge* concern. He was sorta limping, but that didn't seem to stop him and he hacked through another three soldiers.

"Mari, get down!" Peony screamed, her voice was hoarse and faint from how loud she screamed. She was up in the trees, suspended up high like some pop star on a stage. I turned to see another wall of fire in the distance. It wobbled and flickered out; the spell was already collapsing in on itself, and it wouldn't be able to hurt me by the time it reached here.

Something else had caught my eye as I watched the wobbly flames.

Someone was lying on the ground, unmoving.

"Mari!" Sherwin shouted. He was surrounded. He needed me to keep the fire going so he didn't get overwhelmed by the army. One man versus an army wasn't a bet I'd take, but he was holding his own. I shot another fire blast in his direction, but it was less controlled. I was less controlled. The fire climbed its way up my throat until I was breathing it out again.

Peony's healing spells wrapped around me, tying themselves like little bows around my neck. I felt like I was choking to death, more from the healing spells than the fire. She didn't stop, forcing them to intensify as they wove themselves together over my skin. I pointed at the body in the distance. I knew it had to be Falcon; he was the only one dumb enough to do something to get himself knocked out. I saw Peony's mouth moving and imagined the words *oh fuck*, as she worked feverishly to cast in his direction.

I charged at Sherwin. He needed backup, and I was gonna be the best damn backup he ever had. I left burning footprints behind me, another wall of flame for the soldiers to brave. We were going to cut this army off at the knees, and convince that fucker on the hill to stop this nonsense.

Or I'd burn it all down.

DIEGO

Everything moved in slow motion, like when I was "powering down" on Earth. That's what Falcon always called it: when I went back into survival mode to conserve what little magic I had to keep my body alive. Heart. Brain. Lungs.

But now, everything moved in slow motion. Snapdragon was lost to me. I saw it in her eyes, in the way she held herself, in the curve of her hip. She was thinner and it was obvious that she hadn't rooted herself to the forest in far too long. If she hadn't responded to her name, I don't think I would have recognized her. She raged in the air, screaming and desperate. Her staff glowed a sickening red, and the lost souls rose from their hiding places. The pain in their collective voices made my chest tighten. How many of them were here because of me? *All of them*, my conscience hissed. I struggled to take a full breath; I was no better than Snapdragon now.

Falcon had followed me, of course he would follow me, and he was fighting the creatures that attacked him.

Obius had fallen so far since the Shattering.

Snapdragon had fallen into madness.

The lost souls piled on top of me, and I didn't have the strength to shove them away. I didn't have the right to cast them off of me. I caused this. *I love you*, I'd whispered to Jack before I took off. I hoped the heart link delivered my message, because in that moment I was too afraid to let the words out. I loved her for all that she was; I loved the essence of her star lights and how she held my hand, and how she didn't see me as the beast that I was. I loved that she still believed this wasn't wholly my fault, even when I knew that it was.

Obius felt dead. It wasn't my lack of magic that was magnified here, but the lack of magic everywhere. The lack of life. The look on Snapdragon's face was a twisted version of the look I remember when I shattered the links, when I still believed I was doing the right thing.

She had manipulated me, too.

And for what? To slaughter the world? To run Trellis into the ground, dragging our people through the wasteland she had created? It didn't matter; she wasn't the one that ultimately shattered the link.

Something bit my leg, the teeth sinking deep into the flesh of my thigh, and I didn't move. I could just stop moving now, let the souls rip me into shreds as they ought to. I heard Falcon fighting behind me. Jack and the girls fought on with Sherwin at their side. Jack's devastated face replayed in my mind as I walked away from her. The guilt I'd carried for centuries sat heavily on my chest, and I tried my best to convince myself that it wasn't there because of Jack now.

I'm walking away from someone I love again.

The magic of kings–breaking and binding–also meant that I could tame the elements and bend the binds of gravity. Except fire; not even kings played with fire. Snapdragon hovered in the air, watching as her lost souls piled on me and attacked Falcon. I didn't have enough magic to cast this spell twice. Magnetism. It was ancient, given only to a few families to learn. I hated this spell—I'd only used it once before, right before I ripped the ties between the worlds apart. I had to pull them together, close enough that I could break them as cleanly as possible.

My chest ached. It was the familiar pain I'd gotten used to on Earth, but it seemed to seep even deeper than it had before. My bones were tired. I gathered all of the magic I could hold in my hands, pulling it deep from the core of the planet, from the roots of the trees, from the ground my feet were planted in. I tried to take root and raise the magic to cast Magnetism. I might have yelled, I couldn't tell.

Snapdragon was shrieking. She hissed and flailed in the air. Falcon was doing what Falcon does best—flipping the odds in favor and fighting to the end. A huge, mountainous sized rock flew through the air right at her.

"Diego!"

Jack's voice cut through the magic, knocking me off balance. She launched herself at me, and I caught her before she hit the ground. Lost souls tugged and pulled at us both, but her staff was there, zapping anything that reached for us with Lightning.

"Jack, what're you—"

"I love you too," she said, her eyes were hard. She dared me to contradict her or to send her away. "I'm not leaving you."

"Jack—"

"End of discussion." I saw the wall of fire heading right toward us. Snapdragon kept calling Wildfire to do her bidding, and she would burn everything in her path. Her eyes were wide, angry. She looked rabid as she released the spell again.

I folded Jack into my arms and dropped us to the ground. The wall sailed over us, directly at Falcon.

No–

She grabbed her staff and hopped out of my arms. Lightning sparkled in the staff, and she swung it like a scythe. Bolts bounced across the land again, taking out hundreds of souls. Jack's sadness welled in me like a waterfall, overflowing and loud, crashing through me. This was not what her magic was meant for.

"Go! Go get him!" Jack yelled.

"Where are you going?" I shouted back but I already knew; Jack headed for Snapdragon, slinging Lightning at anything that got in her way. When Snapdragon noticed that Jack was coming for her, she lowered herself. The orb was still wrapped around her, in a protective bubble, but she was back on the forest floor again.

"Please, check on Falcon. I can't feel his energy," Jack's voice sounded through my mind. Her words weren't angry or resentful; she shined with Seer's Blessing, ready for anything, waiting for me to respond to her.

"I can't leave you–"

"I'm coming back. I'll always come back to you."

The outline of her body grew smaller and smaller as she ran toward Snapdragon. I wanted to pull her back, keep her here, but that wasn't my right. She had blessed work to do, and I pushed as much love for her as I could through the heart links, praying it would fortify her.

Falcon still wasn't moving. He was crumpled on the ground and reluctantly, I headed toward my best friend.

Chapter Sixteen

JACK

Snapdragon sank to meet me from her floating orb like I should be thankful she graced me with her presence. She sneered as she dropped the orb, landing lightly on her feet. She was a full-on hot mess. Dirt smeared on her face, the braided vines of her hair were tangled and gnarled, her dress was torn, and her feet still bare. What really put her over the edge was the unhinged smile on her face. It had too many pointed teeth, with her lips straining to open too wide.

This would be the first actual fight that I'd ever been in; my hands balled and released, anticipating the need to throw a punch. Instead I grabbed the shaft of my staff as Harold gleamed green with magic, bright and lovely, like life itself. Snapdragon's staff still had a sickly, deathly red glow. The death magic she used had burned through her magic reserves; Snapdragon wasn't used to having to guard her thoughts, and I heard them so clearly.

False One. Succubus. Stealing the heart of the King. I want to rip the smile from your face and grind it into the dirt.

"Why?" I asked. It was all I could get out; her anger drowned out most of the words in her mind, and it was drowning out my thoughts too. She was practically shaking from her ire. Every ounce of her was rage.

"What do you mean *why!*" She slashed at the air with her staff.

"How could you do that to him?" The words were thick and raspy. I saw Diego's unguarded smile and contagious laugh; I don't know if it was her memory or mine. The heart link hummed with magic, and I felt Diego's fingers trailing down my cheeks and neck and arms. Tears stung my eyes, and I blinked them away; this wasn't the time for crying. Harold crossed itself in front of me again, forever my faithful guardian.

"Control his heart, control the King," she said. She was readying some spell, I could feel it. Probably another wave of Wildfire or conjuring more lost souls from their fitful resting places. The souls called for me to send them home to Sanctum. *Soon,* I promised. I just had to survive this and get the links to Sanctum back up and going.

"Were you ever in love with him?"

"I loved sitting at his side," her voice dripped with venom and fury, words shaking from the will to keep from just lashing out at me.

My staff sensed her impending attack, and Harold moved on its own. Lightning. Snapdragon dodged, but Harold didn't stop the assault. Lightning struck again and again, getting closer and closer to her. She leapt back and forth, drawing us further away from the souls and away from Diego. I needed a second to gather myself. Harold kept casting.

We weren't far from the market square. I could see the edges of the market, and I wondered how I could pull Snapdragon away from it. She didn't need yet another target to burn, and from the crazed look on her face, another round of Wildfire was coming.

The banners over the shops were frayed but still standing. That's how I wanted to keep them. Still standing. That's how I wanted everyone to be after this. My mind wandered for a second to Diego, and I saw him shaking Falcon, trying to wake him up. I saw Peony's spells tying ribbons around Falcon's body, trying to revive him. *Wake* him–he wasn't dead. He couldn't be. I reached for him, and felt a spark of life, but it was tiny. Falcon was in critical condition.

Snapdragon, of course, noticed and took that moment to strike. She swung her staff like a club and it hit me square in the stomach. I collapsed into the dirt, and vines from the tree sentinels cushioned the landing.

Ssseend them home, the trees whispered.

Sssend them home, Priessstessss.

Yesss.

Sssoo many sssouullsss.

One more twisssted than the ressst.

The emerald green magic that I associated with Snapdragon had returned, but it wrapped around me. It was *my* magic, time slowed to a halt and Snapdragon was frozen in place.

The memories of Snapdragon's life flooded through me. Her as a child, growing from such a tiny seedling into a nymph, strong enough to leave the lush forest she called home. I saw her darting through the trees, smiling wide and shining with the joy that only children can feel. She was so small, so young in these memories, as she scaled the trees with no effort at all. Snapdragon launched herself in the air high above the treetops and let herself crash through their leaves, knowing there would be branches for her to fall back on. I saw when her Seer magic activated, and how she started to change. The joyous creature had become quieter as the days marched on. She struggled under the weight of the blessing. It didn't feel like a blessing to her. Her eyes grew distrustful; she studied every creature she came in contact with, reading through their thoughts easily, and judging whether she would even approach them all.

She didn't.

I saw the moment that she met Diego, when he was just a prince. He grinned at her, not a care in the world, and not a single dark thought in his mind. She opened up to him so easily, so quickly. I watched as her skin brightened from a dark, mossy green to a thriving summer jade. Flowers bloomed in her hair and she covered her face in embarrassment. Diego beamed at her like he was made of sunlight, and she really *bloomed*. I saw the beauty in her then; no rage, no withering. Snapdragon shimmered in emerald light, like she was cut from the rarest gemstones.

A pang of jealousy hummed through me, but I stayed in tune with her memories.

She bowed deeply to Diego and her eyes darted to his throne. He didn't notice–there was no way he *would* notice. His gaze was fixed on her completely, and when she rose from her bow, he took her hand and kissed it gently. The words they exchanged were hushed; she didn't remember them now. She didn't really remember Diego either; the features of his face were out of focus, but the golden crown on his head was clear.

Her life fast forwarded in my mind–loads of small moments of her laughing at something Diego said, gazing into her crystal staff, staring up at the stars, wrapping herself in Diego's arms with war written on his face. As much as she buried her love for him, all of her happiest memories were with Diego shining brightly at her.

Then I saw the change in her. She caught a glimpse of the Shattering, of twisted and lost souls raging across Obius. She only saw flashes, little snippets of a future she was terrified of. The Seer's magic made her paranoid, and then the visions of her life ending started. There was so much blood in her visions. She panicked. She retreated. She turned away from Diego, who promised and promised and *promised* that she would be okay.

Snapdragon knew the truth though.

She wasn't going to survive, no matter what happened.

There *was* an attack, but it wasn't the humans like she predicted. She was so sure that the threat they faced was beyond their borders, beyond the reach of this world. And she was so very wrong.

There was no reasoning with Diego. He listened to every vision, every terrifying moment that she saw in her mind, and he took in every gruesome detail. Snapdragon trembled as she spoke, and the fear was real then. Diego decided the links needed to be broken—no invasion could happen, no war, if he *just* took the bridge away. No one knew how horrible the ripples would be from that. Not even Snapdragon, with her blessed future sight.

But then he was *gone*, and that might be worse than dying.

Snapdragon never saw the knife that would embed itself in her back. She never saw who wielded the knife, but she had a feeling, she *always* had a feeling there was a snake in their midst. She just thought it wouldn't be someone from Diego's inner guard.

But I wasn't just in tune with her memories; I followed the flow of time, rewinding and rescaling the visions until I saw the ghastly truth that she had been hiding from. The click of Arturo's shoes echoed through Diego's bedroom. Snapdragon sobbed on his bed, holding his shirt tight to her chest. She cried and cried, until she had felt a presence and got up to investigate.

He stabbed her in the back, around her shoulder blades, and she sagged to the floor. Lifeless. Confusion etched on her desperately beautiful face. She laid in a heap, like someone had crumpled up a flower and tossed it aside. Her long, intricate emerald gown that I'd seen in so many visions before slowly turned red.

Snapdragon had died.

FALCON

I was dead. Had to be. There was no way I could ache this badly without being dead. Although, I guess *feeling* how shitty I felt meant that I wasn't dead. Was it bad that I was a little disappointed?

Shadows fluttered in front of my still-closed eyes. I didn't want to open them yet. Memories of the field came back to me. I didn't want to see another lost soul decaying as it was forced to attack me. I didn't want to see any more fire. I didn't want to open my eyes and realize that I was the only one still breathing.

"Falcon, can you hear me? Open your eyes, please." A hand patted the side of my face gently. Smoothed my hair. Traced the lovely fresh and still tender scars on my arms.

"Look at what's happened to you," he whispered. Diego's voice was too quiet for my liking; he was never a loud person—aside from that roar earlier, I remembered that now too—but this was too quiet. Diego threaded his hands through my hair, trying to gently ease me awake.

"At least I wasn't the one blowing shit up this time, right?" I coughed out as I tried to sit up. Something popped and I groaned. Felt like a broken rib. Or three. *Just had to pick a fight with her, didn't you?*

"Don't move too much, Peony is casting some healing spells. She's gonna get you up and moving again." Diego held my face in his hands, just staring at me. My cheeks were a little squished, and I felt like a fish.

"D, I appreciate the concern but you're kinda creeping me out."

"Oh, sorry. I just. I just thought you were gone," he said, releasing my face, but not completely letting go of me. I thought I was gone too.

"Nah, I'm pretty indestructible."

"You're not looking very indestructible." His voice was completely deadpan, but purposely so instead of his normal-Earth deadpan. He was making a joke. Diego was *joking* with me, so I knew I was going to be just fine.

"Yeah, well I'm getting too old for this shit." My back creaked as I sat up fully. I took a few deep breaths. None of that felt great. Diego kept glancing between me and the general direction Snapdragon was before I blacked out.

"Where's Lefty?" I asked.

"Jack?"

"Yeah, I can't see her."

"She's with Snapdragon."

"Alone! What the hell, D–"

"She asked me to check on you–"

"Help me up. She's gonna get her ass kicked if we don't hurry." Peony's magic wrapped itself around me and I felt a little lighter. The pain slowly but surely eased off, which was great, because otherwise I was going to black out again. If we made it out of this alive, I was going to sleep for a week. A whole week. Lots of painkillers. Maybe an ER visit.

Once Diego got me up, I could see the sparks of Jack's fierce lightning bolts and the savage red coming from Snapdragon. They looked like a Christmas card gone wrong–the reds and greens of their magic mixing in a hideous display. Someone was going to get hurt. Someone other than me; that was a given.

Diego looped his arm around my waist, pulling my right arm up to rest on his shoulders. The healing spell stopped for a second, like Peony relaxed the spell now that she saw that I was upright. I waved to her a thank you, but hoped she would keep the magic going. Breathing hurt and was a little more difficult than it should have been, but I didn't wanna dwell on that for too long.

Mari stood in a pillar of fire, blasting her way through a throng of Fae making their way to her. My heart skipped a beat–she was a sight to see, blazing with magic and not a care in the world. I could see even from a distance; Mari moved with the confidence of knowing nothing could stop her, nothing could touch her. She twirled through the fire like she was born from it, taking aim and cutting a blazing path for Sherwin. She'd be okay, I reminded myself. Mari was safe. Nothing could get through that fire.

But Jack wasn't, so I hobbled along the field with Diego on yet another rescue mission.

CHAPTER SEVENTEEN

PEONY

The vines around my waist started to squeeze too tight; it wasn't intentional, these trees were alive and sentient and unbelievably brave. They stood up to the Wildfire. They protected my sister when I wasn't able to and saved my life, so I damn sure wasn't going to complain about a little squeeze.

But it would be nice to have a branch to stand on.

The trees responded to me as if I had said the words out loud, and I was a little spooked. I was fine with trees that had a consciousness, but psychic trees were a lot to process.

We will help you, healer. Sssaave our King. Sssaave our Priessstess.

I focused on the magic that followed through my body, on creating bridges between me and the others. Falcon and Sherwin were the weakest–I wasn't even sure how Falcon was standing. I tried to push as much magic to him as possible. He had broken ribs, bruised lungs, severe scarring and nerve damage in his arms, and a fractured collarbone. The list kept going through my mind and I tried to focus on someone else, before I had a panic attack for Falcon's health.

Sherwin hacked and slashed his way across the field and it made me sick. The Sherwin I knew—the man from Earth, not some fancy court advisor or whatever from Obius—was gentle and sexy and full of mischief. The man I saw here wasn't a man at all; he had horns and feathers, and fought like a warrior from ages past.

Mari had burned enough of a path through to the guy at the back of the Fae. He stayed there, not moving. The giant things next to him stayed close, sniffing and howling from time to time. Each moan or howl sent a shiver down my spine. I wasn't brave like the rest of them, so I stayed in the trees and kept casting. I was exhausted, but I didn't stop. They weren't stopping, and they were all *fighting*.

Pull energy from usssss, healer. We can help you.

I didn't know what that meant, but I tried my best. Wrapping my hands around the vines that held me, I tried to connect with the trees. This was more of Jack's thing—she was blessed with a green thumb more so than me.

The trees still responded though.

Ssend the ssspellss through the rootsss.

Instead of pushing the magic out through my arms, I imagined it flowing through my body, through my fingers, through the vines and branches. I pictured my healing spells weaving between the fibers of the trees' trunks and racing down through the roots.

Yesssss, good work, healer.

The land glistened with my magic; the healing spells seeped into the ground and ribbons of soft blue light popped out of the dirt. It looked like I had planted little sprinklers around the wasteland; healing magic spraying everything in sight. Little flecks of green popped up, and my breath caught in my throat. The grass was *growing*! It was coming back! The relief I felt was immense; I was so damn thankful that it wasn't just gone for good.

The sharp clang of metal caught my attention and I turned to see Sherwin spinning through some elaborate spell using his swords to channel it. It was blinding; the light that poured from him was too bright to look at directly. When it began to fade, I saw that he had rained rocks down on the advancing soldiers.

The guy at the back let out a weird bird call–high, piercing, chirpy–and the soldiers all stopped. They stopped mid swings, mid step, and turned back to him. It was like they were under a spell too.

Maybe they were. The soldiers were too in step, too in sync to be natural. They were just like the twisted souls that Snapdragon was manipulating, except they were still alive. Sherwin grabbed and pulled at them, trying to get someone to engage with him. They didn't. They didn't even seem to notice that he was *there* grabbing their arms and shoulders. I felt the groan he let out from my perch in the trees. Whatever spell was on the soldiers, it forced their bodies to move against their wills, marching and fighting to whatever their master demanded.

"Please, let me down," I said.

No, healer. Keep you sssafe.

"Please, they need help."

Ssstay clossse.

The trees placed me on the ground, the vines checking that I was okay before letting go completely. Little vines curled around my cheek, patting it like I was a child. I probably was in their eyes.

Mari hadn't stopped casting. She blew fire across the fields, at the retreating soldiers. Sherwin stopped following them. He angled his body toward the man that controlled the soldiers movements. Being closer, I saw the anguish on the soldiers' faces, moving not of their will, and that lit a fire in my chest too. What kind of controlling, manipulative sack of shit would force his army to fight like little toy soldiers while he watched?

Sherwin heard me approaching and turned. His face lit up when he saw me. He dropped the swords and scooped me up. He smelled like sweat and maybe blood; there was a tinny scent to him that I tried really hard not to zone in on.

Mari hadn't stopped casting.

"Pea," he said. I felt depleted and weak. Sherwin still had some of the goop he had cobbled together earlier, and he pulled out a folded leaf and applied it down my arms. It wasn't a *pleasant* smell, but it drowned out the bloody scent that filled my nose.

I followed the path his eyes traveled and watched as Mari kept spinning fire. She didn't stop; her body was manic, and the look on her face was drunk. I wrapped myself in as much healing magic as I could.

Mari stood in a pillar of fire. Right in the center. She burned and burned. I doubted there was anything in either world that could convince her to step out of the flames. I'd known her all my life; I had a few vague memories of when she was born, her mama letting me hold her all wrapped up in cottony blankets. I'd seen the woman she grew into, wanting to be more than she was, wanting to be fuller. She thought that Jack and I didn't know, or couldn't tell, how unhappy she had become since her mama died. But she was smiling now, manic and wild, full of the life she so desperately wan ted.

"I hate this plan," I whined.

"I'll go–"

"No, she won't listen to you. She probably won't listen to *me*, but there's a better shot–"

Sherwin kissed the top of my head, holding my face in his hands, and for a second I thought he was going to tell me that he loved me. I wanted him to. I wanted to hear the words tumble out of his mouth in a hurried truth, that he couldn't hold in any longer. I wanted to be someone's first priority, instead of just the problem solver.

But not here, standing in the scorched forest with blood and souls soaking into the dirt.

I sucked in a deep breath and marched over to Mari. She twirled in the flames now, dancing like she was dancing in the rain. She didn't look hurt at least–not physically. Emotionally I was sure she was all fucked up, but that wasn't the pressing issue. I could pour her a cup of tea and let her cry when we were firmly alive and back on Earth.

I had to get her out of the fire, willingly, and get her to drop the magic.

When Mari realized that I was there, she grinned, more flames shooting from her hands. I ducked before anything hit me, and she erupted into a fit of laughter.

"Darling, can you hear me?" I shouted.

She nodded and did another spin. The fire responded to her every whim, and when I stared at the flames, they were detailed and complex. It reminded me of lace.

"Mari, drop the spell. The fight is over, you can come out now."

She stopped for a second. Her brows furrowed and she frowned. "Fight?"

My stomach dropped again, and I took another step closer. I hated this. "Yes, there was a fight, you were helping Sherwin..."

"Ohh!" Her eyes widened and the reflection of the fire was too bright in them. She rubbed her hands together then cracked her knuckles, looking around for the next opponent.

"Mari, it's over. It's done. You can release the spell. You did great–"

"No," she said, her whole body going stiff and rigid.

"What do you mean no?" I swore that my heart stopped; the trees moved closer to me, and I felt the vines snaking around my legs and up my waist–they were ready to snatch me up should things go south.

But they wouldn't. Because this was Mari, my second little sister. Mari was my family, and she wouldn't hurt me.

"I'm not ever letting this magic go," she sang, twisting around in the pillar. That drunken look on her face tied my stomach more in knots, and I desperately wished for my antacid stockpile. I felt like I was breathing my own kind of fire now.

"Maybe just drop the pillar then? I think I need to heal your hands a little." Her hands looked like shit. They were blackened, like she had charred them. I was terrified that I'd touch her fingers and they would fall off. She didn't even notice, and that scared me even more.

Mari dropped the pillar. Heat poured out from around her and I felt myself break out into a sweat immediately. It was like coming out of a sauna and into a burning building. I held my hand out for her to take, so I could examine her. My fingers were quaking, and the intense desire not to get burned simmered in me.

Her fingers didn't fall off when I gripped her hand, and I let out a shaky breath.

"Did you see it, Peony? Did you see my magic?" Her voice was ragged, like the fire had burned through her vocal cords.

"Yep, couldn't miss it," I said, running the strongest healing spells I could over her charred hands. The charring flaked off and that was *all* that flaked off, thank the Goddess. Under the charred pieces was her normal, dark brown skin. No weeping or oozing wounds. No blood. Just her normal self.

"I think I finally found my gift," she whispered.

"What?"

"Wildfire. I can control it. Didn't you *see* it?"

"Mari—"

"I did it, Peony. I really did," she said awestruck and raspy.

She flung herself around my neck and I thought I might burn up from the contact. Mari felt like she was a thousand degrees and I gently pulled myself off. Hugging a volcano didn't feel great.

"You did, darling. But for now, let's quiet that storm a little. You're gonna singe my hair," I said, careful to keep my words light, airy. She nodded, and the heat around her evaporated. The fire burned in her eyes still, and I shot a look over to Sherwin that I hoped said, *we are fucked*.

"Wait, where's Jack?" she asked.

"She went after Diego, don't you remember?" I rubbed the backs of her hands, something I'd done a thousand times before to calm her nerves. She watched my hands curiously, confusion etched on her face.

Then Mari shook her head *no*, holding her forehead like it was hurting. Holding that much magic in probably didn't feel *awesome,* but I didn't want to dwell on that. She wouldn't hear me, that much I knew.

"And Falcon?" she asked, her head snapping up to search for him.

Really could use some of those precious calcium tablets right about now, "He's with Diego. He's been injured, but he's gonna be okay." I kept my voice even and my face neutral. She blinked at me a couple times, the words not clicking. Injured. Okay. I hoped she focused on the okay part.

"He's okay, Mari. I saw him walking around," Sherwin chimed in. She flinched at his voice, confused about where it came from.

"Okay," she said.

"Yep, let's find you some water. You look... parched," I finished lamely. Sherwin's eyes went wide and I groaned. Sherwin made some flappy arm gestures that vaguely said *really now, parched?*

"Water sounds good," she said.

"Then we need to find Deign and the others. It's too silent for my liking," he said. I was decidedly not thinking about the silence. Nothing good would come from it, that much I knew.

The trees again eavesdropped in the conversation, and produced three large leaf bowls filled with water. *Drink,* they hummed. We drank, and I felt lighter. My organs were parched and drained, and the water tasted like heaven. It was perfect.

A shriek in the distance made me spill the rest of the water down my shirt, and I swore. The trees supplied another leaf of water.

"That wasn't Jack," Mari said, another fire igniting in her palms.

"No, it was Snapdragon," Sherwin said. We downed as much water as we could take, and headed for Jack.

JACK

Snapdragon was speaking to me, but I couldn't hear her words yet. The visions and memories faded slowly. I didn't know how to face her now. Snapdragon's face, no longer the beauty that I saw in her memories, hissed and twisted in rage as she snapped at me. Her staff tried to attack me, but Harold blocked and blocked again, like it was fencing. I pulled myself up and just watched her for a second. I was covered in dirt now too. My dress—*her* dress—was ripped and I couldn't bring myself to attack her any longer.

"What are you doing! Get up!" she jeered, her staff still wildly trying to make contact with my face.

She was running out of magic now; between the lost souls and the double round of Wildfire, she had to be running on fumes. The gemstone on her staff blinked in and out, but she didn't notice. Snapdragon was losing her connection to this plane as she whipped herself more into a ball of fury.

I had to end this.

Holding my hand out, Harold settled in my palm. Snapdragon tried casting something, I'm not sure what, but nothing happened. The glow in her staff became duller by the second, until it faded altogether. The gem was rough looking, like it was more of a rock than anything precious. The staff was mangled. The charms I saw in the visions were long gone, and I wondered if she even knew what happened. The blue feathers that were a gift from Diego, the metal sigils, and beads were long gone.

I wondered if she even knew what happened.

I stood just inches from her. She breathed heavily, the anger plainly etched on her face, and I felt the tears well up. I had to stamp down all of my sympathy; she was still trying to attack me.

She had no idea that she had died.

I touched the side of her face, and she hissed, moving away from me, like I was the insane one. Maybe I would be too if I had held onto my broken spirit for half a millennia.

"Snapdragon," I said.

"Don't you *dare* touch me!"

"It's okay–"

She punched at me, but her hand glided through my face. She looked less grounded, less real. Diego took that moment to arrive, hoisting Falcon along like he was cargo. He didn't look fully conscious, really. I still sensed a pulse, though. He tried to lift his head up, but the injuries were catching up to him and Falcon was doing good to be awake at all.

"Snapdragon," Diego breathed out, sitting. Falcon down on a slightly burnt tree stump. She jerked away from me at the sound of her name, at the sound of Diego's voice. When their eyes met, I saw that Diego was crying. He swallowed, the tears rolling down his face, and he didn't take his eyes off of her. The heart link swelled with his emotions, hot and painful, wanting to tear us both apart. He reached for her, but pulled his hand back.

"Snapdragon," he said again.

"I barely recognize you, Deign. You seem so much *less* than you were." Her words dipped with disdain, but there was no bite left in her. There wasn't enough of her to have any strength to the words.

"I could say the same to you," he whispered.

The spell came from my lips, flowing before I could fully stop it. My staff was emerald green, and she tried to snatch it from me.

"What's going on?" she cried, frantically trying to grab the staff from me.

I glanced at Diego, words passing between the heart links. ***Do what you must, my Blossom.***

"I'm so sorry–"

"As am I, but you have nothing to apologize for. Please help her... this is no longer the woman I loved."

"I'll try."

His shoulders shook, and he switched from looking at me to looking at her.

"Rest, be at peace–"

"Stop it!" she screeched, her staff spinning fast with no other magic in it. She grabbed at the staff, and her fingers passed through the shaft. Confusion was etched so deeply on her face that the urge to soothe her nearly overwhelmed me. Snapdragon stared at her own hands, seeing how translucent they were and stilled. She turned her hands over and over, trying to piece together what this meant.

I chewed on my lip and tried a different spell. I didn't have a name for it, and I didn't really understand the mechanics. I twisted the staff through my fingers, rolling it between my palms, and released the alchemy threading itself together. An orb surrounded the four of us–Snapdragon, Diego, Falcon, and me–and I let the scene unfold.

I replayed Snapdragon's true death. I showed them all how Arturo crept up on her when she was alone in Diego's bedroom, clinging to his shirt for comfort. I showed them how he plunged the knife into her back, and how she fell.

Diego sank to his knees, and Falcon pulled him close, an arm wrapped around his shoulders.

"I don't understand," Snapdragon whispered. "This can't be right–"

"It is. You... you just couldn't let go," I said. The truth of it flowed through the spell, showing how she had slowly changed through the centuries, shriveling up more and more. She had fewer flowers blooming from her hand, more twigs instead of greenery. Her magic slowed as she needed more and more souls to keep herself going.

Snapdragon tried to comb her fingers through her hair, and they passed through her. She had a hard time reaching for her staff now, too. It faded, getting harder to see.

"I don't want to die," she said, crawling closer to Diego. He opened his arms for her, but there wasn't enough of her to hold. She sank into him, through him, trying to kneel in his lap, but she faded more, her body passing through Diego's outstretched hands.

"Shh, it's okay," he said. He rocked back and forth, trying to stroke her hair. Falcon scooted away to give them some space. I felt like an intruder, a voyeur, as Diego tried to comfort her. Falcon motioned for me to come over to him, to give me something to do other than watch their final goodbyes.

"Don't go down that path, Lefty. He needs to do this," Falcon said.

"Should I–?"

"Give him another minute." Falcon wrapped an arm around me, and I hugged him back. I dug my fingers into his torn and muddy shirt. A tear rolled down my cheek, and Falcon thumbed it away.

"I've got you, Lefty," he whispered and the hair on my arms stood up. The magic to send her to rest was building in my chest, and I wouldn't have a choice but to cast it soon. I turned in Falcon's arms, looking at Diego and Snapdragon because it wouldn't be long before the spell would overwhelm m e.

"Diego?" I said in hushed tones. I didn't want to break this moment, but it was time.

"Yes, sorry," he said quickly, and I saw the embarrassment and shame on his face. I felt it through the heart link as it burned against my wrist. *"Say goodbye, Diego. It's her time."*

"Don't let go of me, Deign," Snapdragon desperately tried to grab his arms, his shirt, anything, but her fingers simply went right through him. She tried to touch his cheek, her hand hovering just next to his face.

"I won't."

I moved away from Falcon slowly, making sure that he could stand on his own before I started casting. Green and gold bands, shades of my magic and Diego's, flowed around me, each step I took lifting me in the air and holding me there. The bands of color tied themselves together, a harmonious bow, activating the spell in a way I didn't know possible. This was how it was meant to feel, this was how I was meant to cast the Resting Call. I swung the staff, twirling it in the air, as the magic hummed to life. The words were desperate to come out, but I kept moving through the dance of it, for as long as I could give them. Diego needed to say goodbye, and I wouldn't take that from him.

"Rest, be at peace. Return to Sanctum to be born again," my voice rang out, echoing around us, grand and ancient. I sounded more like myself than I ever had before, taking up all of the space around me, stretching and extending with the Seer's Blessing across all of Trellis, all of Obius.

The small, fading orbs of light rose from the ground everywhere around us from the lost souls. There were so many of them. They all heard the call of the spell, the promise of rest, and they followed. There was a mass of them around me, circling around the crystal of my staff. Snapdragon faded and faded, until she was nothing but star lights. Diego placed a hand on her face as the lights slowly went out. Her soul orb was emerald green, just as I expected it to be, and it rose up.

"I'm sorry, Deign," Snapdragon said as she faded away completely. Her soul was absorbed into my crystal ball with the rest of the other souls. As the spell waned and I came back to the ground, I hugged the staff to my chest.

"I'm sorry too," I said to Snapdragon. I saw the hundreds of souls contained in the perfect crystal. One spark of bright green swirled brighter among the rest.

Diego came over to me then, crushing me in a hug to his chest. His breathing was ragged and he dug his fingers into me. I grieved with him; he said goodbye to Snapdragon, and I prayed for peace over her and the rest of the souls. We grieved together for the state of Obius. Pressing my forehead to his, I cupped his face, getting him to focus on me again. His feathers were ruffled and puffed out, and I tried to soothe them back down, back into place. Diego slowed his breathing, and I brought his hands to my lips, pressing kisses into them to stop the trembling.

His thoughts gushed through my mind in a jumbled mess. Apologies and heartbreak. Fear of losing me and Falcon and fear for the state of Trellis.

But more than anything else, I felt his love, and not just for me. I felt the love he still held in his heart for Snapdragon, for his homeland, and the home he made on Earth. Diego pressed his forehead to mine, not saying anything.

"Once we fix the links, I'm going to send all of the lost souls to rest for good," I said.

"Yes," he said. His lips were white and he was trembling.

I wrapped my arms around his neck and Diego squeezed. He let go a little when I squeaked, the first small laugh I heard from him in what felt like ages.

"I'm sorry you had to see—"

"Diego, it's okay."

"I just—"

"You had to say goodbye," I said, tucking a lock of his messy black curls behind his ears. He ran a hand through his hair, forgetting about his horns, and bumped his fingers against them. I rubbed my hands down the horns as they curled back to his head, and played with his hair.

He let out of a shuddering breath, still trying to get some control back. "I had to say goodbye," he said.

"Is it okay to turn around now? Mushy shit is over?" Falcon said.

"Yes, Falcon, the *mushy shit* is over," I said.

"Sweet, because I'm gonna need some more healing spells, stat. And we need to figure out how to get home. D, this place is *lovely*, but I need to see a legit doctor. Gonna need more than tree paste to fix all this," he said, gesturing to the state of his body. He really did look awful.

"How do we get home?" I asked Diego.

"Well, first we need to contact Mama," Peony said as she approached us. Her, Mari, and Sherwin were together, but something was *wrong* with Mari. Her essence was different, and I was immediately on guard. Mari kept looking at her hands, turning them over and over, looking for something. I caught a glimpse of Wildfire from her, and shook the image away.

"What's going on with–" Ice formed in Peony's eyes and I stopped talking. Mari looked dazed.

"Nothing. So I think Mama would be listening for something, right? That would make sense. Any ideas on how we can switch to speaker phone?" Peony said. Her thoughts were loud, and she pointedly looked in my direction. *Yes, something is wrong with Mari. Leave it. She's likely to go off if we talk about it. Let it go.*

"She pulled magic from a sunstone and opened the link," Diego said. He kneeled where Snapdragon was before the Resting Call, and picked up the small pouch that she was wearing. Inside was another sunstone, except this one was a piece of his heart.

"No, you're not gonna potentially break–" Falcon was cut off when Diego held a hand up to shush him.

"No, but I need Jack to help me put this back where it belongs. I think with three pieces, I'll have enough juice to tether a tiny link back together. Long enough for us to get back, anyway."

"You really think so?" I asked.

"I hope so. That's sorta my ace in the hole," Diego smiled. "***Trust me, my Blossom.***"

"Well, I guess let's do this thing," I said. The last time I bound his heart together, I was holding the locket he made for Snapdragon. This time, I didn't have anything to latch on to–

"Use the heart link, my Blossom. Connect to it, and use it to fuse the pieces together." I nodded, and reached for Diego's hands. He held me gently, and I tried to shake the image of how terrified Snapdragon was just moments ago from my mind. Diego was trying hard to be in the present with me, to let go of all of the heartbreak. He was offering his heart to me, broken and fragile, praying that it was enough.

"Focus on me, Jack," Diego whispered in my ear, "Focus on me." I nodded again, and before I made any real effort, my magic flowed again, wrapping around the heart links and Diego, tying us together.

> ***Holy Goddesses,***
> ***Creation, Judgment, and Vision,***
> ***The brokenness in front of me needs to mend,***
> ***To join joyously, righteously, and with precision,***
> ***Tie together the ends that frayed,***
> ***Tie together the paths mislaid.***

His eyes were a brighter gold, like the color of the sun.

Diego stood a little taller, squaring and rolling his shoulders, grinning and the magic that coursed through him was deafening. The gold of his eyes matched the aura around him, gaining more energy by the second. His magic rolled off him in waves, and I turned to take him in. The faint golden glow of his aura made him seem almost angel-like and my breath caught.

Diego stretched his arms like he had forgotten he had them and his feathers spread out wide. He was giddy and his joy was infectious. I wanted to reach for him and hold him in my arms after everything that happened, but he needed just another moment to feel the vitality coming back. He needed to enjoy remembering he was still alive.

Morning started to dawn, and the brilliant sunrise only made Diego shine more. A smile blossomed on my face and I couldn't wait any longer so I hugged him, and he lifted me in the air. The heart link pounded on my wrist, matching the beat of his heart. It was already beating together, the pieces all working in harmony like they were supposed to. I did that.

"Let's cast that one more time," he whispered.

And so we did.

Chapter Eighteen

DIEGO

Jack held my hands, our fingers interlaced, and we started the binding spell. The heart link's magic tied us together and I sucked in a breath. Every time we used this spell together, I felt another piece of myself coming alive. The magic worked like a skilled surgeon, carefully stitching all of the broken pieces together.

I had a lot of broken pieces.

Snapdragon's face was so confused as Jack replayed her final moments. It was everything I worked so hard to prevent. She sank on my bed, before collapsing on the floor like a doll. She was withered and brittle when I finally saw her again in Obius, and I realized that wasn't the woman I loved. It was the shadow of her, the darkest parts that clung to life for hundreds of years, and the leftover fear that she had carried so close to her heart. Were the visions of her death even real? Did she lie about that or had the Seer's blessing corrupted her mind? I'd never really know, and I didn't want to. I didn't want to believe that the years we'd spent together happily were just a façade. Memories of us lying together under the stars or hiding in her rooms as the Trellian Guard marched through the halls filled me. We'd laugh quietly behind our hands as another guard would walk on by, not knowing there was an *intruder* in the Priestess' bedroom, or that it was the King. The days would pass in a blur, until the days stopped passing altogether, and I was left without her.

I surveyed our little group; these people had become the family I thought I'd never find again. My best friends, Falcon and Sherwin, were worse for wear. Falcon needed medical attention and Sherwin could do with a long sleep to rest and heal. The girls, Mari and Peony, leaned against them and I smiled. Falcon leaned more on Mari than she did on him; the faraway look in her eyes was worrisome, but she seemed more grounded with Falcon near. Everyone, including myself, gave her a wide berth.

And then there was Jack.

She stood steadfast in front of me, her gaze never wavering. The corners of her lips turned up in a tiny smile, and I felt the question coming from them. **"Do you still want me?"**

The magic of the binding spell intensified, and the words came back to us, coming from our mouths. The link came together; I saw the neutral point between the three realms–Earth, Obius, Sanctum–where the links tied themselves together. This small space was where it was said that the Goddesses lived, spending Their time with each other and watching over the worlds.

Jack brightened as the spell worked; we saw the thinnest thread between Earth and Obius knitting together with the image of Jazzy and Puddin on the other side, waiting. Jack's magic flexed its might at the sight of them, and the link was rebuilt.

A small portal made of sparkling darkness opened between our hands. Jack and I reluctantly eased our hands apart and watched as the portal grew. It was larger than me now, standing at least a full ten feet high. The binding spell worked so much better here in Obius, with my magic fueling it, and Jack's guiding it all together. With my heart gaining another piece, my strength returned too. I knew I could command my magic again. It was gold and bright, and I felt like I did before the Shattering. Mostly. I could sense how the well of magic in me was filling up, and I wanted to climb the trees and shout that I was here.

Everyone was smiling and hooting with joy–*we did it! We can go home!*–but I felt no joy at seeing the portal there. I glanced back at the razed forest, at the empty market center of Treis in the distance, and at the towers of Trellis Castle that seemed to wobble. Maybe that was just my eyes tearing up.

There was so much that needed to be fixed here.

My heart fractured all over again because I realized then, that I wouldn't be leaving with them, with Jack. There was work to be done, and I refused to wreck my homeland again.

She saw it written on my face, and I could only meet her eyes. She winked at me, and turned back to everyone. Jack took her sisters' hands, and I felt the intent in her movement. I could sense her emotions even more now, in a way I never could with Snapdragon.

"I think what you meant to say–err, think–was that we have work to do." Her glorious magic bounded around in my head, too loud and too strong and I winced. She bit her lips, tampering the smile.

"Mari, Peony," she said. The girls stopped their cheering to listen. "Take care of Puddin for me. Peony, can you handle the house stuff? I know it's asking a lot–"

"Jack–" Peony started.

She held a hand up firmly, "Nope, listen. I... I can't leave yet. I can't leave these souls lost and wandering. I promised them."

"You can't stay here!" Mari shouted, fire erupting from her hands. Sherwin and Falcon stamped out the little flames as they popped up. Mari was unstable, and she wobbled. Peony caught her by the arm.

"Take care of her, too," Jack said, words wobbling as much as Mari.

"How long?" Falcon asked, his voice thick with emotion and pain.

"I don't know," I said. Until it's done. Until I know what happens next.

"You're staying too, Diego? Of course you are," Peony huffed. She glanced between us, seeing a battle she'd fought with her sister several times before, and blew out a sigh. "You're sure?" she said to Jack.

Jack turned to look back at me, the aura of the Seer's Blessing enveloping and embracing her. She looked like she was finally home, too. Dressed in clothes from my homeland, wielding a staff, with the Seer's Blessing swirling around her, Jack felt more Fae than human now. She was more beautiful than the Goddesses, but I kept those thoughts as privately as I could. The mischief in her eyes told me she'd heard it anyway.

"Yeah, I'm sure."

"I'm not leaving you here alone, Diego. I won't leave your side unless you don't want me there."

Peony and Mari hugged Jack, kissing the top of her head with tears in their eyes. Mari picked at the beads in her hair, now a lot more tangled than when we left for Obius. They were weary, exhausted. This was not the welcome I wanted for anyone to experience in Trellis.

Sherwin hugged me, his feathers brushing against mine, and I held him tight. The embrace was longer than the girls had held each other, but I didn't care. Sherwin had been to hell and back, always walking behind me. I'd never be able to repay his kindness.

"Diego," he said.

"For you, I will answer to any name," I said, bowing my head to him.

Sherwin grinned, "Alright, *Buttercup*." I nearly choked from laughing. Buttercup was the name our nursemaid would call all of the children she watched. The memory warmed my heart, and I wondered where she was now, if she survived the fire.

Everyone stood around, not wanting the moment to end, not wanting to say goodbye again. I stayed silent; as much as I loved them, I hadn't earned the right to intrude on their goodbyes. Jack gently shooed them, but she linked her arm through mine, holding me steady. The portal glimmered, and Peony took the first steps toward it. Jack squeezed my bicep and I tried to soothe her by rubbing my thumb across the back of her hand.

"See you soon?" Peony asked. Jack nodded. Peony blew one more kiss, and held Sherwin's hand. He nodded one more time to me, and they stepped through the portal.

"I don't want to leave you here, Jackie," Mari said as her voice broke. She wiped a tear away but it evaporated from the fire magic still in her chest.

"I know, but I'll bring you a souvenir. Listen for us to call again."

"No frogs!" They laughed and Mari stepped through the portal. Her body disappeared into the glittering darkness.

Falcon hung back, heavily favoring his right leg. He watched and waited until everyone had fully faded before speaking, "I'm sorry."

"Falcon–"

"No Lefty, I need to say this. I'm sorry. I'm sorry I didn't see what was going on. I'm sorry for uh, dosing you, D. I'm sorry for all of it."

I crashed into him, hugging him. Falcon nearly fell over, wincing and grabbing his ribs. "No more apologies," I said firmer than it needed to be. He did not need to beg forgiveness, not when I was already willing to give it for free.

"Yep, all good. I mean, this whole thing is literally your fault but–" Jack said. She started to elbow him, but stopped, remembering the ribs.

"Hey!"

"Truth hurts!"

"You really gonna stay? I can stay with you–"

"Falcon, you need to *heal*. You look like death warmed over," Jack said.

"We're gonna be okay," I said, and I was shocked to realize that I believed it. We would be okay. Jack and I would put things right here. Now that there was a real, living Priestess and a washed up King, we could put things back in order.

"I suck at goodbyes," he said as he walked backwards to the portal, "Deuces." Falcon held up a peace sign and stepped into the portal, sucking in a breath and holding his ribs as he faded.

Jack and I closed the portal, thanking the magic for responding to our call, as we rejoined our hands. A bright, emerald green speck caught my eye in her staff and I knew that it was Snapdragon. I swallowed down a wave of grief that threatened to wriggle free, and refocused my attention on Jack. The heart links thudded heavily against our wrists. Jack ran her fingers through my hair, scratching at the base of my horns, and held my face gently. How did I get this lucky to be back in Trellis with Jack in my arms?

She was perfect.

"I'm gonna need a bath, some clean clothes, and something hot to eat. Then we get to work."

I kissed each of her fingers and down her wrists. I bowed deeply at the waist, and she laughed. I'd do anything to keep hearing that laugh. "Yes, my Blossom."

EPILOGUE

HOLY GODDESS OF VISION AND TIME

THE SEER

It had been too long since I'd been back to the mountains. The energy and life of the ocean was enticing, but standing on solid rock that held the history of the land etched in its formations was timeless. The cabin I'd spent so many years in was worse for wear, much like me. The logs were faded and peeling. It could do with some fresh paint and fresh flowers to bring it back to life.

But it would have to wait, because there were other lives to watch.

I had three glass bowls filled with crystalline water from the mountain lake just up the way. The water glistened as sunlight filtered through the dirty kitchen windows. I sat at the table, peeling potatoes while I took my time to scry.

There was much to see, thanks to my latest Priestess. Much to be taught too. I rocked back in my chair, my sweater catching on the chair arm, and fished the handful of bracelets out of my pocket. They would sell nicely at the next crystal market; the lake water here charged them with more magic than any human could ever hope for, but it was always so nice to see them hoping.

Jack Hawthorne's pretty face appeared in the center bowl with King Deign behind her, swaying to some tune. He was smiling again, and I was surprised at how pleasing that was. He was reckless, too emotional for his own good, but maybe the years had taught him something.

Marigold Groves and Falcon were back to back in the left bowl, and I didn't need to peek any further to feel how their hands had laced together. Falcon finally did the right thing; he listened better without my dear sister's tattoo on his skin, leaving only my own. Marigold looked like this cabin: worn out but still so full of life. She had swallowed the Wildfire, like I knew she would, like she was born to, and I smiled so fondly at my girl.

The other Hawthorne girl, Peony, and Deign's Shadow stood heart to heart, in the remaining bowl. *Go on, child*, I urged her, *take a leap while you still have time.*

The portal from Obius had opened and returned four of the six of them. Four would be enough for now. Marigold needed to tame the fire in her heart before she could be trusted out in the world, and Falcon had many wounds to heal.

And the King of course, needed to find his replacement and continue his journey of penance. The little sister covered in cerulean feathers would wake soon to find her world collapsing. I sighed happily, starting now on the onions. It was good there was a Priestess back in Trellis to guide her.

Best to prepare some more empanadas for the children.

Their road is still very long ahead of them.

TO BE CONTINUED...

DEAR READER

Thank you so much for reading *Visions of Fire*! I sincerely hope that you enjoyed the next adventure for Jack and the rest of the crew as they explored Obius and faced some major demons of the past.

If you enjoyed it, please consider leaving a review and spreading the word! This helps other readers to find this book; chatting and posting about it on social media, blogs, and forums is an absolute blessing for indie writers. This is how we connect with our readers, and every review is so appreciated! Look me up on Facebook and Instagram; I love hearing from readers!

Also, if you'd like some exclusive content and teasers for the next books in Jack's world, you can always sign up for my **NEWSLETTER** too!

Love,

Jana

Acknowledgments

Visions of Fire was a whirlwind for me. I wrote the first draft of this book in about six weeks of crazy, inspired writing fervor. It was so much fun, and I had loads of support. My wonderful husband, Glenn, who faithfully put our kiddos to sleep each night so I would have time to write. My lovely friends: the Em's, Emma and Emily, KK, Joshu, and Lena who listened to my constant blabbering about these characters and this world. My parents, Jim and Shirley, who tell every human they meet about my books and my journey. My kiddos too for seeing me write and having the understanding that I was following my dreams; hopefully it'll inspire them to always follow theirs too.

Then the professionals that got this book to where I wanted it to be: my darling editor, Andrea Davidson, **the Ardent Editor**, whom I can't thank enough for her skills and insights, and Candis Frey-Curry, my **eagle-eyed proofreader** who saved me tons of heartache of digging for typos.

Thank you from the bottom of my heart.

The last book in The Seer's Blessing Trilogy: Visions of Kings, will be coming soon. Stay tuned, folks!

About The Author

Writer. Wife/Mom. Servant to 4lb Chihuahua with a Napoleon complex. Avid coffee drinker. Travel junkie. Book devourer. (Not, *literally*—too much fiber.)

I've been writing most of my life, but my heart has always been drawn to magic. Urban Fantasy--mixing magic with real life--became the perfect genre for me.

Born and raised on the Southeast Coast of Virginia, when I'm not writing or momming, I'm heading for the ocean.

Come join my newsletter called **"The Magic Shop,"** where I'll send you monthly emails to tease upcoming books, provide flower, crystal, and character bios, and *of course*, pictures of His Royal Highness, Prince Babar, my chihuahua.

Feeling social? I'm on Facebook and IG, and I'd love for you to come say hello!

f facebook.com/profile.php?id=100091558147127

instagram.com/jana_sun_books/

tiktok.com/@jana_sun_books?_t=8nZvXwxUsCV&_r=1

amazon.com/stores/Jana-Sun/author/B0CLSBT8VH?ref=ap_rdr&isDramIntegrated=true&shoppingPortalEnabled=true

goodreads.com/author/show/42798427.Jana_Sun